Hood Misfits Volume 2:

Carl Weber Presents

Hood Misfits Volume 2:

Carl Weber Presents

Brick & Storm

www.urbanbooks.net

Urban Books, LLC
97 N18th Street
Wyandanch, NY 11798

Hood Misfits Volume 2: Carl Weber Presents

ISBN 13: 978-1-60162-640-0
ISBN 10: 1-60162-640-1

First Trade Paperback Printing January 2015
Printed in the United States of America

10 9 8 7 6 5 4 3 2 1

Distributed by Kensington Publishing Corp.
Submit Wholesale Orders to:
Kensington Publishing Corp.
C/O Penguin Group (USA) Inc.
Attention: Order Processing
405 Murray Hill Parkway
East Rutherford, NJ 07073-2316
Phone: 1-800-526-0275
Fax: 1-800-227-9604

Episode 3:

The Showdown in London Town

If you know the enemy and know yourself you need not fear the results of a hundred battles.

—Sun Tzu

Prelude

Introduction to Dante

"You got my ends, bruv?"

Dante sat at his long cherry wood king-style dinner table where he often handled his business. The hardwood floors had been polished to a mirrored shine. The muscles in his arms twitched in annoyance as the toothpick in the corner of his mouth flicked up and down. He liked the dining room. He'd called it that for several reasons, reasons no man, woman, or child wanted to ever find out first-hand. The man he was talking to stood in front of him with glossy eyes, ashy lips, grinding teeth, and trembling hands. Robes knew the moment he was snatched up into an unmarked van and driven to Dante's mansion what was about to happen, but he was high enough to hope that he could talk his way out of the jam he was in. Dante had the best blanca, bings, and drone in the Bricks. If you wanted a hit of the good shit, you came to Dante's crew to get that. Blanca was cocaine, bings was crack, and drone Mephedrone in London slang. Robes had gotten a biscuit from Dante on the strength of his word alone. Said he was going to sell that shit and bring the money back to Dante. Only thing was he knew he shouldn't have taken that shit when it was offered, but he needed a hit bad and was willing to do damn near anything to get it.

To be honest Robes had been watching his back in all codes. He knew soon as word got back to Anika that he had been buying from Dante and bringing it back to the Bricks she was gone split his bloody skull. Robes was a part of the Jamaican Lords who held shop in the Bricks, which was Anika's codes. They called that nigga Robes because he was always walking around in long robes looking like a knotty locked Jesus and shit.

"I don't 'ave it yet, bruv, but if you just give to the end of the day, yeah?" Robes begged.

Dante sat not moving. The look on his face was stoic as he stroked his cleanly shaven chin. Dante hated hair anywhere on his body except his head. That stemmed from childhood trauma. Anytime Dante's daddy would get drunk and fuck his mother he'd make his twin sons, Dame and Dante, more like force them face first into his crotch to smell his dick. He'd wanted to make sure they knew what pussy had smelled like on dick. His father had been hell in the streets and even more hell when he was at home. Dante didn't like that shit then, but now he understood the method to his daddy's madness. Humiliation was better than death. You take a nigga's pride and you had him by the balls.

"You know, Robes, you said that same shit exactly three hundred and sixty hours, thirty minutes, and ten seconds ago, bruv. You think I got time for the run around about my ducats, blood?" Dante questioned coolly. "You took a biscuit from me. That's fifty racks of crack."

As Dante talked he motioned with his hand to one of his henchmen. The boy left the room quickly. Dante then stood, unsnapped the top of his cane and pulled out a sword so shiny that you could see your death on the blades.

Robes backed away with his hands in the air. "Don't kill me, Dante. I got kids, bruv. Let me 'ave 'til the end of dusk. I'll—"

Robes's words got stuck in translation when the double doors opened and his three children were led in the room with guns to their heads. His two fourteen-year-old twin daughters looked at him with tears running down their faces and fear in their eyes. Gray duct tape covered their mouths and their hands were tied in front of them. They had been stripped naked. Robes's whole body started to hurt at the thought of what had been done to his baby girls. It almost weakened him to his knees.

"Jah bless mi soul," Robes spilled from his lips when he thought of the monster he knew Dante was.

Dante was more feared than respected throughout London. Nobody, not even coppers wanted to be on that nigga's bad side. Only Anika and Phenom were equally revered. Those were the three faces in London you never wanted to see if you had wronged them.

Robes looked to see his fifteen-year-old son's face had been beaten and bloodied. He knew his son was a street warrior so he could figure out that the boy had fought hard not to be taken, but was outnumbered. He too was taped and restrained.

"Get down," Dante ordered.

Robes looked from his children to the sword Dante had leveled at his side. His daughters' loud sobs tore at his insides. The look in his son's eyes begged him not to bow to any man. His son, Deeks, was street like that. He'd die standing before he bowed in humiliation. That was just the way the boy had been wired. Robes had been wired that way too, before drugs. Drugs broke the strongest of men down to the core, down to nothing more than a shell of what they used to be. Drugs had taken his wife from him. Drugs were what had him kneeling before a man named Dante to be beheaded in front of his children. Jah only knew what that nigga Dante would do to his kids afterward. He didn't want to, couldn't stand to see the fright on his kids' faces as they looked on so he closed his eyes.

Dante laughed loudly and then chuckled in a sinister way. "Oh, nigga, you think you 'bout to die, eh?" He laughed again. "You owe me, bruv. You can't give me what's mine if you dead, yeah?"

Robes opened his eyes and looked up at Dante after glancing at his children. He didn't know what that crazy nigga Dante was about to do, but was glad death wasn't in his near future. If only Robes had known that what Dante was about to do would forever be worse than death in his son's eyes, he would have begged for death a lot sooner.

Dante unbuckled his belt and then dropped his pants and underwear to the ground. "You're going to pay me back one way or another and no way you or your kids leaving the dining room until you do."

Robes swallowed then almost threw up at the thought of putting another nigga's dick in his mouth. His face screwed up and defiance swelled in his chest as he shook his head and moved to stand up.

"Nah. Fuck that shit, Dante, bruv. Nigga, you can kill me first before all of that—"

Whatever else Robes was about to say never made it to fruition. Dante's fist connected with his mouth. Robes fell backward spitting up blood. He'd obviously forgotten who the fuck Dante was, where the fuck his pedigree came from. Before Dante's father, Lu, was killed in prison, he thrived on making niggas, the hardest niggas, into bitches in a matter of seconds. Same as on the street. As above, so below. Dante stepped out of his shoes, kicked his pants and underwear off before charging at Robes. Dante's dick swung like a pendulum as he went after Robes. He grabbed the disheveled man by the collars of his robes and punched him over and over again until at least ten of his top and bottom teeth came flying out his mouth. Deeks cringed more at the thought of his father sucking another man's dick than he did at his father dying. He'd rather his father die than go out like that.

There would be no such thing as physically dying for Robes that day but he would die internally and he would be dead in the eyes of his son and one of his daughters. The man they'd known as Daddy, the man who had stolen to feed and clothe them would never be the same man as they'd seen him before. His grunts and groans of pain would never be erased from their minds.

Dante snatched a bloody-faced Robes from the floor of the dining room and made him kneel again. Robes fell back over. Although he had taken a good beating and was weak he could kneel. Yet, there was still no way he would suck another man's dick. He'd rather die. Dante saw this. He could peep the game and knew the man's pride wasn't going to allow him to kneel down and suck dick. Didn't matter to Dante. Somebody was going to pay for his product, with the emphasis on some*body*.

He walked over and snatched Deeks up from the floor. The boy wrestled and tried to jerk away from Dante's grasp. If his hands hadn't been bound he would have swung on that evil nigga. But he couldn't do any of that. He was bound and gagged just as his sisters whose sobs were now louder than they had been before. Dante slung the boy over on the huge, thick wooden table onto his stomach then snatched down the jeans that were already sagging, and boxers that covered the boy's hairy ass. The boy already knew, had already heard that Dante was like those boys in the cells. He'd ass rape a dude just as he would a bitch. The bitches he raped and fucked for pleasure, the niggas for the pain and humiliation it brought them. Although Deeks knew he couldn't get away he still struggled and tried to speak through his taped mouth.

"You or your son, nigga," he told Robes. "Your mouth or your son's asshole. And your daughters got three holes each. Who's paying? You or them, blood?"

The thought of Dante doing something as vicious as sexually assaulting his three children was enough to bring Robes to his knees. Robes prayed to Jah that he wouldn't ever have to see this fate again. It was already breaking him down mentally as he eased up onto his knees. Dante wasted no time dropping his hold on the son and shoving his hung dick into Robes's mouth. Dante was the animal his life and his father had raised him to be. He gave no fucks about anyone except his money and his power. Even as the thought of taking the people out responsible for his brother's death encouraged the rage in the way he mouth fucked Robes, Dante's face never changed. That stoic look stayed planted there. The evil in the eyes of the man never left.

As he tried to choke a now almost toothless Robes with his dick, Robes's son sat with his head bowed in disgust and hate. He didn't know who he was most disgusted with or hated the most, Dante or his father. Robes's eldest twin daughter was feeling the same. She'd never respect her father again for sucking a nigga's dick. For what it was worth, she would have let Dante fuck her in every hole she'd owned not to see her father on his knees like that. When Dante pulled his dick out and shot his semen all over their father's face, all three children simply wished they were in another place and time.

Hours later after Dante had gotten his fill of bloodlust and humiliation in for the day, he sat in the back seat of a steel gray Mercedes as his driver drove him through Hackney. Robes had been dropped off for his whole codes to see. He was naked, bloody, and still had Dante's semen on his face. The madman chuckled in the back of the car at his own lunacy. He thrived on it. Dante had kept the man's daughters but left his son with him in the middle of the street. Robes still had a debt to pay and since he didn't have the money or the product, his daughters would suffice. Dante was sure word around the way had been spread about what Robes had done. Sooner or later his own hood would take care of him for the affront to his manhood.

It was time for Dante to move on to other things. He smoothed the front of his designer black dress slacks and flexed his fists.

"Did you get her location?" he asked his driver.

Dante had laid his cane on the tan leather seat as he leaned over to one side, hand stroking his chin.

The driver nodded and looked at his boss through the rearview mirror. "Yeah, boss. She's in Phenom's code, heavily protected. You ain't getting in or outta that shit without death coming for you."

Dante grunted deep in thought. He'd done some slick shit to get Phenom's and Anika's attention. It had worked, had worked so well that the nigga was willing to negotiate. That made Dante smile a wicked one.

Chapter 1

Ray-Ray

Same day, three hours later

"I'm so happy to see you all right now. Y'all just don't know," I said once we had all gotten back to my flat.

It was my birthday and the best present I could have gotten was Trigga, Big Jake, and Gina. I had thought all them niggas was dead. Gina's voice was a little hoarse because of the injury she had given herself. She still had some visible scars on her chest, legs, and arms, but my girl was alive. I couldn't stop hugging her and crying. Dame had made all our lives a living hell. We had all been chess pieces in his game. He'd killed Trigga's folks, Big Jake's grandma, my parents, and abused Gina like she wasn't even human. Then to think that nigga had somebody shoot Jake in the legs so he wouldn't make it to the NFL was even crazier. I was happy that nigga was dead, but I didn't tell nobody I could still hear him in my head, taunting me.

"Where y'all niggas been for the last three months?" Ghost's little voice rang out. "Trigga you said you wasn't ever gonna leave me. I thought you was dead for a while."

"Told you to trust in a nigga. I always keep my word," he told her, pulling on her thick pigtails. "Niggas got shot up and injured so we had to heal and get right."

"Y'all couldn't call?" I asked.

"Shit was crazy back in the States and we couldn't even leave right away like we planned. Alphabet Boys were all over the place. When we did leave out, we had to head to Nigeria with the African queen, Anika. We had to lay low for a minute. Gina had to heal. She cut herself up good," Trigga explained.

I looked at Gina who had her head lying on Jake's big arm. I knew Alphabet Boys meant the FBI, DEA, ATF, APD and any other law enforcement agency that had taken interest in Dame's empire.

"Then this big nigga got some burns and shit on his back, another bullet in his leg, and one in his back.," he kept going. "We knew you were safe because Phenom had eyes on you."

"Yeah, but outta all that shit, Dame is fucking maggot bait right now," Jake spoke out. "And that alone had a nigga sleeping good at night."

They all laughed at that. I didn't. Dame still tortured me in my dreams. I still couldn't shake the fact that I'd sworn I saw him when me and Ghost were at the park that day. I didn't voice my opinion though. I didn't want to kill the feel good vibe they were in. We all sat around and talked for a good while. From time to time I would glance at Trigga. I realized that I was still scared to look at him all because of the fear Dame had instilled in me. As I stood in the kitchen mixing cherry and grape Kool-Aid, I finally just really looked at him. It was rare he smiled so every time he did my pussy thumped. There was always something about that nigga's smile that got to me. I shook off my infatuation of what I couldn't have and watched them laugh and talk with one another.

Ghost was right in the thick of things, looking on and talking like she was one of us older Misfits. At times I wanted to tell her that she was too young to be talking that way, but I couldn't really. She was just like us. Had been through a lot like us. Both her parents dead just like mine, Trigga's, and Big Jake's. We may as well say both Gina's parents were dead too.

"Li'l shawty, what'chu looking at?" Trigga asked me breaking me out of my thoughts.

"You," I answered before my brains caught up to my mouth.

He stared at me for a long time before he smirked like he was amused. I didn't even realize Ghost, Jake, and Gina had all turned their attention to me because I was caught up in Trigga. I averted my eyes not sure what else to do with them. My cheeks heated up and I still had to wonder if he would be interested in me. That day Dame made me suck his dick and then nut on my face came flashing back in my mind. Why would he even want a girl like me after that?

I finished fixing the drink then took everyone a glass. For three months I had been living on my own like I was an adult and shit was still kind of surreal to me.

"So, now what?" I asked as I sat on the couch next to Trigga.

"What'chu mean?"

I looked at Gina when she asked the question and smiled.

I answered, "I mean what do we do now? All I know is the streets. All we know is the streets. I ain't even finish high school. Don't know if I can."

"You can and you will finish."

I jumped up from the couch when Anika walked through the door. I could have sworn I had locked that shit. My nerves were on edge as I grabbed my gun and aimed it at her by rote. For the past three months I had always kept it near me for easy access. I was used to protecting me and Ghost so it was a natural reaction. She stood in front of me in an all-black cat suit that contoured to the curves of her body. Black combat boots that came to her calves. Her long, braided hair cascaded down her back as that knowing smirk she always carried painted her features. She wasn't fazed by the gun I had aimed at her face.

"How does it feel to have your family back?" she asked calmly. "And put the gun away before you accidently shoot yourself, niece."

Although her words were pleasant, there was something about the way she closed the gap between us that said even if I pulled the trigger it would be me that ended up laid out on the floor. But before that thought could resonate within me, the man I knew as Phenom came through the door and snatched the gun away from me so smoothly I didn't know I had it.

He tossed the gun to Trigga who stood and caught it midair. "Keep this away from her before she accidently shoots herself," he told him.

I glanced back at Trigga who gave a slight head nod like they were all communicating about something I didn't know. Phenom's British accent was rich. The black suit he had on put me in the mind of Idris Elba if he was to ever play James Bond. I could easily see some of Trigga's features in him. He was tall like Trigga but slimmer. Haircut was tapered and lined to perfection and although that nigga was fine, he moved slowly and stealthily like he could kill you quicker than you could blink.

I didn't like how they had just tried to play me. That whole head nod and "get the gun before she shoots herself" thing made me feel inadequate, out of the loop.

"Don't be snatching shit outta my hand," I snapped.

I didn't care who he was. I didn't want to be put back in the mind frame that I had to lie down and take shit from niggas anymore just because they thought they had the upper hand.

Phenom's gaze found me. He didn't flinch. Didn't smile or nothing. I couldn't read that nigga. A look passed between him and Trigga again, pissed me off some more.

"Children shouldn't play with guns unless they are going to use them, Diamond. Is what I'm saying comprehensive to you?"

"Don't talk to me like I'm stupid either."

I may have been a child according to him, but if Anika had been any other nigga, they would have been dead, no questions asked.

"Diamond," Anika called my name softly as she stepped between me and Phenom. "It's okay. We're not the enemy. Phenom is a bit overprotective when it comes to me is all. One day, you'll have a man who will feel the same way about you."

"It's okay, Ray-Ray," Gina said as she stood and took my hand. "We ain't gotta be all angry all the time now and defensive. Dame is dead. We safe now."

I turned to look at Gina. If it hadn't been quiet in the room, we wouldn't have been able to hear her that well. Her voice went in and out mostly. At times she had to clear her throat to speak. I shrugged. I guess she was right though. Wasn't a need for me to be up in arms about anything with Dame dead. Guess I was still paranoid.

"You're not safe," Phenom spoke gruffly.

That nigga's voice carried a lot of bass when he spoke. I didn't even know his whole story, only what I had read in that text that said he was Trigga's uncle and Anika was my aunt. I had so many questions but none came to mind at the moment.

I shook my head. "Huh? Trigga killed Dame. I saw him do it."

"That's why we're here," he continued. "Dame is the least of your worries."

I was still confused and looked to Trigga for some sort of sign that he at least knew what Phenom was talking about. There was a scowl on his face where a smirk had been just a moment earlier.

"Dame has a brother," Trigga stated coolly.

My face frowned. Chest got heavy. "What?"

He repeated. "He has a brother. Here in London."

Ghost had recoiled on the couch. She'd balled her little self up with her knees to her chin, arms wrapped around her legs, like she was trying to disappear. Gina turned to look at Big Jake trying to figure out if someone was playing a joke on us or like me, trying to see if anyone would break out into a smile and tell us they were joking. But there was no smile on Jake's face or Trigga's. I looked at Anika and that all-knowing smirk was gone. Phenom's face was something akin to a frown and looking like he had walked into a room full of decomposing bodies. Everything about what had been said was confusing me. If Dame had a brother who was in London, why the hell would they send me there and leave me all alone for three months?

"If he has a brother here, why y'all send me here by myself?" I asked, voice slightly raised and shaking.

I had asked that to everyone in the room, but my eyes were trained on Trigga. I was two seconds away from slapping that nigga. It was him who had told me to board that plane no matter what. If that nigga Dame had a brother over here, Ghost and I had been in more danger than I had thought. My gaze was unfocused when I looked around the room again. Posture slumped as my neck bent forward. I was feeling like I was about to pass out from exhaustion.

"I didn't know until last week," Trigga voiced like he knew the answer I was looking for.

“Doesn’t matter anyway. I had you protected. All of those niggas you see out there every day protected you and the little one. No one was coming in or out of here without getting past them,” Phenom explained.

That still didn’t make me feel no better. I kept thinking about all the shit that could have happened to me and to Ghost.

“I don’t know them niggas.”

“Doesn’t matter, Diamond. Nothing was going to happen to you,” Anika told me as she stepped forward and laid a hand on my shoulder.

I shrugged it away. “It does fucking matter because if it didn’t none of you would be in here looking and acting like something was about to pop off. So if the shit didn’t matter and nothing was going to fucking happen to me or us then why y’all telling me now that he has a damn brother?”

“Because the rules of the streets are different here in London,” Phenom said. “Dante has done his homework. He’s nothing like his brother. They’re only alike in looks. Dante is wiser, more cold and calculating than Dame was. Dame was a saint compared to Dante. If Dame was a killer then Dante is Hitler. I’ve been watching and waiting to see if he would make a move. I got word he went to the States doing some talking and looking around, finding out things on his own. He wanted to know who offed his demented-ass brother.”

“I don’t care. I don’t care. I don’t care about none of that shit,” I screamed. I was beyond belligerent. “Why am I here? Why did you niggas leave us here?”

“Because it was the safest fucking place for you to be,” Trigga finally spoke up with a little too much bass in his voice. “All you’re thinking about is this nigga retaliating, Ray-Ray. There was other shit that had to be handled. Like our names and faces being shown around. Did you forget that nigga Dame had cops on his payroll? Did you forget they know what the fuck we look like, li'l shawty? Did you not think they were going to question why we weren't found dead or alive? I know you're pissed about being left here alone. Damn, I was pissed when I found out too, but shit is what it is."

As Trigga talked he briskly walked up to me and got in my face forcing me to take a small step back.

"Come on, Ray-Ray. You gotta start using your head. You're no longer the little girl you used to be. You can't get that shit back. It's gone," Phenom added in. "You've had your fun, your relief." He clapped his big hands twice. "It's game time."

"Fun?" I repeated looking between him and Trigga. "You call me being scared shitless for the last three months fun? That shit wasn't fun for me, nigga. Every day I had to live in fear—"

Phenom cut me off, grabbed me by my arm, and started pulling me to the door. It was nothing for him to snatch me up because he was way taller than me and a helluva lot stronger than he looked. I tried to struggle against his hold and was surprised that as soon as we left my flat the outside of the building was lined with Anika's female guards and black males, young and old all armed to the nines, weapons very visible. Some were the dudes I had seen every day since I had been in London. Some were complete strangers. Phenom kept yanking me forward until we got to the parking lot.

It was a gated area, but just outside that gate sat cars lined all up and down the street. Males of all races and nationalities hung out of the windows and stood by the cars. Loud reggae and rap music drowned out my breathing. Baggy jeans, durags, and bandanas were displayed on male bodies. When they saw Phenom emerge from the walkway they all stepped outside of their cars, music was turned off, and it was all hands on deck. At first I thought he was just showing me that he had me surrounded. Thought he was trying to calm my nerves, but it was when the steel gray door opened to the Mercedes that I realized what was going down.

The first thing I saw were the red bottom male dress shoes and the bottom of the black wide-legged dress slacks. Then as the man exiting the car stood at his full height my heart started to hurt. The world and time stood still as I watched in horror. His hair was like Dame's. Skin tone the same color as Dame's. Same height as Dame. Only difference was his build was thicker. Instead of a red cane, the one on his arm was a platinum one. There was a smile on his face that contrasted with the murderous intent in his eyes. A scar was on the right side of his upper lip in the shape of a cross. Just like Dame, he had light eyes and was heaven to look at even to my young eyes. But I knew from experience with his brother that the looks were only to draw you in for the kill.

"Nice of you to bring dinner, Phenom."

When Dame's twin, Dante, open his mouth I swear the air around me chilled. The hairs on the back of my neck and arms stood up. His voice was deep making him sound way more man than Dame could have ever been. His accent was rich and told that he had been in London for a long while. It was a mixture of old world English and Caribbean dialect. Smooth like it could talk you into doing anything he wanted. He kept his eyes on me and in that moment I was back in Dame's control scared to look at another man for fear of what he would do to me. I looked away and down at the ground.

"You're on the wrong side of the codes, Dante," Phenom coolly told him.

"Eh, I am?" Dante shrugged. "And yuh on di wrung side of di war, my man. Where is di boy that murder mi brudda?"

Phenom casually shrugged. "Don't know which you speak of."

"Is that the game we're going to play, bruv?"

"I ain't cha brother, nigga. It is what it is."

"I don't believe in turning the other cheek, Phenom."

"An eye for an eye, Dante."

"Vengeance is mine and that bint yuh holding is mine."

I ain't know what bint meant but I knew I had just been insulted, called out my name.

"Cut the bullshit, yo. You're on the wrong side of the fucking codes. I suggest you pack up your bloody nancy boys and get the fuck off my block, bruv."

Phenom's voice told that he wasn't in the mood for playing games. The way some of his boys hand flanked him with weapons drawn said he wasn't going to tell Dante to leave again. Next time he would show them the way out. Phenom's men and Anika's guard didn't hold their guns like the thugs in the movies. No, their shit was aimed like they were the cops or military. I felt like I was standing in the middle of a movie theater watching a movie while everyone else watched me.

My palms started to sweat, fingers were moving fast because someone else was controlling my nerves. I felt like a puppet whose strings were being pulled every which way but loose. I didn't know why Phenom had dragged me outside for that clearly delusional nigga to see me. I made the mistake of looking directly into Dante's eyes and I swear his straight-faced, unblinking gazed chilled me to the bone. I didn't want this shit again. I thought we were done. Thought this shit was over and there I stood looking at my worst nightmare manifested. Dante's lips eased into an amused smirk as he stared at me dead on.

I hadn't even realized Trigga was standing next to Phenom until he chuckled like something was humorous to him. He stood wide legged with his arms folded across his wide chest, hoodie up over his head. The look on his face was the same it had always been. That nigga was never afraid to die. For some reason that scared me more than knowing Dante knew who we were.

"I didn't come here just to make noise," Dante spoke sternly. "Ah come fa mi just due. What's more important to you? That bitch you holding? The killer of my brother? I hear it's yuh fam, innit? Me and yah fam get real close these days, yeah, bruv?"

Dante stared Phenom down then laughed manically like he knew something that Phenom didn't. I looked over at Phenom and the saw the slight tick in his jaw.

"Yo, son, I don't even know whose fam you're speaking of, bruv," he said then chuckled. "So, once again"—Phenom gave a hand signal and I heard guns click—"get the fuck on or you're about to be fertilizer just like your punk-ass brother, nigga."

Sirens could be heard coming closer, but I didn't have time to think about that. Phenom was pulling me back toward my flat.

"I wanted you to see that this shit wasn't a joke," he growled out at me. "Wanted you to see that the shit was real. This is your life now and you gotta live that shit and play this fucking game to survive. No need to run from that shit until we've wiped out every enemy. If you keep running they keep coming and gunning for you. That nigga will kill you and eat your fucking heart, I swear down, yeah?"

As he talked he lightly shoved me back inside. Gina had sat down on the couch and started rocking back and forth shaking her head.

"I ain't going back to that shit. Never fucking going back so y'all gotta tell me what to do because I ain't going back," she whispered.

She tried to talk louder but it wasn't happening.

"You ready?" Phenom looked at Trigga and asked him. "This nigga is a part of the reason my sister and brother-in-law is dead. I been waiting years to take this nigga out. Started in prison when I popped his pussy-ass daddy. I took a bloody case just to take that nigga out. You did your pops justice with that nigga Dame. Dante is a different breed, which is why he's survived for as long as he has. It's war and it's now. You down?"

Chapter 2

Trigga

Was I down? Clearly he still had a lot to learn about Trigga. The fact that I was there was answer enough.

"If I go make me a mask no one see who boyed off the ting. Run up on man I'll boy off the ting. Hop the railings and boy off the ting. Woyyyy! Make me a mask. No one see who boyed off the ting. Run out the bush and boy off the ting. Your screaming please don't boy off the ting!"

Some new type of music I was jiggin' to blasted all around me as I rode my BMX bike through the borough of Hackney with my skull-printed black hoodie hanging low over my head thinking about how my unk came at me. Like I told that nigga, don't question me about my fucking loyalty, fam or not. Nigga, you new to me. No new friends feel me? We came London to get away from those niggas in the A after lighting that shit up. We didn't come here for some new shit, but I'm a hood nigga and I never back down from a fight. So like I told him, I'd educate myself because I was in a new area, like anyone with brains would do and I did. I bashed some niggas heads in first day I landed in London.

I cut up some palms, faces and stomped niggas, just to see how real this place was. Just by doing that I learned a lot, but shit wasn't always how it was supposed to go. Just like the States, London was on some straight hood shit with parts of it trying to gentrify just like how they did South Chicago or every borough in NYC that rich cats wanted to take over. Shit like that got people mad. Shit like that put people out of homes, works, and community, and shit like that was what bred us Hood Misfits.

Check it, let me hit the rewind and come correct. Three months ago a nigga had planned to die and take down all those who had wronged me and mine, and eventually those who wronged my fam. ENGA was the motto. ENGA was what took down a foul nigga name Dame who thought the world belonged to him simply because he had the power and money to make people bow to his demands. Yeah, fuck that Scarface wannabe nigga because in the end, he was dead and no amount of money and power was going to bring him back..

At the same time though, Jake and I got roughed up mad hard. Niggas came out like roaches, from all levels of the streets and law sweatin' us, trying to take us out. Jake got lead through him, and I got lead in my side, shoulder, and thigh. I had a feeling that shit was going to happen which was why I sought out Phenom. Turned out Phenom was my blood so that shit worked out like heaven, feel me?

Like Sun Tzu said, hit them with annihilation, and then they will survive. Drop them into a KOBK (killed or be killed) situation and then they would do all they could to live. Reason for that was, when we fell into danger, we then aimed for victory. ENGA. That's what happened to us. Wasn't pretty, wasn't simple but the plan did what it was supposed to, and on some real shit, it also revealed more players to the game. That was how my mind worked. For every objective, there was a reason and a countermeasure.

London was my life for now. Figuring out the streets, the codes, the people, and me and my fam's place in it was my MO. That shit included hashing out a new plan to finish up this blood vengeance with this new nigga,

Dante, Dame's older brother. No lie, when my unk hit me with that knowledge, I spazzed out. Like where they do that shit at?

We came out of death, only to get our freedom snatched away again when hitting up London? Fuck my life, feel me? Was a nigga scared? Naw, but a nigga was definitely tired, know what I mean? A nigga was also not feeling that fear that was put into my fam 'cause of that nigga Dame and now his Darth Vadar returning from the dead–looking twin, Dante.I had my last week at the hospital to get my mind wrapped around that Dame had a twin brotherwhere I had sent Diamond and Ghost. I had talks with my uncle who helped me accept that this shit was what it was. Like who would have fucking guessed that the demonic spunk would spread overseas and grow into massive evil? The devil sure as fuck knew what he was doing and was one step ahead of even my own uncle.

Shit got real. Especially when I got to see that nigga. Before stepping to Diamond, letting her know we were alive, Phenom had us checking his endz, where his legit business was and how the gangs were coded in London. When we pulled up outside of Dante's codes, shit got really real for me and took me back. It was like staring Dame in the face all over again, except for that cut on that nigga's upper lip. Seeing him up close like that had my finger itching. Nah, it actually had me squeezing my Glock and aiming to pump lead into him, but Phenom stopped me before I could. Something that would come back to haunt me later.

Afterward, we chilled at his other spot in London's South Kensington Estates residence where he hipped me up on things. I learned that he and my pops, after taking down some OGs on their block to keep the family safe as a whole and get my mom down to ATL, made a code to protect each other always. Phenom headed to

London to get a new life with our Trinidadian family out there, aunts, uncles, and cousins. My pops followed my mom down to the A. Before I was evenborn, they dealt business. Both worked the streets to stop this gang shit, but both kept their hands deep in it at the same time to clock their enemies.

Finding all of that out had me trippin', and everything started making sense with why my pops was gunned down. It wasn't just that my pops still had his hands in the game, but that he was about to pull the plug and get ATL clean. He had some shit, some good shit too, which would have made that truth come to light but then, like a ghost, it was gone with him. Or so I thought, until my unk let me know he knew everything my pops was planning, but it didn't matter then because ATL was too locked up in chaos. Just like London.

Yeah, life was different now. Safe, but not so much. My unk had Diamond and Ghost stashed up pretty fresh. She had her own apartment, or flat as they say out in London. Right next to a barber and beauty shop, that he and the African queen Anika owned in Hackney. She had hands over here too. Her crew ran Brixton, another borough. Every borough had specific crews who ran the codes. So just like back home, you could have niggas claiming game on any street, or block, all in the same borough, or zip code. Every crew had to respect the law, or codes. You step into the wrong spot and your shit was got. That was how Phenom hit me with that, and basically, shit wasn't different at all; we all just spoke with a different lingo.

Back to Anika though: Phenom didn't tell me much about how they hooked up, just that she was his woman. I saw they sported tatted rings, but he said they had a relationship where she did her, and he did him, but at the end of the day they stayed loyal to each other and that he'd kill anyone who fucked with her. Told me she'd do the same and that it was my mom who got them together when they went to Spelman. That was it. So, she was my aunt, but I guess they had some open shit so it was what it was. I guess in this game you had to do shit like that. Because if you both were bosses, you had to use whatever you could to get where you wanted to be.

After that, Big Jake and I spent our time healing and learning Anika's zones in Nigeria, then their spots in Trinidad, Jamaica, Dubai, and back in the States before coming back to London. My unk had Jake and me learning his empire, little by little. I was good with it. I knew Jake and I wanted to keep our shop back in the States and maybe even bring a shop over here. My unk was down for that legit move. So once we got here, he showed me around like I said. Had me watching Diamond and Ghost. Checking out their patterns. That's when I also noticed Dame's brother watching them. He sat on his boundary so I couldn't murk that dude like I wanted. Had to respect the codes.

Now, I was out checkin' the codes while riding bikes with one of my cousins Speedy.

"Oi, Trigga, blood, you feelin' that Tempa T? Suma these dickheads dun know non'ting 'bout dat grime ey? Don't know shit, man, they don't know shit! Chav's coming into our zones trynna spit talk like . . ." Speedy started rapping.

His words came out fast as he hit me with some lyrics to the rhythm of the song I was listening to. But what made that shit funny was how he slowed it, then chopped it up, sounding like a nigga had bumped his head. Words were inserted at wrong times, fucked-up slang used. I found myself cracking up laughing while he rapped with his hands as he rode his bike next to me to a socca beat.

"Fucking tossers man, eedjits!" He shouted to set off folks who looked around our age, walking down the street, smoking joints and huddled up.

On his back was his bulky book bag. Inside were his various forms of hidden shanks. Some in small hand bats, others hidden in pens or books. He sported a fitted that covered his dark brown eyes. He had a crooked nose with a gash over it from it being broken and a wide, dimpled, smirking grin, as if he was always thinking of a fucking joke. I never would have thought this cat was my cousin but he was. Nigga was light bright, almost white. Mixed up he said and that nigga looked it.

Said his mom was Bangladeshi and white, while his pops was Trinidadian. He sported wild long hair that he wore in two braids down his back. Rocked a trimmed goatee only on his chin and even though he was about the gym, he forever kept a piece of candy in his mouth. Sometimes that shit had shanks in it, too.

Nigga was crazy as shit. The fact that he was leaning on his bike, right now, bobbing his head, running a shank against the street, while he spit rhymes let me know that. Dude reminded me of Gina sometimes with how he would spit random things out. But on some real shit, Speedy was mad cool. He was my unk's eyes. My unk had us meet him in Nigeria, so we could learn to trust him. The fact that any nigga was calling me blood didn't mean that they were to me. My unk got that 'cause he knew I still was learning to trust him. Anyway, Speedy was cool as fuck and crazy. Ready to fight anyone and not afraid to die.

The booming laugher of Jake behind us on his bike had me laughing even harder. "Nigga you stupid as fuck," he said as he held his heart laughing, and then pulled out his cell.

"Right, Jake, nigga sitting here flapping at the mouth on swoll sounding like Busta Rhymes after throat surgery and lookin' like a Teenage Mutant Turtle," I laughed out.

Speedy shifted in his seat laughing his ass off. “Fuck off, blood, I swear down I gotta get you two in this London street life music, ’cause wha’ comin’ from the States now is trash.”

Still on his cell, Jake’s shoulders shook with laughter. Looking like a grizzly bear on a too-small bike, I checked him maneuvering it like it was a breeze before singling to us. It was kinda dope that my homie, a nigga who was now officially like blood to me, was sporting a smile. The three months back when we were healing he learned about Gina carrying what could have been his kid. Had fucked him up when she lost that baby, too; on some real shit, had fucked me up too. Dame had literally stomped a baby out of Gina. Both Jake and I almost went back to Atlanta just to piss on his fucking grave. That shit broke my bro down deeply to the point he hadn’t said shit until we got to London. Even when Gina was around, he just held her, got more protective, and only said maybe two things to me.

Now he was speaking and laughing and it was a relief. Nigga was still torn by that but the prospect of having a second chance was giving him hope while he cracked jokes.

“We got some grime niggas back in the States, too, man; don’t forget that shit and I’m feelin’ that Ghett nigga. Straight real shit coming from him. Hey, check it, swing us back around to the crib. Gina hit me up food is ready. A homie is hungry than a motherfucker.”

Covering my face while I laughed, I leaned back and slowed my bike down to ride next to Jake. “Nigga, you stay hungry, even though that shit turns into muscle.”

It was getting late and the sound of our stomachs let us know it was time to eat. Anika was going to cook for us while my unk continued to school Diamond and Ghost on the way we needed to handle things. Shit wasn’t easy for any of us, but none of us had time to gripe or be pussy about it. On some real shit, I was just happy to be away and able to have some peace right now, even though Dante was running in my head.

After circling around the block, we hoisted our bikes up on the bike rack and headed inside. The whole flat smelled like the islands and Nigeria; my stomach was hurting for some food in that moment. As we headed upstairs, I could hear talking. Diamond had been kinda quiet after Phenom had let her know how it was in London. She had sat listening while he and Anika let her and Ghost know that they were going to take up classes soon to finish their education.

They then let us know that we all were considered citizens of both England and America because of some pull Phenom had with changing our records. It helped us out since we were young and needed to work. Dropping my keys at the door, we all spoke to everyone in the spot. Jake quickly went to Gina and pulled her into his arms to kiss her. Speedy dropped on the couch and flipped on the PS3 as I took my unk's hand and clapped shoulders, giving him respect.

"What did you see, nephew?" Phenom asked of me as I stepped back.

With a push of my hoodie to uncover my head and face, I noticed Diamond was standing next to Anika watching everything she was doing. It reminded me of being back at Dame's house when she was checkin' for Anika at the boss table. Same shit was going on now, but it was different. Fam recognized fam and I could tell Diamond was trying to see how to trust her and even my uncle.

"Everything, nothing, and more, unk. Saw my routes to take. Routes to escape through if shit goes down with law or other gangs and saw where we could hide out if we have to. Gained that insight like you wanted," I explained.

"Good; next time you go out, hit up some of the shops so they can learn your face and you can learn theirs. We have a lot . . ."

As we quietly spoke in codes, Diamond came out of the kitchen and came my way. "Trig, hey."

I noticed a note of excitement in her voice and it made me smile when she tried to smooth it over and act like it was nothing. My unk gave a nod letting me know we would finish the talk later and walked into the kitchen. Taking off my Glocks, I set each one down in their usual spot in the living room.

I slid my arm around Diamond's waist as she hugged me. "Sup, li'l shawty. Got the place smelling good even outside. Where's Ghost?"

"'Sleep. Should be up soon. Anika did her hair so she's happy about that. So, what we doing, Trig?" Diamond quickly asked, glancing away and pushing me slightly backward.

Ever since stepping back in she had been asking that and I told her each time that we were going to follow out with the rest of this plan with taking out Dante, before he came for us.

"It's the same shit, Diamond. We doing this, taking care of family. I got the streets down now, and I can show you where to move. Hook you up some crew of your own to take out with you if you go into main London. I got you," I quietly said, checking out how her eyes darted and how she shifted on her feet at times.

"I don't need no new crew. I got y'all. I'm good," she said.

She wasn't trusting no new faces. I could feel her on that. I knew she was still feeling like Dame's ghost could come out at any time because Ghost told me Diamond had bad dreams at night.

"Look, let's just walk up to that nigga and cut his throat or something huh? Do him fast like we did Dame," Diamond rushed out, while holding her arms around herself.

My mouth opened to hit her back with reality but before I could my uncle stepped up to us.

"Young one, check it, if Dante and Dame's mother couldn't handle them and if that nigga Dante could kill his own mother what the fuck do you think you can do guerrilla style? Use this time for peace and educate that brain even more. You're a young queen. Once whose mind is stronger, you will be able to command and take out whoever you want, when you want it, like your aunt. But right now, you have to stop operating in fear."

Stepping in, I nodded, continuing, "Because to live in fear is to be locked in it, which only makes you a bigger target, shawty."

Phenom gave me a nod again and went back to Anika, picking up a knife and standing behind her as he chopped and kissed on her neck.

My gaze focused back on Diamond. She had her hair up in that bun I liked. She wore an oversized shirt that showed her shoulder with tight leggings that looked like she had the Nigerian flag wrapped around her. With the new set of Nikes on, I knew she had gone shopping.

My hands slid in my pockets and I shrugged. "We good?"

"Yeah, I guess so. My bad, just seems like shit isn't real," she quietly explained.

I could get where she was coming from because a lot of times I felt the same way. "Well check it, this is real, and now you get to do some things different. We ain't slinging and I ain't out doing murder. You can decide what you want to do with this life now here, feel me? And you can do you, while me and Jake protect this fam. It's up to you. Me and Jake are going to open up our shop and get to working on that, so you don't have to work much and focus on school," I offered in support.

"Phenom wants us to think about going to college here, so me and Jake are thinking on that shit, but at the same time, we're also handling this street business. We're making this life what it is. I got Ghost to look out for and protect too, get her back in classes and make sure she grows up right too, so see, we got an agenda that can make you feel good yeah?"

While I spoke, I walked up to Diamond where she was toe to toe with me, hoping something in what I said was giving her some strength.

I was about to say something more when Gina stepped up and moved between us to give me a hug. "Trig!" she squealed.

Warmth filled my chest as I held her tight. This girl right there was my heart, my little sister in spirit. It was hard seeing her laid up in the hospital like she was. When she had slit her own throat like she did, she had moved away from our plan and took it in her own hands. It had pissed me off. Baby girl was supposed to drug herself and make it look as if she had ODed not slice her throat. But knowing that she was pregnant, and with the way that Dame had abused her, I guess she did what she thought was best.

So I held her then stepped out of her grasp to grab Speedy's book bag, I opened it and pulled out the Happy Meal box I had got for her and watched her eyes light up.

"Yeah, they got them here too, li'l shawty. Took our bikes to get you something special."

Gina quickly snatched the box out of my hand then tore into it. "You know you're so dope. I love you, Trig."

Big Jake's chuckle behind me had me laughing too, especially when she got up and moved to sit right next to Speedy to annoy him. We all watched as they started up a deep conversation about the game and shanks. He handed her a controller; she took her time in talking and began to murk him in what he was playing.

I felt Diamond stand next to me and it had me thinking. We didn't really talk about everything that went down at Dame's. About how I left her and died basically. I figured girly would be ticked about it, but shit, it was what it was. Every nigga had a sob story and now we had a new one. It wasn't something I was really wanting to get deep into a conversation about but, I knew, I owed her a sorry.

So I took her hand and glanced down at her. "Look, my bad for how that shit went down between us. I had to do what I had to do."

Diamond kept her eyes on Gina, and smiled when Jake sat down next to her and got in on the game.

"Yeah. You got Gina back so it's even," she quietly stated.

The way her voice softly wavered had me thinking otherwise, but I didn't feel like questioning shit, so I left it where it was. Anika's sultry voice chimed around us and I let go of Diamond's hand to go get Ghost so we all could break bread and eat as a new family. Ghost was hyped the moment I woke her up. Baby girl hugged me tight and I let her ride my back as we walked into the living room. She sat on my left and Diamond sat on my right. Gina sat on Diamond's right and Jake sat next to Ghost. Down the table, Phenom sat at the other head of the table, Anika was at his right, and Speedy was at his left.

Like Jake always says, that one supreme being, whoever a person may call it, doesn't make mistakes, and gives you a family sometimes that no man can put asunder. This is mine and that nigga Dante can come for us like he wants, but we always got an advantage, ENGA.

Chapter 3

Ray-Ray

Use this time for peace and educate that brain even more? Was that nigga serious? Like I knew Trig had said that Phenom was his uncle and could be trusted but I wasn't hearing that nigga talking about using this time for peace. Everybody was treating me like I was the weakest link, like I didn't or couldn't have no say in what was going down. Just shut up, Diamond. Do what we say Ray-Ray. But these niggas were from the streets right? Had been in the streets all their lives, right? So they knew there was no motherfucking peace when it came to blood feuds. So why the fuck were they trying to play me? Trigga asked me if we were good and I said yeah just to keep the peace, but no, we weren't good, nigga.

He fucking left me all by my damn self with some fucking psycho nigga looking for me, for us. At first I was happy as hell to see them, thinking that we were going to lay low here for a while and eventually go back to the States. I was cool with that until I saw Dante. Dame and Dante the two most evil names a parent could give their sons in my eyes. Dame was a fucking *Omen* type nigga and I could only imagine that Dante was about to unleash an inferno. I was never going back to that life again. Never. I'd kill myself first.

I guess Trigga and them didn't understand what it was like for me having to endure the kind of shit that I did. Guess they ain't understand what it was like to have someone shoving a dick up in you when you didn't want them to. None of them understood what it was like to have a nigga try to strangle you while raping you. Not one of them knew what it was like to watch your best friend get the same thing done to her, have guns held to your head and knives held to your throat just because that nigga was high or feeling like fucking your day up.

"Why you so quiet, Ray-Ray?"

I looked up and saw Gina walking into my bedroom. I didn't know how long I had been sitting on the bed looking out of the window. Dinner had been good, but it was over and I'd walked into my bedroom just to get a moment to myself.

"Just thinking about shit," I answered.

"Like what?" her hoarse voice asked after she had closed the door and sat down beside me.

"How to kill a nigga."

She grabbed my hand and laid her head on my shoulder. For a while we just sat there and held hands. She hummed as she rocked back and forth.

"I ain't going back to that life ever, Ray-Ray. Never ever going back. So whatever you thinking, I'm down. I had my baby stomped outta me. Losing my baby was worse than the pain of what else happened to me. I ain't ever going back to that shit."

A sad, depressing feeling washed over me as I remembered Dame's big foot crashing down into her stomach. Before Dame was killed, Sasha, another girl who used to work for Dame, set me and Gina up with the help of two other niggas in the house, Pookie and Blackout. Sasha had tricked Gina into believing that Dame had wanted her to take me to the strip club so I could be trained on how to dance. Although something in my gut was telling me some shit was off with it, me and Gina left anyway.

To make a long story short, Dame found us and took us down to the basement, the Underworld. He damn near beat me and Gina to death down there and when he found out Gina was pregnant, he stomped the baby out of her.

"These niggas talking about peace and education. How the fuck am I suppose to focus on that with the threat of this nigga looming over me?"

I didn't even realize my hands had started to shake.

"Shhh. Relax, Ray-Ray. You know Trigga gon' protect us and we got more people who care about us around now. And we both know that we gon' ride or die in this so shit don't matter. It's okay to be scared. I've been scared most of my life," she said as she lifted her head then moved to stand in front of me.

"Yeah, but a bitch tired of being scared, Gina. I wanna live life. I wanna fucking be normal. I wanna go to college and parties like a normal kid. I am a fucking kid. This shit ain't how life was s'posed to be."

My breath caught hard as I realized I had started crying. I was deep into my feelings, I knew that. And I knew that people were going to be telling me to pull it together and think smart, but goddamn it, sometimes I wanted to think dumb like a dumbass kid. Like the dumbass kid I was.

"Shhh, don't cry, Ray-Ray," Gina said softly.

Her soft hands came up to wipe the tears away from my face then she kissed my lips. It was unexpected but I didn't stop her. I'd missed her, I couldn't lie. I knew we weren't in love or no shit, but I did love her. Not like a sister because we'd had sex, but not as deep as a lover because she had Jake. Still, when her tongue parted my lips, I gave in to the sensation she always gave me. Kissing Gina was like an energizer and a tranquilizer all in one. It was nothing for my arms to enclose around her when she straddled my lap and took the kiss deeper. Her hands massaged my scalp as she tugged at my hair. When she moaned out it stirred something in the pit of my stomach and settled between my legs. My moan joined Gina's as we fell back on the bed.

"I missed you," she told me as her hands found my titties underneath my shirt.

My back arched and legs fell open so she could fall between my thighs.

"I missed you too."

My head was a fuzzy memory after that because Gina had taken my shirt and bra off. Her warm mouth and velvety tongue were on my nipples. She took her time with those then she would kiss around the soft parts of my breasts. I'd never had enjoyable sex with a man, but Gina had always given me pleasure. My tights and underwear came off next. She did all of that while tracing a trail of kisses down my flat stomach. When I tried to take her shirt off, she shook her head and stood. I was confused until she smiled lightly and slowly removed her shirt. I could then see why she wanted to do it. I remembered her right titty had been sliced open from being in the Underworld. I could still see that it was healing.

I sat up and moved to sit on the side of the bed, pulling her to stand between my legs. I planted butterfly kisses up and down the still-stitched breast. She hissed a bit then arched forward encouraging me to keep going. My hands found her waist then I slid them around grip her plump ass. Gina's ass was the kind people paid for. It wasn't too big and wasn't too small. It had just the right amount of firmness. I slid her skin-tight jeans over her petite hips and helped her pull them off. My lips kissed her belly button. She still had visible scars there too.

That nigga Dame had done a number on us both mentally and physically, but just like before, we found comfort in one another. When she urged me to lie back and got her on knees, my mind went to Trigga. I couldn't deny I wanted that boy. Wanted him to want me. I remembered the kisses he gave me when we both lay on that dead nigga's bed. The way he moved his hips like we were fucking gave me chills. And when Gina's lips kissed my pussy, it was Trigga's name that almost escaped my mouth.

"We're about to make a run to the Bricks," I heard Phenom saying as me and Gina walked from my room.

We were holding hands. Our sexing had gone from the bed to the shower. Big Jake's eyes found mine. The way he looked from me to Gina then to our intertwined hands and grunted low told me knew we did more than talk. I didn't even really think about how he would feel with me and Gina sharing that kind of intimacy. Before I knew about her and Big Jake I was used to us touching, kissing, and sexing one another. Didn't know how to stop or if I should. I saw Trigga leaning against the wall, but looking at him would only anger me so I kept my eyes on Anika and Phenom.

"Ghost, put ya headphones on," Trigga said before Phenom continued to talk.

Ghost jumped up from the couch. "But I want to hear what he's saying and I want to go where y'all going."

Trigga stood straight up. There was no emotion on his face and his mood was undetectable. "Put ya headphones on, Chas. This wasn't a debate."

Normally when I told Ghost to do something or called her by her name she would fight me or argue me down until she got at least part of what she wanted, but with little to no fuss she plopped back down on the sofa in a huff and slammed her headphones on.

"'Preciate it. Now volume up," he told her again.

Next thing I heard was the faint sound of some song about pumped-up kicks and kids running from a bullet.

Phenom started talking again. “We’re headed to the Bricks. That’s my woman’s side of town, son. We gotta pick up some shit. Drop some shit off, eh? We in and we out. I don’t really fuck with the Jamaicans like that since they started dealing with that dickhead Dante, too. So this is my last shipment with them.”

“You guys can tag along see and hear what goes down and how it goes down. These Jamaican nutters nothing like in the States. These niggas don’t come equipped with nothing but evil intentions. Remember that going in. Don’t trust nothing you see,” Anika added.

“So, we’re not really using this time for peace?” I asked sarcastically. “It was just some bullshit to pacify me with, basically?”

Phenom cut his eyes at me and placed his gun away so quick it was like he never even had one. His long black trench coat matched Anika’s as they both were dressed in all black. They had turned my flat into a situation room for the time being. The way he looked at Trigga then nodded his head back in my direction telling him to “handle that” pissed me off even more.

Anika stepped in front of me as Phenom walked out the door. “Listen to me: that attitude you got, niece, use it in the streets against the enemy who will be coming for you, yeah? Don’t toss that shit at him, me, or anyone else in this house. You got some shit to get off your chest, I really don’t give a fuck right now,” she said stepping closer until we were face to face. “Nobody got time for your childish pettiness now. Get in the game or stay the fuck back because you’ll only be in the way.” With that she turned and headed for the door behind the man she called her husband.

“Well the fuck y’all want me to do? Be at peace or get in the fucking game?” I yelled.

But it was to no one because she was gone. I looked around the room a little embarrassed at being snapped at and more ashamed that I was feeling like I was about to lose my mind. Jake brushed by me next. I could have sworn he did that purposely. I looked up at Trigga as he walked toward the door.

"We'll talk later," was all he said as he walked out. He stopped as he stepped out the door and look back. "Move ya ass, li'l shawty. Let's go."

I looked at Ghost who was sitting looking like she was about to cry.

"What about Ghost?"

"I'm staying here," Gina said. "I can't really do shit in the street 'cause I'm still fucked up, but I can stay here and bust a cap in any nigga who steps in here and he ain't supposed to be."

"And Speedy gon' be posted outside, so they good," Trigga added.

With that said, I followed Trigga out the door. We all piled into a black Hummer and made the drive over to Brixton, which was no more than ten minutes away. Really, the streets of Hackney were no different than the streets of Bankhead or Godby Road in Atlanta to me. In some places trash littered the streets. Young boys, black and brown mostly, walked around with their pants off their asses. Chicks who looked to be no more than teenagers giggled and cackled as they hung around sets trying to claim a spot as the main bitch. Shit was no different. I really didn't feel safe with night falling. Especially when we pulled into a back alley that led down to an empty set of garages. The garages took up the whole back alley. Heavy island reggae blasted. I was surprised any of the men could hear as they all talked to one another.

"You ready to die?" Phenom asked when the Hummer stopped. "Because these niggas in here wake up every day ready to die. You gotta wanna die more than you wanna live to survive these streets, yeah."

"Since linking with Dante these motherfuckers done cock up my money and my product. They turncoats and I don't do turncoats no matter who they are," Anika said.

"Then they tell tales that be fulla loads of bullocks. Now we take the blighters out. So again, who's ready to die?" Phenom asked again.

He was talking to everybody and none of us at the same time. I had no idea what some of the words he was saying meant at times, but I guess it was just something else for me to learn.

"How many units we getting today?" Trigga asked.

"Fuck the units, nephew."

"I meant of blood, nigga. How many units of blood?"

Trigga had zipped his hood to cover half of his face. The crazy side of that nigga was back. I knew he was on that bullshit earlier. There was nothing but the look of death in that nigga's eyes. Big Jake was chuckling in the back as I heard his gun click. Anika was the first to step from the truck. I noticed she was quiet and I was wondering why they were going to let her walk into that place alone. About six or so dingy-looking dirty dread heads stood there waiting for my aunt. What tripped me out was the one with red dreads standing off to the left like he didn't want to be seen.

"Y'all gon' let her walk in there by herself?" I asked in total disbelief.

"It's her work and her units, eh? Mi gyal can hold down she self. She no bombaclat," Phenom spat out as he watched.

Anytime the Caribbean in him came out, I had to wonder if Trigga could speak that way too. Phenom could talk that shit all he wanted but I saw the way his hand gripped the steering wheel and the way he took long pulls of the gonga cigarette he was puffing. *Fuck that,* I thought. I already had on a trench; I grabbed the Mac 10 in the black duffle bag on the floor of the truck and jump out. I knew it was a Mac 10 because Jake and Trigga had been talking about the beauty of it on the way over. Trigga wasn't fast enough to stop me. For the first time, I caught him off guard. Although I ain't really know her, she was the closest to my mama I would ever get again. So I needed her to come out alive. I still had a lot of shit I needed answers to. Now, for the life of me I didn't really know anything about pulling the trigger on that gun, but I was gon' learn that day. I slowly walked up and flanked her. I couldn't lie; I was so scared my pussy was trembling.

"Aneeka, yuh brang me young gyal fa di ramping shop, yeah?" one of the Jamaicans taunted.

My aunt didn't break a sweat as the Beenie Man–looking nigga kept eyeing me up and down.

"I ain't bring you shit. Where is my money, Pras?"

The dreaded man gave a hearty laugh. "We 'ave fi tek a trip inside di shop, eh? Yur money's dere."

"Bring my money here. Bring my money now. I won't say it again."

"Why so hostile, gyal? We no fi do business anymore?"

Anika pulled two machetes from her sides so smoothly that all could be heard was the swish in which they sang against the air. Because I didn't know what else to do and instinct had me in fight or flight mode, I drew the gun that I wasn't even sure I knew how to fire. That shit didn't have time to register though. All I heard was a loud male yelp and then a black ashy hand hit the concrete.

"Ahh, bruv, this bitch is crazy. She cut my fucking hand off," a boy cried from the corner.

He dropped down hard to his knees yelping. His face was screwy, turned upward as his eyes shut tight and his breathing got rampant. Anika then rushed forward, hopped on the top of the small table that sat between us and the men.

"I won't say another fucking time to get my money." She leveled the bloody machete at Pras's neck. "Where is my dough?"

"Irie, irie," he said with his hands up in the air. "Dante—"

As soon as the name Dante left his mouth my aunt kicked him square in the face her thick army boots drawing blood. When his body fell back, she jumped from the table, and stalked him until he hit the ground. Guns cocked around us. One was leveled at my head. The rest trained on Anika as she stood over the Jamaican Lord ready to end him. My gun was snatched from my hands. The nigga's gun that was at the base of my skull also had his hot breath on my neck and his dick pressed against my ass.

"Preety gyal like yuh should be coming fi mi ramping shop, eh. So say when we finish off di rogue bitch yuh and me have us a lit'ul fun?" he said against my ear, the British accent mixed with his Jamaican one making his spittle fly into my ear.

I didn't know what the fuck a ramping shop was, but I knew I wasn't about to be taken anywhere else against my will. That was what had me swinging my hand back and grabbing a handful of that nigga's nuts. When he bowed forward I elbowed him hard enough to back him up off of me. He dropped his gun and mine. The Mac 10 slid across the way but as I rushed for his gun he grabbed my foot, tripping me. I hit the ground hard almost slamming my chin against the pavement. I heard another male yell; gunfire had me recoiling then fear made me use my Nike-clad feet to kick the redheaded dread square in the face again. My aunt's grunts could be heard as I used my elbows to crawl backward. I continued to kick at the man trying to get control of my feet again. Red the Dread fell back, but I could see him reaching in his pants for another gun. I frantically turned and grabbed the butt of his 9 mm Sig Sauer. I didn't even blink when I turned around and fired. My aim had never been perfect but I shot that nigga square between the eyes just as he was aiming at me.

His blood splattered in my face as he fell forward and almost landed on me. I squealed and jumped up. Heart thumping and breathing rampant, my vision went toward the Hummer wondering where Trigga and them niggas were, then back to my Anika who had just finished hacking a nigga until all he looked like was carved turkey. She was covered in blood with a scowl on her face. I briskly walked toward her to see she had cut off both Pras's hands. She moved from the nigga she had just carved up and then stood wide legged over Pras with her machete aimed at his face.

"I know you told Dante about my shipment." When she spoke her voice was calm as if she was talking to a friend, like she hadn't just cut up about five niggas.

"I swear down, mi told no one about ah ting, yeah," Pras pleaded.

"You lying to me, Pras. I told you when I found out you started doing business with that nigga on my turf that I was coming for you."

Pras was sweating and trembling. "I swear down! Dante tell me you and Phenom about fi be making moves wit di Jews in Hackney near Springhill Park, yuh? He telling all di boroughs wit di blacks that yuh bout fi be teking money elsewhere, yeah? So mi tink about mi family and started doing business where mi money stay flowing. Was never meaning to turn on yuh."

"And where is Chyna?"

"Mi dun know. Mi swear down, eh. Dante tek her away from here when him heard you be buk."

I didn't expect my aunt to look at me and ask, "What would you do?"

"Kill him," I answered without thought.

Anybody batting for Dante's team was any enemy of the ENGA state. We all had motherfucking agendas and mine was to stay alive. Fuck what Phenom was talking about wanting to die more than the next nigga. I wanted to live. I didn't know who Chyna was and didn't care to know. Whoever she was must have been close to my aunt because water rimmed her eyes.

Pras started pleading as he used his bloody elbows to try to back away. "Don't kill mi, Anika. Mi help yuh find Chyna."

"You been knowing where she was and you ain't ever said shit before now."

Without blinking, Anika raised the blade and brought down square between Pras's eyes. His wig split open like a melon. She yanked the machete out and turned to walk away. For a moment all I could do was stand there and look at the man who used to be Pras. That nigga had died with his eyes open. That pleading look was still in them. I finally turned and jogged to catch up with my aunt. Just like before I knew who she was, when I was under Dame's lock and key, I was amazed and awed.

As we walked back to the Hummer, my heart thumped so hard against my chest I felt like I was having a heart attack. My throat swelled like I was becoming short of breath. It was the same overwhelming feeling I had when I smashed that nigga, Pookie's, brains in. Once we got to the truck, all the contents of my stomach came rumbling out.

Anika snatched the driver side door to the Hummer open and hopped in. I took my bloody shirt off and wiped the rest of the vomit from my mouth then climbed in the back expecting to see Trigga, Jake, and Phenom, but they weren't there. I panicked when Anika cranked the truck.

"Wait, where Trigga and them?" I asked.

"They'll meet us back at the flat," was all she said as pulled off.

We rode in silence. No words passing between the two of us for a moment.

"Who's Chyna?" I finally asked.

She glanced at me. "Nobody."

I could tell that was all I would get out of her on that subject, so I left it alone.

"You did damn good back there," she then said.

"Thanks."

That was the gist of our conversation as we pulled in the parking lot. Nightfall was upon us. The hair still stood on the back of my neck. Maybe that was the reason I exited the truck with a bat in my hand. I grabbed it from the back seat as soon as we stopped. I found that anytime I killed somebody with a gun or knife, it sickened me. Still, I grabbed another 9 mm anyway. Then stuffed a small shank into my bra. Fuck dying. I wanted to live. Nobody was going to take my life away from me anymore.

Chapter 4

Trigga

Diamond's words played in my mind while chaos popped off around me. It had the night air feeling like electricity and the fine hairs on my forearms stood on end. Phenom and me had watched Anika and Diamond disappear into the darkness of these British Jamaicans' spot. It was tripping me out how she was popping off at the mouth. Just yacking. Shit was starting to piss me off. Be mad and shit, but fuck. Me, Jake, Gina, and Ghost, ain't Dame. Naw, scratch that, 'cause her anger felt like it was pointed at me. I wasn't Dame. I ain't did shit but bring her in this and protect her ass and she popping off all foul. A nigga ain't a fucking psychic. A nigga can only guestimate the future and flip it to a nigga's need. That's it. Fuck the rah-rah.

I wasn't down with the shit she said. I wasn't bullshitting. People live every day in the streets, ducking from bullets, but they're still able to find a touch of peace, that's all a nigga was meaning. Shit was deep but don't fucking get in the way of what the fuck a nigga was doing, why? Because now, she was becoming a liability and that shit wasn't cool.

Never give niggas ammo to use against you, period. That was an old-school rule, one Dame tried to use against me, but shit didn't work out in his favor. Now, I had to get back to doing me because if I slipped up, that meant I was weak and could get played, which I wasn't about to let happen, or let that nigga Dante get a sniff of. So, fuck the bullshit; back to the agenda. A nigga was not about to let pussy drive him crazy, especially since I ain't ever hit.

The Bricks, I had learned, was a hot zone, kinda like the Southside of Chicago, or Watts or the Trap. Peeps of all ages and colors were running the streets. Some hood, some not, but mainly thugs was strumming the streets. From my perspective, it made sense to run business in this hood if you were on some criminal shit. Was a lot of people to manipulate, and a lot of ways to get people to run your dirty shit.

So, there we were for my unk's woman. We had waited only about five minutes before we jumped out the whip. My unk wrapped barb wire over his leather fingerless black gloves while shifting his shotgun against his back. Jake checked for his Glock and two metal pipe rods he had strapped against his back. Me, I had my Glocks with two silencers. The hit of weed with the scent of food filled the air while I sat on top of the roof of the restaurant building next to the Jamaicans' spot. Music thumped and I watched my unk blend into the darkness.

Ever since we had gotten to London, I saw a change in my uncle. Nigga was more tense and on edge. That cool and collected business owner back in the A seemed to slip slightly away. Shit, the same was with Anika too. They probably didn't think I could catch that vibe but I did and it had me feeling like this shit was deeper than a blood feud, that there was another agenda going down. Either way it went, a nigga was just here to be done with the bullshit, and get some kills.

Checking on the numbers that were down below, I could see that killing these goons was going to be simple from the outside. Crouching on the ledge of the building,

I smirked when I saw one of the Jamaicans look up at me. Nigga stood there looking forever. Smoke circled him like a dancer, his matted chunky locs stuck up in the air like nigga needed dryer sheets pressed against him as he shifted on his feet digging his hands in his pockets. From where I sat I could tell that he wasn't sure what he was looking at and how I sat had it looking as if I was nothing but a part of the roof. So, I was chill. I watched him watch me watch him, until a silver BMW rode up. Turning, nigga threw his blunt to the ground, curiously looked back up at me while stepping closer to get a better look then shoved it off.

He walked right past where Jake was hiding. Nigga must have had glaucoma or some shit because he was a fucked-up watcher. Or he was on that good shit. Little Kevin Hart with locs–looking cat gave a chin up to his homies, one who called him Ditz. Ditz moved at a clearer angle for me and I focused my Glock while I waited.

For whatever reason I always had a good sense of hearing and in that moment, it was coming into use. I could see Jake hiding and I signaled for him to remember faces while I listened. The spike loc'd-up cat walked to the car and greeted the person who stepped out of it. Dressed in a gray trench coat, this dude tucked his shades away and crossed his arms over his slightly muscled chest. Something about him had me feeling that he was five-o or whatever the Brits called cops. I knew my intuition had been right when he moved his trench back to show his Glocks and badge.

Shifting where I sat, I listened as this Iron Man–looking dude asked Ditz if he had his payment I had to assume.

"You pricks tryin' to shive me. Eee?" he asked Ditz.

The rude-ass busta turned to the side with a loud snort before spitting on the ground then snapped his fingers and pointing in the Jamaican's face with a stretched-out finger. I swear some niggas were extra. Let that had been me and that fool would have been dead. Nigga, I don't know where your hands been.

Anyway, this cocky bastard continued poppin' off at the mouth as Ditz kept his eyes on that finger while dude drawled low in a thick British accent, "Cor! Listen, I don't like waitin', an' you and yours 'ave had me waitin' for months, dim."

The end of a steel Glock pressed into the rude cop's chest; both men stared each other down before the Jamaican spoke up. "Now yuh don't be wanting to do that eh? Get irie with all that and remember that we got yuh gen. We run dis shit, not yuh. Now mi man dun said to check yuh spot tomorrow. It will be dere, bruv, on mi word. Swear down, yah."

Malicious laughter from the other guy had Ditz stepping back before a bullet went straight into his skull. My eyebrow rose up when I saw that shit; nigga dropped a card on Ditz's dead chest then hopped in his ride pulling out his cell speaking loud as he shouted on his cell while leaning out his window while other Jamaicans came out.

"On your word, mate? You act arse about face and you get done proper. Like I said, don't fuck with my stuff. Get me my boon, or the protection is done. Your note is . . ." With that, that nigga drove off and I didn't hear anymore.

A crowd of those goons spilled out in the small alley like roaches. The scene below was interesting as fuck, something I tucked into the back of my mind. For now, I had other shit to handle and get down to. Quickly aiming my gun, I shot off clean rounds. Jake stepped out to use his pipe, sending it into the stomach of approaching goons. I knew Phenom was already inside handling business because the sound of nigga's screams spilling out from the opened back door.

Shifting onto my feet, I stepped back, ran forward, then jumped off the roof onto their main rooftop in a roll. Bouncing back up, I kept sprinting until I got to the roof's ledge where I swung down to scale the side of the building and land on the ground. Phenom had told Jake and me to take the stash of money that they had taken from Anika. So that was what we did. Ducking reaching niggas, I let them know I was a different type of thug as they whipped out their homemade shanks.

My fist found the face of a Rasta horse-looking dude. His bucking teeth almost scraped my fist but I shifted my stance and sent my elbow into his temple stunning him. The tip of his shank tried to slice at me, but I was too quick. I leaped back then shifted behind him to sharply pull his neck back toward me, folding him back in an arch until I left his neck exposed and gripped his shank-fisted hand.

Snatching it up, I connected metal to his jugular, piercing it and watching blood gush out like a sputtering geyser. The high-pitch yell he gave had me almost dropping him and looking sideways at him. Yo, I wasn't ready for that soprano sharp scream he gave. Dude looked like he'd have some bass, but yo. Anyway, because of that, I twisted his shank from his hand and sent it slicing into him like a Thanksgiving turkey, before pushing him into a wall.

Thumbing my nose, I laughed when I saw a white guy with thick caterpillars of locs rush toward me sporting a bat with a machete in it. I kind of liked that shit, so I made a note to cop it once I had his head on a post. Cocky I never was. Clever and assured of what I was going to do was who I was. So, it was nothing to me to let that nigga body block me. The purpose of that was to get close enough to send my knife into his ribcage, which I did. I twisted it deep into his side, where the quickness of it had him staring at me with shock before hitting me with his fisted hand. Pain ripped through my skull but I bit down hard, and kept my balance turning to slam his head into the side of a brick wall. Teeth and brick dust went everywhere with trickles of blood.

Sweat dripped from down my hooded face. My heart was pumping in overdrive. Though I wasn't a big dude like Jake, I still had muscle and could handle my shit, like using my speed then relying on my power and strength. Like now, my fist rested on the pavement of the street holding the bat I had taken from the cat I had just taken down. It was batter up and the goon who was rushing me down, his chin met the end of the bat.

Velocity had me holding tight as the blades sliced through that nigga's chin. I rammed him, dug in my pocket quickly to bring out my keychain blades made by Speedy and I finished the job. My blades tucked between each finger were now coated in blood. Hair from that dude's long beard went flying and my Glock finished the rest, walking away at the sound of his gurgled hiss falling to the ground.

More guttural grunts sounded around me and I saw Jake body slamming dudes. Though he got shot up in his legs and it missed paralyzing him, for some reason, it seemed like it only helped him move better. Jake's thick, muscled arm jolted outward to snatch a passing Jamaican by his throat. We both locked eyes on each other as he squeezed.

"What you see, man?" I asked.

The struggling grunt of the dude Jake held had Jake's face contorted while he squeezed. A vein popped from his forehead as he bore his teeth like a pitbull under stress. "Got that punk's numbers from his plate. The card I kept there . . ."

Pushing my locs out of my face and tucking them back in my hood, I nodded so Jake could know I was still listening. "What it say?"

"Shit, this nigga is a fighter, hmph," Jake hissed and kept squeezing until he heard a snap then pop and the goon he held stopped his struggle. "Had cash amounts on it and just the letters S.B., whatever that shit means."

Dropping that dude, Jake paused to breathe for a moment then wiped a hand down his glossy face. While slightly bent with my hands on my thighs, I noticed out the corner of my eye at the same time as him another enemy coming our way. Tiredly, Jake reached behind him, pulled a pipe, and threw it at that cat, as I hoisted my Glock and let off a round. One round between the eyes, and a pipe in his head killed him in mid-run and we kept on talking.

"Dude looked and smelled like five-o or a business dude with a fake badge, what you think?" I asked.

Jake tilted his head to the side and paused thinking before hitting me with knowledge. "Nah, not a business dude because at my angle I got to see that nigga's badge. It was real. He flashed it too hard for it not to be. Nigga was really feeling himself before taking down little Mikey or whatever that fool's name was."

Scowling as I thought. I wondered what the fuck was up. So the Jamaicans had a cop in their pockets? It had me wondering if Anika or Phenom knew what was up.

"A'ight, man, that's business, let's break, and finish this shit," I said while pounding fist with Jake giving him dap.

He adjusted the black bandana mask he wore around his mouth then disappeared around the corner heading toward the ride.

My back covered thanks to Jake, niggas pushing up daisies at my feet, I pulled out my Glocks and walked into the back office. Light washed the whole room, causing me to blink for a second before seeing blood and more bodies everywhere. To my left was a corpse who lay against a pillar. The pillar I could see through the gaping hole in his stomach.

Phenom was nowhere to be found but his art was everywhere, so I took the time to retrace his tracks and look for the safe box. Bloodied papers stuck to my feet while I cautiously walked through. It looked like the Jamaicans were on that drug shit, but from what I was seeing as I crouched low to see their notes, they had units growing in something marked S.B. BONDS. Whatever that shit was. The only reason I was tripping off of it was because Jake had just mentioned that S.B was on that nigga's calling card and second because it was serious ducats on the papers. Since Anika had her ducats ripped from her, she just might be interested in returning the favor and taking these bonds, so I snatched up the notes and tucked them in my jeans.

A sharp whistle from outside let me know Jake had it covered, and a second had me following it into another room where my uncle stood. A huge bank safe stared me in my face, framing the wide-legged gait of my unk. Blood dripped from his barbwire-gripped hands onto the linoleum gray floor as his shoulders rose up and down. Getting closer, I saw it was empty. Powder covered the floor, random dollars lay around, but the bulk of it was gone.

"They cleared shit out," he greeted me once I got closer.

The tone in his voice was that of a man who lost something greater than money and it had questions forming in my dome.

"A'ight, so let's bounce. I got more bodies to take down and Jake is still in the alley," I told him as I pushed at a desk and looked through it for whatever I could.

"I don't like being fucked with. See, that's that kinda shit that makes what they thought was fucked up even worse, nephew," Phenom growled low.

Something in how he said that had me glancing up for a moment. My unk looked like he was on one. I noticed in his other hand that he had a black USB flash drive and I wondered what that shit was for or came from because all the computers here looked like they came from back in the old days.

"Whaddup with that, fam?" I asked as I walked up to him to see just how fucking crazy this nigga was.

Maybe the apple really didn't fall that far from the tree. The barbwire move was pretty dope, one I planned to use myself since working with my hands was more so my vibe.

Phenom tossed me the drive, stalking away from the huge bank safe. "Part of the game. The second in command had it on him as I ripped that nigga's head off from his shoulder. I know you good with tech shit, so it's time you show me how good you are with it. I'm not even going to call my own team because I want to see you work, nephew. So check that shit out and show me what you find out a'ight?"

My mouth opened to ask him how he even knew that I could work some tech shit. Damn, not everyone knew that and Dame wasn't even hyped on the fact that I could hack some shit sometimes. I wasn't the best, but it was something I learned back when I was going through foster homes. Used to jack phones, reprogram them, and sell 'em back to other kids. Then I used to take over the computers at school just because I was bored and wanted to play around. But the fact that Phenom knew had me tripping on how long he really had been watching me.

Stuffing the flash drive, I walked up to my uncle studying him from under my hoodie. My eyes narrowed and I fisted my own hands, standing at my full height while I addressed him.

"A'ight, but check it, this shit ain't really about money is it? I know it's not so come correct. I'm your blood and I guess your right hand and shit but this ain't about to be some Dame shit again trust. I got a stake in this shit too so don't fucking use a nigga just because I'm young."

His low chuckle surrounded me as he pushed me to the side. "We'll speak on that shit later, just trust in an OG a'ight? Now get ya body count."

The sound of feet approaching had me realizing what was about to go down, as I went sliding into a nearby wall. Quickly maneuvering around, my Glocks came out with a swiftness. Bullets ejected from their barrels while opposing bullets came my way causing me to duck down.

In front of me lay a broken table, so I reached for it, used it as a shield then threw it at a group of renegade Rastafarians while shouting out, "A'ight, I got you!"

I realized music was still thumping and it had me suddenly hype as fuck. Phenom was in front of me, landing blows to niggas' heads. Every Rasta who came into the room was of different shades and hues, which tripped me out. London was very eclectic and it seemed that sometimes with these thugs, color came second unless they were out-and-about racist skinheads or some crap, but even with that I heard they had other races in it sometimes, too. Shit was rainbow over here, but I didn't give a damn at all, because my Glock, blades, and bat never discriminated.

Moving from where I sat, I ran forward and worked up some cats getting bashy at the tune of the music thumping with a sardonic expression on my face. Phenom threw a nigga my way and I took that bat and let the blade slash his side open. Blood and pieces of skin, clothing, and guts burst out to hang like a backpack. Nigga was so dazed that he slipped on his own blood, fell backward, and cracked his own neck. My uncle gave off a laugh that sounded like me then brushed his coat off and stepped over dude.

He hunkered down low with a glowering stare, moved back and forth as if he was dancing then sent his leg straightforward, swiping upward then down on the neck of another goon. I watched that dude jerk back then try to hit my uncle with a left and right hook, holding a blade in hand, and miss. Phenom quickly moved to his side. He stopped his hits and just stood there, letting that guy slice him across his chest before he countered back and grabbed the goon by his neck. He lifted in him the air with a loud growl then slammed him down into an exposed pole.

“Damn!” I said as my uncle’s aggressiveness distracted me for a moment. I had no idea that nigga was that strong but he was.

“Dodgy bloodclaat nigga’s are neva to be trusted you know that. These rassholes turned coat on mi woman. Did her dirty, so I’m making sure to remind ’em not to fuck with my power. Chaos law,” Phenom growled, his British accent fusing with his NYC and the island. It sounded crazy as fuck but it was dope.

What had me respecting what he said even more outside of living what he had just said was that he calmly cleaned off his coat with one of the dead cats in front of him, and then coolly strolled out of the room. Dude was reminding me of my pops and once we talked, and we got level with this, I figured that he could be one nigga I trusted. Moving around the back office, I signaled to Phenom that it was clear, noticing that his eyes was still scanning the office. Something had that dude’s focus for real but that talk would be later. For now, it was time to roll the fuck out.

I didn't have time to be played and now that my interest was in this cop dude, the shit that the Jamaicans had going down, and taking Dante's life, new plans were formulating. I was banking on a lot of heads rolling after all this shit finished. Just how I liked it.

Chapter 5

Ray-Ray

I was sweating, running through some unknown part of London. I was barefoot and naked. Headlights behind me lit up the path to run. I had to get away. Needed to get away. He was not going to get me again.

"Aww, come on, my Diamond. Don't make me chase you," Dame called out behind me.

I started crying harder, running faster. Tears blinded me. Glass and the broken road cut up my feet.

"Di gyal got speed, brudda. She fi mek me lots of pounds, eh? Yuh kill mi brudda, bitch, and now I kill you, but not before mi tek back what'chu owe."

That was Dante. His voice chilled me. It frightened me more than Dame's because I didn't know what he was capable of. I kept running but it felt like I was going nowhere. Felt like I was stuck in place. I started screaming frantically. Looking behind me caused me to trip over my feet and I hit the ground hard. I tried to crawl away but couldn't. Something was holding me down. When I looked back up, Dame and Dante were standing over me. Two devils with the same face, one with the shape of a cross above his lip from a scar. I couldn't even talk. All that would come from me were the screams that I had become so used to. Both men were dressed in white suits, only Dame's wounds had bloodied his. The beating that Trigga had given had his face drenched in blood, too.

Both of them had those canes in their hands and brought them down to start beating me. The pain was unbearable. Felt as if once again, my skin was being pulled off with each hit. I felt bones breaking in my fingers as I held my hand up and tried to lessen the blows, but they kept coming. Fear had me panicking, and I made the mistake of using my legs to kick. Dante grabbed my feet, unhinged his cane, pulling out a shiny silver sword. My scream got stuck in my throat when he brought it down and severed my foot. The pain was crippling. My whole body heated up like I was feverish. Slobber hung from my lips as my tongue felt like it had swollen and was choking me. That nigga laughed with a guttural growl that told me he wasn't finished. He yanked me closer to him then, spread my legs as far as they could go and then some. Felt as if I had tried to do a split and couldn't but was forced down to the ground anyway. The shit hurt so badly that I didn't even realize he was about to shove his sword clear up my pussy.

"Payback's a bitch, my Diamond," Dame said as he grabbed my throat and placed a gun against the temple of my head. "And then you die, bitch."

That was all I heard before the heat of the lead split my skull and the sword rip my pussy from the inside out. I was trying to breathe, trying to fight, trying to scream, but I was only chocking on my own blood. More hands grappled at me. I didn't know where the strength came from but I was trying to fight back too.

"Diamond," a male voice rang out.

I kept screaming and swinging. My nails clawed at his face.

"Ray-Ray! Wake the fuck up, li'l shawty."

"Get off of me," I yelled out.

I heard feet running toward me. It wasn't until the male picked me up and I melted into his hold that I became lucid enough to realize I had been having one of my famous nightmares. When I came to, Ghost and Gina were standing at my bedroom door while Trigga had gripped me in a bear hug from behind as he dragged me out the bed.

"Wake up and calm the fuck down," he growled against my ear.

I finally took a deep breath and realized I was home in my flat and that I was safe.

"Diamond, you okay?" Ghost asked me.

I caught my breath and nodded. "Yeah."

"You sure?"

"Yes, Ghost. I'm fine. Now just leave me alone for a minute, okay?" I snapped at her.

I hadn't meant to. Ghost looked like her feelings had been hurt by my tone of voice. She looked from me to Trigga. I guess she was trying to understand why I had snapped at her. I didn't even know myself.

"Gina, take Chas to the front for a minute," Trigga said from behind me.

Gina averted her eyes like even she was embarrassed to see me in the state I was in. But she took Ghost's hand and did what Trigga had asked of her. When the door closed, Trigga lifted me from the floor and tossed me on the bed. I bounced clumsily but didn't have time to focus because he had moved as slick as a panther and caged me between his arms on the bed. It was then that I could see the scratches I'd given him to the face. And I swore it seemed like the spot that I clawed him in when we first met when Dame had killed my parents was one of the same spots I had clawed him again. The corner of his left eye had a slow trickle of blood leaking from it.

"I don't give a fuck what'chu going through right now; you ain't to never in your fucking life talk to Ghost like that again or take that tone of voice with her. You don't fucking lash out at the people you call family, li'l shawty. Like it or not, we all we fucking got. So fuck yo' stank-ass attitude and fuck you being mad at the world. And motherfuck you being mad at the people who ain't never did shit to you. Talk to her like that again and watch you be dead to me."

He'd said most of that through gritted teeth. I couldn't figure out what scared me most in the moment, the fact that I had hurt Ghost's feelings or the fact that Trigga was looking at me with same look he gave an enemy before he put them out of their misery. That blank, empty look of death, kill or be killed, was in his eyes. He left me there lying on the bed with my ghosts and future demons.

I probably would have stayed locked in my room all day if I could have, but Trigga wouldn't let me and neither would my aunt. Trigga didn't even knock on the door; he shoved it open and told me I needed to come eat. He didn't move away until I had dressed and was making my way from the room. Ghost wouldn't look at me. Normally she would sit by me at the table but this time she sat closest to Trigga. I felt like shit. I did. I ain't ever want Ghost to feel I didn't love her. Didn't ever want her to feel I was her enemy. So I made it my agenda to apologize to her because I did love her like she was my little sister.

"Nice of you to join the living, Diamond," Phenom said to me.

He was sitting at the head of the table like usual with the *Times UK* newspaper in front of his face. The front page showed the face of a soldier who had been hacked to death in a place called Woolwich, South London.

I didn't respond to his greeting. I felt like all eyes were on me as my aunt set trays loaded with pancakes, bacon, sausages, homemade biscuits, eggs, and grits on the table. The radio was playing. The same music they played in the States they played in London. Phenom dropped the paper on the table.

"We make moves today. We're looking for something," he said.

I noticed the way he and Anika made eye contact when he said that. Something was going on that we didn't know about with them. The way Trigga smoothly looked between the two let me know that he had peeped game too.

"Check it, before we get to that though," Trigga started as he snatched a piece of bacon and bit into it, "me and Jake scoped some of them Jamaican cats talking to some dude who looked like the law yesterday."

"A copper?" Anika asked. The way her eyes seemed to widen showed Trigga had told her something of interest.

Trigga shrugged. "Yeah, a cop or whatever y'all call 'em over here. Nigga was jawing about his boon or protection was gon' be over or some shit like that. Anyway, when a nigga hacked into the drive, I found more shit to match the notes and receipts I copped from the floor of those Jamaican cats' place."

Anika completely stopped serving and rushed to stand by Phenom. Her hand squeezed his shoulder and she looked like she was about to cry. *What the hell?* That wasn't the woman I was used to seeing. She wasn't the cool, calm, and collected African queen who even had Dame in check. That wasn't the woman who made every nigga in Dame's house grab his dick and want to bow before her. I didn't know who this fragile-acting woman was.

Phenom had placed a hand over his mouth then rubbed it aggressively up and down his face. I was starting to think this shit was about more than money and drugs.

"Show me what'cha got, nephew," Phenom casually said.

Trigga grabbed my laptop and then went to his hoodie where he pulled out all these receipts and cards and dropped them on the table in front of Phenom and Anika. The way they both didn't hesitate to start looking through them told me my assumption had been right about it being more than money that they were looking for. Yeah, they looked at the money transactions but it was the locations and maps that they took most interest in.

Trigga set the laptop on the table and started to talk again. "A nigga couldn't get that far because like I said I ain't no tech head but I can do some shit. Some of the other codes gon' take a nigga a minute to get in, but this shit right here shows that money been passing through this network like water and then this shit," he said as he clicked the mouse. "This shit shows a list of gangs I'm guessing. Something about code wars or some shit. Then you got some more names from something called Trident. Whatever the fuck that is a nigga know they ain't talking about gum."

As soon as Trigga stopped talking a movement by the window then a loud bang and the yell of a kid made us all grab weapons. Even Ghost grabbed a bat as Gina grabbed her .45. Gina was quick in her movements. She grabbed Ghost's hand and headed for the hidden hall closet. Jake's big, hefty ass didn't even stop chewing as he grabbed a pumped-up shotty from underneath his chair while Phenom and Anika both flanked either side of the window. Trigga was the only crazy motherfucker to go to the window. I guess that was what Phenom meant when he said you had to want to die more than the next nigga. If this was about to be a gun battle then Trigga had placed the target right on his chest. That nigga was clearly out of his mind.

I was cocked and ready to shoot as soon as I saw the shadowy figure approaching the window. Before whoever it was could make a move Trigga's gun was at their temple.

"Aye, yo, wait a minute, bruv. It's ya blood, yeah. Caught this lit'ul young-un snooping by the window," Speedy said, quickly pushing his hood away to show his face.

There was a little dirty boy who looked to be spooked out of his mind. He looked no older than Ghost. "Please don't kill me. I was a lit'ul hungry and Ghost my friend. Was only wan'ing ta see if she would give me grub and munchies like before. I swear down," the little boy pleaded with his little dirty hands in the air.

"You know this kid?" Phenom asked me as he put his gun away and snatched the kid through the window.

"Ay, you were right going to kill me were you, bruv?" Speedy asked wild-eyed looking at Trigga. "You're mad, man. Madder than a hatter ya are, blood."

"I shoot first and ask ya name never, nigga. Better be glad you spoke up, bruv," Trigga cajoled.

He and Big Jake cracked up laughing at the look of terror on Speedy's features. I knew Speedy was a killer like Trigga. Anika had told me. Only Speedy didn't use guns; he was a shanker. But to be on the same level as Trigga you had have more than one way to kill because that nigga knew a hundred ways you could die.

"Yo, Gina, bring Ghost in here," Phenom called out.

When they came from my room instead of the closet they had gone in, I knew Ghost had schooled Gina on the secret passages in the house. Ghost rounded the corner first then stopped.

"Dillenger, what are you doing here?" she asked the little boy.

"I only wanted munchies, swear down," Dillenger said again. The look of fright on his little face showed he was scared shitless. His light eyes were watered and if he could have I was sure he would have pissed himself.

"You know him?" Trigga asked her.

She nodded but there was something else on her face that I couldn't read. "I give the li'l nigga food sometimes because he told me he ain't have no place to live," she answered.

"You better not ever let me catch you snooping around here again. You get me?" Phenom said to the little boy. "You want grub, you knock on the door, eh?"

Dillenger nodded frantically. "I will. I swear down."

I was beginning to guess that "I swear down" in London was the same as "I swear to God" in America.

"Get him some food, Chas," Trigga told her.

She did, but it was the way that she hesitated that gave me pause. I looked at Trigga and saw that he was watching her too.

"I don't think we should let him go. We shouldn't let him leave," I said to Trigga in a low tone, but all the adults could still hear me.

"We don't kill kids," Trigga said to me.

"Yeah, but—"

"No buts, Diamond. We're not killing a kid," Anika said.

"You gon' kill the kid because he's hungry?" Phenom asked with raised brows.

"No, we can feed him, but we shouldn't let him leave," I said.

"Why not?" he asked me.

"Because who knows how long he was hiding there and who knows what someone could pay him to tell what we've been talking about?"

"Pretty gyal has a point, Uncle. Street gangs pay lit'ul ones ta snitch all the time, yeah? You know this," Speedy spoke up.

I looked at Trigga to see if he thought I was crazy, but the fact that he was eyeballing the kids in the kitchen let me know he was thinking hard about what I had said.

"Chas, take him to your room and let him eat. We'll come get you in a sec," Trigga told her.

I breathed a sigh of relief. Even though I had been a total bitch to him at least he was taking into account my theory.

We didn't say too much else out loud with the kid in the house. We spoke in codes; although sometimes Speedy didn't understand what we meant, he quickly caught on. He reminded me of Gina. A little dense, but smart where he needed to be. Instead of leaving the house like we had planned in the beginning, Phenom wanted to wait until nightfall to move, so we did. Throughout the whole thing I would check on Ghost from time to time. She and Dillenger were playing her game most times. Strange enough, the little boy almost looked like he could be her brother or something.

He was a cool kid. Head full of curly hair with gray eyes. It was no secret he was a rainbow baby, mixed with a little of everything. His clothes were a bit dingy and dirty, but oddly enough, his sneakers looked like they had just come out the box. Everything was going as planned until I went to Ghost's room to check on them again. The window was up, curtains blowing in the wind, and they were gone. It was nothing for them to trail the metal ladder down the wall.

"Ghost is gone," I ran to the front room yelling.

Trigga was the first to jump up from the couch. "What?" His eyes narrowed on me. He was angry but I could tell behind that anger was something I had never seen in him before: fear.

"She's gone. Ghost is gone," I said again.

Chapter 6

Ghost

I may not know a lot of shit, but I was raised in the game. All I knew were tricks and schemes because that was all that had been taught to me. Even though Trigga was like my dad and shit, he even taught me ways to get over on people. But he only did it because he knew the game wasn't gonna be nice to no misfit like me. I ain't have no mama really and my daddy wasn't shit. My mama woulda been a good mama had that nigga Dame not turned her out. She was still good enough to hide me so that nigga wouldn't get to me. And she was friends with Trigga. My mama knew Dame was about to kill her because she gave me all my stuff like social security card, birth certificate, and stuff like that. She told me to give it to Trigga and I did.

I cried when she died but not really 'cause I knew Trigga was gon' take care of me, but I was still sad 'cause I knew she ain't ever had no real chance at life. That nigga Dame had taken her when she was fourteen. She was twenty-four when she died. 'Cause of the shit I had seen I ain't never been to trusting of any nigga 'cept Trigga. And especially not no bitch. Diamond had snapped at me this morning. It hurt my feelings, but I wasn't tripping no more. My mama used to wake up screaming in the middle of the night too because of that nigga Dame. So I kind of felt sorry for her.

Trigga had taught me to always pay attention to shit like my surroundings. That was why I knew Dillenger was lying about being hungry. We was walking down the block now. Had just jumped the gate to Springhill Park. Nobody was in the park that time of night but hoods and misfits like me. So nobody was paying attention to us hopping the gates and walking around. I told that li'l nigga that Trigga had hid some money down by the river. I knew he would go for it 'cause Dillenger liked to steal shit. He was always stealing stuff when we went to the stores around the area.

"So, they hid money, eh?" he asked me, trying to hide the fact that he was excited.

I kept my head low so the fitted cap I wore could keep my eyes covered. Had on my baggy jeans and Timbs so niggas would keep thinking I was a little boy. My braids were hid under the cap.

"Yeah, I saw 'em do it. Where you get'cho new Jays from, Dill? Them shits is boss."

He grinned. "Did some runnings for e8 boys. They paid with the kicks, yeah?"

"Oh yeah. How I get down with them niggas? Trigga don't be really giving me no money."

"Oi, it's easy, yeah. Just show them that you can move wif'out being seen by the coppers and ya sweet in there like nothing. Been doing it for a while, yeah," he boasted.

"Really?"

"Yeah. So what were you guys talking about when they pulled me in? Are those your parents? Anika and Phenom? Is that lot your family?"

"Why you asking all them questions for, Dill?"

He laughed low and shrugged. "No reason, just never seen them around you before."

I knew he was lying. I'd seen him with dudes from Dante's crew a lot. Had seen the li'l nigga even get out of Dante's car before. I remembered that shit as soon as Phenom took Diamond outside and Dante was standing there. That was why I ain't been talking to him like I used to, not since I knew that niggas was out to kill my family. If I ain't know nothing else, I knew I wasn't gone go back to living like I did with Dame. And that Dante nigga looked just like Dame. They was brothers, twins. I wasn't going back to living in no walls and sneaking around. I was never gon' let my family be snitched on so they could get killed. Never.

That was why while Dillenger was busy digging with his hands where he thought money was gon' be, I pulled out a small iron bat that I had been wrapping with barbwire and hit that li'l nigga right in the back of his skull. He had been spying on us for somebody because he kept asking me too many questions. All in my room, he kept asking me questions. There was one thing that Trigga had taught me and he ain't even know it. Dead niggas told no tales.

Dillenger cried out after that first hit. His voice was shrill as he fell face first, rolled over, and then kicked my legs from under me. I hit the ground with a loud grunt.

"You bitch. I'm going to tell my dad all the shit I heard them saying and then I'ma ask him to buy you for me," he snarled as he jumped up and tried to grab my hair.

Blood was soaking the back of his shirt. I ain't know what that nigga was talking about having his daddy buy me, but I knew he was stronger than I thought. The bat had fallen from my hand. He jumped on top of me, grabbed both sides of my face, and then slammed my head into the ground. I was dizzy but could make out as he reached into his back pocket. He was going for his shank. I knew he carried one just like most of all the misfits around the way did, even those our age. I wasn't stupid though. The man I called my daddy, Trigga, was a killer and he always told me to have more than one weapon. He had to teach me that shit 'cause he knew what kind of world we was living in. That was why I could get to my shank first. I stuck my hand in my front hoodie pockets and janked Dillenger in his side.

He fell back crying like a bitch. He was rolling from side to side holding where I had stuck. I stood and rushed for my bat. I had to catch my breath as I walked back over to him. My head hurt from where he had slammed it.

"Who the bitch now, li'l nigga?" I asked as I raised the bat then brought it back down over and over again against his body and face.

The blood didn't scare me. Nothing scared me more than my family being killed and me being without Trigga. He was the only daddy I knew. The only person who loved me. Him and Diamond and Gina and Big Jake was all I had and nobody was gonna take them from me. Dame had taken my mama before she even had me and he ain't never let her love me openly like she should have. Nobody was taking my family no more. Yeah, I was crying, but I ain't stop swinging my bat until Dillenger's face was unrecognizable. It would take a minute for the cops to identify him.

"Hey, what in bloody hell is going on over there?" I heard someone asked.

I grabbed my backpack and my cap and took off running. I never looked back. I didn't stop running until I made it to the other end of the river. I needed to get rid of my bloody clothes. So I made sure nobody was around before I started pulling them off. I wiped the blood off my face as best as I could and quickly changed into clean clothes. Out of all the things Trigga had taught me, paying attention to my surroundings was the most important. I was so amped and in a hurry to get back home that I didn't see the detective in the plain clothes watching me as I killed Dill. I didn't even hear as he followed me. Once I had pulled on my clean clothes and shoes, I was headed back to the flat. I knew Trigga was gon' be mad at me but I had to do this so Dill wouldn't go snitching.

Dead niggas told no tales.

Just as I was about to hop back over the gate, a pair of hands snatched me. It was a grown man, I knew that. The fear I ain't feel while offing Dill was real now. A hand came over my mouth.

"Shhhh. There, there, you little killer. You're going to go for a pretty penny," he taunted me.

I tried to scream and kick but it did no good. He was too strong. I could hear his shoes clack and scrape against the street as we headed to his car. The trunk was already open and he tossed me in like trash. I tried to jump back out but he punched me in my stomach; at the same time he snatched my backpack off. I fell back into the trunk of the car as he put his phone to his ear.

There was a wicked smile on his face. "Oi, do I have a prize for you," was all he said as he slammed the trunk with me in it.

Chapter 7

Trigga

Talk about some liability shit. The moment Diamond hit me with the knowledge that Ghost was gone, a nigga was already out the door strapped up and moving down the streets. It wasn't nothing for me to realize that little nigga had something to do with all of this. Like Ray-Ray had said, that little nigga shouldn't have been left out of our sight. Second, I shoulda put a bullet in the middle of his skull, fuck not killing kids. Kids who carried the same eyes as a nigga I done seen twice, one dead and the other alive, a little nigga who had the same type of characteristics needed to be gunned the fuck down. Only because of how he played himself. He wanted to be caught and being caught was making a coded statement. Little dude was part of the streets through and through and I knew that game because I came from the game. I was just smarter.

The distant low shouts of my fam behind me didn't stop me as I passed through the tower blocks, or what we call in the hood the projects, something like how Cabrini Green's towers used to be. Ghost was trained by me, so I knew wherever the fuck she would go, it would be somewhere she could hide. It would be somewhere she could maintain her surroundings, so I knew she wouldn't walk through the projects but around it. But, even that still kept me on point in tracking her.

"Trig, man, slow the fuck down. Where are you going? Do you even know?" Big Jake's voice sounded behind me.

I stood counting the balconies before I turned around, "Tracking my girl. Hey, Speedy, this shit is our endz right?"

Speedy jogged up to me and nodded; concern had his brown eyes darkening as he pulled out a cell while watching me. "Swear down, wut ya need blood, I got you. Phenom and Anika are on di other side of the 'set' lookin' for her and Gina packing up da flat. No one is trustin' that young-un bruv, so we got you. Whut you need?"

"I need eyes. Hit me up a spot on the high rise. I need to see from the skies," I calmly commanded. If Ghost was still walking around, best bet to see her was by balcony view from the towers.

"Give me some addys so I can hit up some people and talk to them about seeing her," Jake also relayed.

Speedy was on it. He spit out flat numbers for Jake to hit up then had me follow him inside of the towers.

"I'm gud wit' a bossy gyal at the top. She hold mi nigga's stash sometimes. A propa chick, she'll hold us down blood," Speedy explained while we took an elevator that felt like a cage to the top of the towers: floor nineteen.

Time was all I was thinking about, so the faster we could move, the faster we could make sure Ghost was good. I had hit up her cell, but there was no answer and she knew how I was about that shit. No text meant she wasn't near her shit and that was a problem. Pushing open the gates of the elevator, we strolled down the tower hallways. Everything was washed in a dingy green shade of paint. Scribbles of gang signs sporting both Phenom's and Anika's cliques let me know that this level of the towers were theirs. Here in London, though I called this shit projects, it really was a mixture. You could get all levels of people living in this shit, from low to middle class. It was crazy.

Hustling down the hall, we stopped at 19LH. Speedy shifted on his feet and rapped his knuckles against the steel door. Music could be heard bumping, with the scent of cooking food. We waited, and got nothing. Frustration had me tilting my head at my cousin before he put his blue and black Js against the door kicking it then banging on the door again.

"Ei, open this door, gyal. Dun be playing no shit come on," Speedy yelled. He glanced at me with light humor in his eyes then whispered, "Sometimes a nigga gotta act nutters with these gyal's ey?"

Jokes stayed coming out of his mouth and it had me shaking my head. The angry clack and grunt of the steel door in front of us drew my attention as it snapped open with an annoyed bang.

"What! Don't be pissin' me off with all that banging and shit on my door areshole!"

A tall, brown-haired chick stood in front of us with a scowl on her face. Upset, she pushed strains of her silky hair behind her ears and her face was flushed bright red reflecting her irritation. Recognition hit her features as a light smile spread wide the moment her fist suddenly connected with Speedy's shoulder.

"Heeeey, Speedy, come in, my bad. Thought some twat had a problem or that it was Tunez," she said moving to the side.

From what Speedy had explained on up, Tunez was his boy from the block who was a local DJ with him and was this chick's nigga. Personally, I really didn't care but I listened anyway just in case it was some info in the mix that I needed. Stepping into her flat, I watched her check me out while I checked her out and I almost found myself inwardly laughing. She sported a simple jersey and jeans with white kicks. Her hair was pulled back into a pony and the sound of a kid in the far back of the room let me know why she also was standing in a protective stance.

Glancing around the medium-sized flat, which held toy cars in one area of the room and a table full of plates with a waiting dinner on it, I saw the balcony and glanced at Speedy.

"Ei, chill wit that, L. Look my bruv here needs your deck, you down?" Speedy explained keeping everything simple. He had already told me her name was Laura on the way up. I guessed L was her nickname.

"There it is; go use it. Just was getting my son in. The endz is on some piss today. Bloke's acting all loony and shit." L motioned while she locked the door.

Heading to the balcony, I slid the doors open while Speedy and L spoke. They both clowned around talking about everything and nothing as I took in the whole block. I saw the marshes and wondered if she'd go there since it was that close. My eyes trailed from the flat we were sharing with Diamond and I tried to see if any suspicious rides were speeding out of the endz.

"Oh shit, Speedy, for real? Sometimes the snakes in the grass are closer than you expect. I don't play wit' kids, so yeah, I think I saw her on the other side of the towers with some other kid," I heard L say.

The concern in her voice had me turning around and coming back into her living room, "She always has her pink and purple backpack; did you see that, ma?"

L's gray eyes glanced up thinking. As she turned to get a bottle of Coca-Cola she spoke to us in thought. "Oh yeah. I've see her 'round 'ere going to primary. Yeah, saw Dante's kid wit' her. Thought that was suspect since he only comes to the endz to snitch to that bitch Dante, but yeah, saw her and she was wit' him again. Didn't know she was yours."

Speedy spit out exactly was a nigga was thinking: "Dante's kid? When dat 'appen, yo?"

"You stay gone, Speedy, workin' the endz and whatever the boss got you doing, bruv. We keep the word for when you all need it, cha?" L raised both eyes brows in the air, as if saying "duh" and walked in the kitchen.

"People been missing, mainly kids and us young-uns. Misfits, bruv. Wondered when attention was gonna start getting paid," she went on.

I listened, and I thought, *damn.* All this shit was deep but at the same time, Dante's kid? The fuck was this and why did everyone know this shit but Phenom and Anika? Had to be because they had been gone for so long, only thing I could think of. But, the fact that little nigga had been around my baby girl had me pissed all the way off. My family was becoming liabilities. This was fucked up.

My hands slid in my pockets and I urgently moved to the door, "Hey yo, L, baby, thank you for hitting us with that knowledge. A lot of shit was going on but we got you, mama."

"So you're one of the Yanks who moved in huh? You got us? Make sure you do 'cause Dante is nutters. I got a kid and I ain't got time for all of that other stuff, so protect us now, too. Phenom and the African queen have been good to us, so don't muff up the system."

I chuckled at her brass balls. I could jig on this chick. I gave her a curt nod and rolled out as Speedy passed her some dough then followed me. We made it out of the towers just as Jake was hitting my cell with numbers. In code, it meant that people saw her near the marshes like I thought. So, Speedy and I headed that way. My mind was a mosh pit. Like, for real a nigga hadn't been that bent out of shape since finding out Dame had murked my mom and pops. But I couldn't let that shit deter me. I kept my eyes open then stopped dead in my tracks. Footprints let me know she had been here. I followed each one until I got to the marsh's edge. Turning, I saw another set of footprints. Looked like a struggle.

As I followed, my cell vibrated and I picked it up since it wasn't a text. "Yeah."

"Found a body. That kid Dillenger. Close to where you are. I see you, brah. Just walk backward and go left close to the bank," Jake explained.

Though it was dark, Jake's huge, muscled frame could be spotted surrounded by a bunch of trees. She had picked a good spot. Because she was so little, it was perfect to do some dirt but also still see her surroundings, which had me wondering what the fuck was really going on.

Dillenger lay in front of my Timbs mucked the fuck up. Blood was everywhere, with pieces of his skull and brain matter. I knew the cops were going to have a good day with this shit. *Damn, baby girl, what was going on?* I wanted to act confused with the whole scenario but after hearing what L had told us back in the towers, I could only guess that she figured out some shit with this little nigga and took him out. No doubt, I was proud of her, but where the fuck was she?

"I hit up Gina, but she said Ghost ain't come back. Ray-Ray is buggin' out," Jake explained as if reading my thoughts.

I turned around backing away to go back to where I came from as Speedy and Jake followed. From where we were, even if you were at the towers, you couldn't really see due to the angle they were at. So it was no point in asking if anyone saw shit, unless it was people who were walking by at that same moment, so I keep it moving. Her feet tracks left out of the marshes and back on the block toward a gate next to an alley. My eyes kept scanning until it stopped on a side alley where Phenom and Anika stood.

Something wasn't right with how they were looking and it had my temples suddenly pounding and my pulse pumping. Everything around me suddenly got hot. I kept walking until I was right upon them.

"Nephew, I'm sorry," was all Phenom said.

I wasn't sure what the fuck he was sorry for until I saw Anika with Ghost's book bag and her broken jeweled cell phone. I had got her that, when we got here. It was her favorite colors, pink and purple. Now that shit was broken and I knew my face was frozen in a blank mask as my mind processed.

"What was seen?" gruffly came from me as the sound of the city ebbed behind me.

All I heard was the thumping of my heart with the sensation of heat rising in anger.

"Some of our eyes said they spotted a white car pulling up out of here, hon. When we got here, this was on the ground, next to a kiddy bat. I figured it was hers," Anika softly explained.

Lights from the intersection and houses behind her cast an eerie glow, one that had my stomach clenching in the seriousness of the situation. I began nodding my head thinking, then thumbing my nose as I contemptuously spoke, "So you saying, what huh? She was snatched up? That little nigga led her out here to get got?"

The sound of a pair of familiar all-white wing-tipped oxford shoes came close with that of the grip of a strong hand on my shoulder. Anger had me seeing red and I brushed the hand off.

"Fuck this London bullshit. Never should have brought any of them here, man, fuck this. I know who did this shit and I'm about to handle it right now; clearly they don't know who the fuck I am," I spit out.

"Kwame, step out of that and think—" Phenom offered in comfort but I wasn't hearing it in that moment.

"Fuck that. They put me in chaos and best believe I'm about to bring 'em just that, fuck the other shit," I heatedly cut in.

I heard the sound of a Glock and intuitively knew that was Jake backing me up. A cold sneer slowly spread across my face in knowing that. My locs spilled haphazardly over my face and I stared deep into my uncle's eyes speaking to him without saying shit. He knew I wasn't on some delusional "get myself killed" stupid shit. Naw, anger always kept me levelheaded and clear of mind and right now, I was into a plan.

"You either with me or against me. If you with me check my next move," was all I said as I walked off.

The sound of feet following me let me know that they were with me and flanking me. I roughly tugged on my hoodie then went to where the body of that Dillenger kid was. Reaching into the pockets of my hoodie, I pulled out a pair of leather gloves with barbwire sewn into it and put them on. Like I said, I was feeling my uncle's style with that, so I made it even better. The tips of each one had razors, too, and I gripped the kid then threw him over my shoulder.

"We heading to Dante's zone. Me and him got some shit to talk about."

Phenom gave me a nod then hit his cell. I could hear doors on the block opening, which meant that he had the whole codes on lockdown and protection. Jake hit up Gina and Ray-Ray letting them know what was up. Ray-Ray rushed out of the house telling us that she was coming too. So we waited as she found me with Dillenger's body over my shoulder and Speedy stayed with Gina to protect her. I could tell she wanted to question what had happened but knew better by the look on my face. Walking with the body, we headed to Dante's "set space," by stashing the body into an unmarked van laced with plastic. A set space was a safe zone for any gang to chat it up. Me, I was using it to prove a point or send a message depending on how you looked at it.

Once we pulled up, I could see Dante's ride waiting at the gate. Nigga sat on the side of his ride with a smile on his face. His legs were crossed at the ankles, while his dark gray business coat–covered arms were crossed over his massive chest. Nigga had the look of boredom mixed with elation on his light sepia face.

The cross scar on his lip was slanted to the side with his malicious grin. Darkness was set in his pitiless eyes. Several street hoods surrounded him, with some of the surviving Jamaicans, some East Indian gangs, Jews, and Asians. I really couldn't give a fuck about who he had behind him. It always only took one bullet to end a motherfucker and, besides, we had just as many numbers as he did.

Slamming the car door as I slid out, I walked forward with a purpose. Death wasn't nothing to me. I had survived it, even as I welcomed it, so if any of them popped me off, it was whatever. I always had a fallback if that ever happened anyway.

"Di nigga, Trigger. I got mi sum calls dat say the killa of mi blood wanted ta speak wit' me? I am amused. What can I kill you for, boy?" Dante taunted.

See, niggas like him and Dame really thought that their words or actions could put the fear of God in me, or respect anything they had to give me but no. Right now, I had to break the code of Sun Tzu. I knew right now that I couldn't attack this cat where he was unprepared, or appear where he would not expect it, because I was purposely in his zone. But in using this tactic, he would also still be blindsided with the fact that where he watched me, others of my uncle and aunt's team were in his blind spot. So I smiled while using Sun Tzu's other code: "all warfare is based on deception."

Locking eyes on him, I said nothing. Kept my mouth shut, returning to my old self, that silent, lethal mute. My jaw ticked and I felt my temple thumping while he waited for me to say something.

“Wut you American niggas be about? Yuh don’t understand wut I’m sayin? Let mi clear it up. What do you want? Word in the endz is that your mob is dying, that true?” Dante smirked.

The accent he owned smoothly disappeared into that of an American tone. He rubbed his hands together then crossed them back over his chest while holding his platinum cane.

My eyes bore into his skull like a 9 mm and I backed up, walked to the van, opened the back, and pulled out the body, wrapping the kid over my shoulder like a coat. Laughter lit up my eyes and I calmly stepped forward, thumbing my nose and putting swag in my step.

Just to fuck with him and give him disrespect, I flipped my language on that dude, all while noticing the whites of everyone’s eyes as they bucked out and stared at me in disbelief, “Who di fuck is Trigger rasshole, cha? Tis sho’ ain’t Tigga eitha. My name is *Trigga,* brah, get ya shit right. Anyway, a nigga look good don’t he? I got that new shit right here.”

Dillenger’s body stayed wrapped around my shoulders like a fur as I did the Cat Daddy, turned in a full circle then stood in place going back to being silent before speaking again, watching Dante from under my hoodie.

“Play me and I play you. Welcome to my world, nigga. I’m done being brand new. This shit may be a new zone but we all from the same pond feel me?” I growled.

Grunting, I forcefully threw the lightweight body so that it landed at Dante’s feet with a hard wet thud. Many of his crew started grumbling, popping off at the mouth like bitches as shock hit them with who it was. I heard some women scream and I saw niggas step forward, but that nigga Dante just chilled where he was. He gave one look at the body. Saw the blood that had splattered on his shoe, and then stood to extend his foot and wipe it off on Dillenger's shoulder.

I found myself laughing at that shit while I stood there. Nigga had no respect for even his own. The comforting feel of my steel filled my hands from under the sleeves of my hoodie. I flexed my arm, pointed forward, and pumped off several rounds, killing the men around Dante including his driver who sat right behind him. I did that move just to prove a point, even though I knew that nigga probably didn't care. And he didn't. Nigga didn't even flinch as he held up two fingers telling his side to remain silent.

Cool with whatever message that came across, I kept my stance waiting.

"Was good to finally be introduced to you, bruv. We'll be hangin' soon," Dante crooned.

Not even the death of his son moved the nigga so you know the death of a few of his henchmen wouldn't move him. He pushed off the car, pressed the end of his cane into the back of Dillenger's lifeless, small body and several other dead niggas around him, and then walked off slowly before pausing.

"Phenom, ya trained him well. I'll enjoy killing ya both, blood," Dante yelled back as he disappeared with the remainder of his crew.

I memorized every face around him and in the set. The sensation of my uncle standing next to me while resting a hand on my shoulder let me know he was just as pissed off as me. I didn't even have to see if he was watching that nigga hard like me, jaw clenched tight with a vein pumping next to the fresh-lined cut of his hair near his temple.

Nah, the tone in his voice as he holla'd at me let me know that. "Let's ride out; your point was made, and we still didn't find her."

My point actually had not been made because this shit was not done. Following my uncle, my mind went back to Ghost. Images of her face flickered in my mind. Any pain he gave her, he fucking was going to experience later, by my hand.

Chapter 8

Ghost

I was naked and cold in a cage in a room filled with other girls and little boys. Some knew English and some didn't. Some were smaller than me, looked like they was hungry, but no matter how much we was different, we was all scared. I could tell by the whimpering and crying.

"What's your name?" a girl asked from the cage beside me.

I looked at her. She was older than me and pretty. Dark like Diamond. Her thick hair was in two plaits like Diamond used to do mine.

"Ghost," I answered.

"Is that your real name?"

I shook my head.

"My name is Chyna," she told me.

"How long you been in here?" I asked.

"Only a few weeks. They're keeping me here, I don't know why. They moved me to this place. Must be because my parents are getting close to finding me."

Her accent was cool. Kinda made me wish I had one. "What they do to kids in here?"

Her wide eyes looked up at me. "Sell them."

My eyes got big as hers and I crawled to the bars of the cage staring at Chyna. "Sell them? Like for money?" I asked. My body started to shake a little bit 'cause I was cold and scared.

"Yes, men come in and bid on you. If the price is high enough, they can buy for the night or forever."

Up closer I could see she was naked like me. She had a bruise under her right eye. "They ever buy you?" I asked her.

She shook her head. "No. I'm too old. They like the smaller children. It's bloody sick. Really it is."

I didn't say nothing else. I was mad at myself for getting caught. Trigga was going to be so mad at me. I didn't want to start crying but I couldn't help it. I shoulda been paying attention like my daddy taught me to and I would'na got caught. When I started sniffing my nose I could hear other kids crying louder too.

"Hey, don't cry, 'kay? I'll protect you best I can, eh? Dante likes me. Sick bastard don't want anybody to bloody know he's got the workings for a minor, yeh?" Chyna reached through the bar on her small cage and grabbed my hand. "It's irie, yeah?"

Dante? That nigga was selling kids just like Dame? He was my uncle but he was just like that punk bitch. Fuck crying. Trigga said you never let the enemy see your weakness 'cause they'll use that shit against you. So I dried my tears quick when I heard feet coming down the hall. Most of the kids started crying louder and huddled back in their cages. I looked over and saw one boy had pissed himself. Fuck this shit. I was gonna get the fuck up outta here dead or alive.

Chapter 9

Ray-Ray

"Why did you do that?" I ask Trigga.

"To make a point."

"What was the point? Aren't you afraid he's going to kill Ghost if he has her?"

He turned to look at me, lips twisted. I knew in his heart there was murderous intent. "My point was to let him know that I ain't afraid of shit he does and I'll always meet him where he comes for me."

I could tell by the way Trigga was acting that he probably was thinking I was just asking shit to fuck with him, but I wasn't. My mind was running a mile a minute and most were images of all the sadistic things I knew could be happening to Ghost. Dame had girls as young as ten in that house sometimes because that nigga sold pussy to the highest bidder no matter the age. I had the jerks like a powder head just picturing some big, overgrown nigga trying to fuck a nine-year-old Ghost. Shit had me on edge. Not to mention I couldn't get the image of that little boy wrapped around Trigga's shoulders like a shawl and dancing before tossing his body at his father's feet.

"We need to get back to the flat," Anika said.

"No," Trigga said and turned on his uncle. "You both need to tell us what the fuck is really up right now."

Phenom didn't flinch. "You heard what my woman said, blood. Back to the flat."

"Fuck the flat," Trigga said. He was pissed. Some of Dante's goons still loitered around, watching, no doubt waiting to rush back and tell Dante our crew was having trouble.

Phenom stepped to his nephew. "You better use your head right now, Kwame," he growled through clenched teeth. "Don't bloody challenge me right here and not right now. Back to the fucking flat."

He said Trigga's real name low enough so nobody heard it but me, Anika, and Big Jake. I knew Trigga so I knew that nigga's mind was working overtime. He wasn't gonna rest until he got Ghost back. Wasn't gonna chill or none of that shit. Phenom had to know the monster that streets and life had made of his nephew. I could tell he knew by the way both of them stood, backs erect, fist clenched at their sides like combatants. But, like I said, I knew Trigga. There was always a method to this nigga's madness.

That night had to be the worst night I had ever been alive. I couldn't sit still thinking of all the things that could have been happening to Ghost. I cried. I prayed. Then I got real. Anika kept Trigga and Phenom from getting downright grimy with one another in the streets. We really couldn't afford for the other niggas on Dante's team to see that shit. So they calmed down enough for us to make it back to my flat.

"So, now are you two going to say what's really going on?" I asked my aunt.

I didn't know what was going on with Anika, but she looked like she was two seconds away from spazzing out. Phenom paced the floor of my flat until it looked like he was crazed. That didn't account for Trigga moving about like he had ADHD. I would have given anything for my mama or my daddy to show themselves and talk to me like before, but even they had been silent.

"We have a daughter," she stated with no emotion in her voice. "She's sixteen, young like you. Your mother was three years younger than I was. Our father was a Nigerian who loved white women and their submissiveness over us. Shanna's mama's skin may have been white but she was every bit a black woman on the inside. That man didn't like that so he left Shanna and her mama just like he had left me and my mother. Shanna's mama had been fucking with my daddy while he was married to my mother. Now you know how we're sisters." Anika took a breather like telling that story was hurting her. "Shanna was pregnant with you and I got pregnant with Chyna a short time later. I knew she was my sister, but Shanna didn't know me until I introduced myself to her. She was fucking with your nothing-ass daddy."

I cut my eyes at my aunt. I didn't care what people said about him; when he was alive, he protected me. Kept me safe and out of harm's way. Anika caught my look but kept talking.

"I don't care what you think. Your daddy was a predator. Shanna was only fourteen when they met. He was pimping her out. That ain't love. Anyway, to make a long story short, me and Shanna were cool for a while but I couldn't take her choice of life. I tried to get her to come with me but by then your daddy was all in her head. He was all she could think about. We had a fight, like a fist fight because I told your daddy I'd kill his ass if he ever laid hands on her again. Almost got Phenom to pop him. But Shanna was ride or die for that nigga. Fought me because I wanted to protect her. He'd used her face as a punching bag, but that didn't stop her from swinging on me. After me and her fought like that, I finally realized that Shanna loved the life she was living because it was what she was used to. She didn't know anything else. I was scared shitless she was going to start doing to you what her mother did to her. Many nights I cried in Phenom's arms because I was afraid she would start pimping you out like her mother had done her. I was surprised to see that she was the opposite of her mother in that sense. Once our daughter was born, me and Phenom, we moved out of the States; well I moved to London to be near him because he had already been in the UK for a while at that point. We sent her to live with family elsewhere because we never wanted anyone to know who she was. We been in this thing a long time, Diamond, and no matter how hard we try to do the right thing sometimes we gotta get down and dirty with the lowest of the low. That causes problems. That makes enemies so we did what we had to do and protected her. We had to. Changed her name to a more common one because we wanted no clues to anyone knowing who she was."

"Somewhere along the way, some wangster found out about my daughter," Phenom chimed in. "See, I stepped foot back into the US just weeks before you found me, Trigga. My only agenda had been to get you and get out. Same with Anika and Diamond. Yeah, I had businesses set up there and came in from time to time to watch you closely, but shit changed the moment my daughter was snatched from her school one day."

My face frowned because I obviously confused. "If you knew Dante had your daughter why not call the cops or just go get—"

Anika waved her hand and cut me off. "I know what you're about to ask. We know he has her, but he keeps moving her so we never know exactly where he's keeping her. Not to mention, we're of the streets. We run the streets so getting coppers to help us would be like inviting them in to arrest us," she said then took a deep breath like what she was about to say next pained her. "When I say this, I want you to listen to me, Diamond, and know that we had some tough decisions to make during these last three months." She sighed hard before continuing. "Phenom is a killer. He's a gangsta, and sometimes a drug dealer just like me. But he's a father before anything, sometimes even before being my husband, he's a father, and the one thing that can take that man and bring him to his knees is something happening to his daughter. That's why you're in London. He was going to trade you for Chyna."

"What the fuck?" Those words left Trigga's mouth before they could leave mine. Trigga jumped up from where he had sat down. My eyes widened and a gasp escaped my lips.

"Listen to me, Diamond," my aunt pleaded as she quickly spoke. "I would never allow that to happen, okay? Even though Chyna is my daughter, you're my blood too and I would never allow anybody to bargain your life."

Fresh, hot tears rolled down my face. My hands began to shake, eyes blinked rapidly, and my head started to swim. "So this whole time I thought you guys were helping me, he was planning to turn me over to the man who wants me dead?" I started rocking back and forth because there was something wrong with that. "And you still rock with this dude?" I asked. At least I thought I asked. I felt as if I was floating somewhere over my body.

"No matter what he does or how crazy he may think in a fleeting moment, Diamond, that's my husband. I will ride for him and die with him before I turn my back on him no matter what," she stated sternly.

"Yo, you niggas played me, right, unk? Now this shit makes sense as why she was in London and we were in Africa," Trigga fumed.

"Ain't this some fucking bullshit?" I heard Jake grumble.

"That ain't right," Gina spoke up. She tried to say more but started choking because of the injury to her throat.

"Yeah, my thinking was fucked up," Phenom bellowed out. "But that's my fucking kid that son of a bitch has."

It was clear he wasn't making any apologies. There was pride in that man's eyes, but also a father's love mixed with a little bit of fear of what may have been happening to his daughter.

"We was somebody kids too, nigga. We ain't got nobody. No fucking parents and the motherfuckers we thought we could trust in the end turned out be like the very niggas we fought so hard to get away from," Trigga yelled slapping his big hand against his chest. "Every nigga got a motherfucking agenda and you niggas ain't no different!"

I was stuck somewhere between reality and a dream. Gina had stood behind me and placed her hands on my shoulders. Big Jake and Speedy had rushed to stand between Trigga and Phenom. Anika's eyes never left mine. Any other time, I knew Trigga wouldn't have spoken to his uncle like he was some random nigga on the street, but Ghost was gone. My life was set to be bartered, and he was feeling like he didn't do enough to protect either one of us. I could tell by the crack in his voice. No matter what that nigga said to me, Trigga was a protector. Once he had you in his heart wasn't nobody taking you out. Look at the way he had protected Gina when he could and all those years he had protected Ghost. I could tell he was feeling some type of way.

"Fuck yo' feelings, Kwame. I don't give a damn what you thinking of me right now. Put yourself in my shoes, nephew. What or who wouldn't you give to get Ghost back right now?" Phenom barked out. "I ain't never gon' say I was right in my thinking, but that's my daughter. That's mine and no matter what I had done to protect her, she still got got. I gotta live with that shit every day as a man, as a father. Gotta live with that phone call and hear my baby girl screaming in the background in my head every fucking night. To know no matter what the fuck I had done or did, I was no fucking closer to getting her back. So I was at my lowest fucking point and Diamond was the only play I had left."

My aunt reached out to take my hand and I snatched it back. I didn't know this bitch, I thought. Every nigga had a motherfucking agenda and theirs had been to hand me over to my enemy. The enemy of my enemy was my motherfucking friend.

"So that whole episode with you dragging her out there for that nigga to see was so he could see you had the merchandise, right?" Trigga coolly asked his uncle. When my aunt dropped her head I knew the answer. "That's why that nigga so cool, calm, and collected because he know your hand, huh, unk? You know this is fucked up. This shit here ain't right. You ain't nothing like my pops, yo. My pops woulda never done no shit like this."

"This is one time you need to think with your heart, nephew," was all Phenom said.

"You was going to let him give me away?" I asked Anika. That quiver in my voice was evident. Gina tried to say something to me but I cut her off.

I stood and my aunt stood with me. "I would have never let him give you away like that, Diamond. He wasn't thinking clearly. You know what happens to girls when niggas like Dante take them. Ahmir was a man conflicted. He didn't even tell me this until—"

I knew Ahmir was Phenom's real name, but I didn't even let her finish talking. I made an about face and walked to my bedroom, slamming the door as my response to it all. For the first time in a long time, I broke down. I hadn't felt that alone and scared since the first day at Dame's mansion. This whole time I was thinking that we finally had somebody to protect us, keep us from the gritty, grimy life we had been introduced to and this whole time we had been played.

I ignored my aunt's knocks at the door. Ignored Gina's too. I took out Ghost's passport, opened it to her photo, and held it to my chest as I cried.

"Lord, if you ever listening to me, please don't let what happened to me happen to this little girl," I whispered as best I could.

My tongue was thick, mouth was like cotton, and eyes burned with tears. I was even worried about Chyna. I didn't know how long that nigga Dante had been keeping her, but I prayed to God that she was all right too. Was there even really a fucking God? Who or what would let these fucking monsters get away with this shit? I knew they could hear me crying, but I ain't give a shit. I could still hear Trigga and Phenom arguing. Their yells couldn't be hidden by my closed door. Sounded like some furniture was moving around. I figured Big Jake wasn't going to let Trigga and his uncle get physical. To be honest, I didn't want to see Trigga like that either.

It was only seconds later that I heard pounding on my door. I tried to ignore it until Trigga made it known it was him. "Ray-Ray, open the fucking door or I'ma kick this shit down," he demanded.

I knew he wasn't playing and I was in no mind to test this nigga with the mood he was in. I walked to the door, unlocked it, and got back in the bed. He walked in the room, slamming the door behind him too. I expected him to say something, but all he did was plop down on the edge of my bed with his head hanging.

"Sorry, li'l shawty. I fucked that up," he said.

"Don't apologize. You got me out of that madman's house, Trigga."

"Yeah, and almost got you put back into another one."

I watched the way his wide back massively expanded with each deep breath he took. I didn't want to admit to him that I was conflicted in my thinking.

"We have to get Ghost," I said.

"I know."

That was all we said for a long while. He sat in silence and I lay back in grief. Eventually, I tugged on his arm and urged him to lay back with me. As hard as I tried to fight it, I fell asleep, but he didn't. Every so often I would be awakened because of him constantly tossing and turning in the bed or his pacing the floor talking to himself. The last time I woke up he had taken his shirt off and it looked like he was reading the tattoos on his arm. I got up and walked over to where he was standing. I didn't know what else to do so I stood on my toes, wrapped my arms around his neck, and kissed his lips.

He stiffened for a moment but then his hands found my waist as he returned the kiss. Until we could figure out a way to get Ghost back all we had was this. I didn't protest when he easily lifted me around his waist and took me back to the bed. It was the moment that I wanted, but I could tell it wasn't going to happen. He wasn't into it because just like me, all he could think about was Ghost. As I lay underneath him I looked up into his light eyes. His locs had been pulled back into a ponytail until I reached up to let them down. His gaze didn't waver as he looked down at me.

"I can't do this right now, li'l shawty. My dick may be hard as fuck but my mind is mush and I ain't trying to fuck you just to be fucking you," he told me.

"I know."

For a while we kissed some more, even touched a little, but eventually he rolled off of me and I moved to lay my head on his chest. I would never tell him what was running through my mind because that nigga would probably kill me. But I was going to leave out of here in the dark of the morning. Since that nigga Dante wanted to make a trade for my life, since Phenom wanted to do it too, I would do it my damn self. By the time Trigga figured it out, hopefully he'd have Ghost back and whatever happened to me happened. I was tired anyway.

Chapter 10

Phenom

A monster had just been created by the actions of my failings and my woman was distant from me, from the choices I had to make. The plight of a father was never easy when it came to living the hood life and my nephew was learning that. I had spent years in the gutta, cutting, and bucking. Taking heads and leaving some mothers without a son or daughter.

My hands were fucking bloody, torn, and emaciated. That's how long in the game I'd been doing this shit. From the bowels of Brooklyn to the pond of London's gang-riddled streets. I was there in the height of all the chaos that reigned in both locations. I ran the streets of the '80s at the birth of this shit, feel me?

Did the same in London and I knew, always, that this life would be my grave. So, I wasn't created outta some kiddy bubble gum yackin' thug crap. Was a nigga ashamed of that shit? No. Through it all I used it for my advantage to thug in the streets then thug in the corporate world. Everything worked out to the point of what I needed and had to do three months back. Then shit changed.

This shit wasn't for the faint of heart and I knew when my nephew found out, any trust we had just built was fucking done. The fact that we just almost took each other down was the proof of that shit and in this reality of everything, my blood was right. I wasn't who he thought

I was, which that's not my fault all the way. I'm a man who never had to bargain for shit in my day, but it took the snatching of my seed to make me turn my back on the very principles his father and I both devoted our lives to. We changed all to be about this life and built this legacy on intellect and power.

Today that shit was just twisted in the truth of what I had planned to do in weakness. My name, my reputation was now looking suspect in my own house. In this shit, Dante gained the upper fucking hand. He weakened the inside of my domain. I stood in a flat that I had planned to set up for them to have in privacy and safety that we wouldn't intrude on as street bosses but as fam. I stared out the massive bay window of the flat, watching a girl who reminded me of Anika slip out and disappear down the streets of a block she didn't know shit about. I observed my kingdom fracturing and it had me gripping the windowsill hard in frustration of the reality of it.

"Ahmir, did she leave?" Anika's sultry voice whispered behind me.

It was the voice that got me the first day we met. It was that ass that had me deep into her curves and that led me on the rocky road of our relationship, which lead us to our unique marriage.

"You know she did," I replied, lost in my thoughts.

Anika slipped up against me, her hand slipping around my waist to hold me as she used the gift of persuasion that was only hers. "Time to play the next card, baby."

"That I know too, ma; they both have been in that son of a bitch's hands too long. Hit up Clip and let's go."

Leaning down, our mouths met in heat. We always could get on one level even in fighting. It was something that we knew gave us power in this type of chaos.

"I love you, baby, and this family will be okay, especially when we get our daughter back," she whispered against my lips.

I gave her back my usual, "Loving you too and that's truth."

We tongued down some more, my hand resting on her belly where we had created our daughter when we were still young, around my nephew's and Ray-Ray's age.

Anika Okoye-Ekejindu was my equal in every damn thing and I was hers. Her curves melted into the hardness of me and my hands slid down to get a touch of her juicy. The soft moan I got from her let me know we'd always be good even in death, so I let her go and we headed out into the night, strapping up and setting in the next plan of the game. Weakening the protection in the streets but taking down the Dirty Cs.

See, everyone thought we were being lax. That we didn't know that kid was Dante's or that he had pull in the lowest and highest of places. Never reveal the true hand to your game, because that shit can tear an empire down at their own weak spot, and Dante had weak spots. It was just time to reveal some of them. The rest me, and mine, would reveal later.

Chapter 11

Trigga

Once trust was broke for a nigga then that was the end of that connection. Phenom was now just another nigga after what he broke down to me. He had his agenda and now I had mine. We were not going to be on that same page ever again. Nigga was now dead to me. And now after this shit, I had to search for my own for the rest of us.

Peace was never going to come to me. That I did take with me from what that nigga Phenom had said to us. For the life of me, him turning on fam who supposedly was to be protected at all cost, in order to barter them off, was not making sense. I don't give a fuck who it was. Ghost was mine. Like, I realized today that girl wasn't turning into a little sister for me. Naw, she was my daughter through and through. And though she was snatched up, was no fucking way I'd hand over anyone in my fam to that foul-ass nigga Dante, unless I had some plan behind that shit and that person knew it.

My thoughts were fucking with me. I tried to stay laid up against Diamond but how my mind was working wasn't letting me. Any other nigga would have hit, since the chance was there but, yo, I just couldn't do it. I was hard as fuck for her, was cheefin to see what she felt like, but too much shit was going down in the moment.

And on some other shit, I wasn't sure if she would have been down because that was what she was still used to: a nigga dumpin' in her and hurting her. To me, she would never be that type of broad, so before I could lie with her, I had to see where her mental was and I needed to get my mental right and get Ghost back for real. Damn, and even get my cousin back, because anyone in Dante's hands were damaged goods day one. That was why I was pacing and not laying up against Diamond anymore.

Was too fucking hard to sleep. Kept seeing my mom and pops go down and my little sister's face as she played in the park before she was gunned down. I sat up and watched Diamond sleep for a moment. Part of me knew she wasn't, 'cause of how shallow her breaths were. But I got up anyway started pacing, and then went to the bathroom to take a piss. Jake and Gina were in their own room 'sleep and Speedy was laid out on the couch. I kept it walking when I saw Phenom near the kitchen with Anika moving to walk up to him.

Just checking how she watched me, I knew she'd gun me down if I laid hands on that nigga. I could see that love all through her, but right now, I wasn't fucking caring. I ain't need no friends at one point in life and now, it looked like I didn't need no blood. I can do bad all by my fucking self. Slamming my hands in my pockets, I kept my head low and walked on back into Diamond's room.

When I stepped in and closed the door, I glanced up and shook my head. I shouldn't have even been shocked about it because I already knew she'd do some simple shit. The window was wide open and the cool night air had the curtains flapping and covering me in its embrace. Diamond was gone, and from how stuff was on the floor, I knew she was moving fast. Slight irritation had me thumbing my nose. Habit had me almost turning to tell Phenom and Anika so we all could go get her, but I had no love for those two anymore so fuck them to hell was the motto right now.

I moved around the room quickly, walking to the window to see where she was heading. I had just made it in time to see her turn a corner, so I hustled around to get my shirt, strap up, and then knock on her wall, in the familiar coded pattern me and Jake had. I waited to see if he heard it. When he hit me with that same rhythm back, I knew he was down and would meet up with me to where I knew Diamond was heading: Dante's codes.

Strapped up and ready, I climbed out the window, pulled my hoodie over my head, zipping it up to expose my eyes, and then sprinted down the block. The endz was quiet, but I still saw random niggas and broads roaming the streets, drinking, smoking, or just fucking off. Catching up with Diamond was the priority, so I wasn't even checkin' for anyone who tried to step to me. Taking an alley, I ran into fence, pulled myself up and over it then landed back to the ground returning to my sprint.

Flashing lights and sirens screeched past and I waited. It seemed like since my time being in the endz that more roadblocks by the coppers were being set up. A lot of them were by schools and the shit had me feeling some type of way about it. The sound of a car coming up had me dipping into the shadows of an alley and waiting for it to pass by. A white van slowly road by, stopping near me. The sound of doors opening had me stepping deeper into the darkness as I listened.

"Oi, this one is a fighter. Wack her good and let's go mate," a pitchy, funky accent sounded. I knew it was British but it was almost too hard to understand for a moment, so I had to replay it slowing my mind again to understand. As I did so, I heard grunts and screams before the doors closed again and the car pulled off.

Realization hit me about that ride. I'd heard from several of the people in the towers that a white car had been spotted in the endz around this time every day. It was the same one that Phenom and Anika told me about when Ghost was snatched. That shit had my fingers itching because if it was the same one, it sounded like some kidnapping shit was going down in the endz and I'd just gotten close to it. Another realization hit me: Diamond was still out here; what if she had just gotten snatched too?

Pushing off the wall, I kicked started on my run again. Snaking through alleys, jumping over gates and pedestrian bridges, my pulse was thumping hard in my ears. Sweat was kissing my skin and heat had me wanting to pull off my hood. I kept running, crossing into Dante's codes until I heard a familiar feminine voice shouting over a group of niggas.

"Fuck you. You think I'm scared about any shit you got to give? Fuck you wack-ass niggas."

Laughter sounded off and I moved closer behind the wall of a community building to see her surrounded by about ten to eleven busted-up niggas of all varieties. Some had locs, some had long hair, other had no hair, some were scarred the fuck up from shanks and others were as huge as Jake. Speaking of, that nigga almost got sliced up the moment he stepped behind me.

"Yo, you know not to do that, man," I hissed low, my own shank pressing against his neck.

Jake's big hands lifted in the air and he gave a lopsided smile. "The Lord is my weapon, bruv. I like how they say that shit, man. Anyway, Ray-Ray being foolish?"

Dropping my hand, I turned back around and saw her swing on a tall, lanky Asian-looking guy. I gritted my teeth and gave a quick nod. "Yeah. Where's Gina?'

"She said she wasn't leaving. Said she's waiting on your fam and going to holla at him for a moment. She's tired of running, Trig," he quietly explained.

"Ah yo, if that's the case, who is that back to back with li'l shawty?" I said with a quirky smirk on my face.

Jake pushed me back to look over my shoulder and his grip got so hard, I had to push that nigga back.

"Yo, not my baby? Nuuu I wasn't readyyyy. Damn, G baby! Fuck 'em up," Jake hissed low in shock and slight amusement.

Gina stood with Ray-Ray sporting her fishtail ponytails, dressed in tights and twin tanks, one pink, one white with the pink and white Js I had gotten her back in the A. Ray-Ray's high-pitch grunt distracted me from speaking on Gina and Jake's low growl almost made me laugh. Both broads' grunts were so high it had them sounding as if she and Gina were in Wimbledon playing tennis.

I focused on what they both were doing and inwardly chuckled. Baby girl Gina had her kicks planted into the face of one of Dante's goons. Blood and teeth went flying with the side of his face turning left. Once she had him distracted, Ray-Ray turned around to help and ducked under that nigga's arms to jump into the face of another cat, using her elbow to slam into his Bubba Gump–lipped face, so Gina could hunker low and punch him dead in the nuts.

I knew watching them work like they were their own clique that they were crazy as fuck. These two bad bitches were going to fucking get killed and for what reason, I wasn't even sure about at the moment. I just knew that both of them were going to be snatched the fuck up had Jake and me not been there. But, right as I was about to push off from the wall, a white van pulled up and two CIA-looking cats stepped out in suits and shades. One of them started yackin' at the mouth and I instantly recognized the voice.

Instantly, I signaled behind me to Jake and I pushed off the wall. "Yeah, they're getting buck as fuck; anyway, strap up, we all about to scrap. These motherfuckers 'bout to take Gina and Diamond, leggo."

Timbs thumped against the street pavement as we ran head long into the middle of Diamond and Gina's fight. The two CIA-looking cats tried to turn and run to their van but they didn't make it in time. Being smaller than Big Jake, I was able to sprint faster as he body dropped niggas by the numbers. I dashed to the van, pulled out my Glocks and let off several rounds hitting each man in the back, and legs. I glanced around noticing that where we was no one who really saw shit, so I rushed up on each fallen snatcher, searched for their cells, then cold blocked each one.

Behind me, Diamond was moving like a junkie looking for a hit. She stomped whoever was on the ground in front of her. In her hand was a makeshift shank. She swung out and stuck whoever came her way in their ribs, across their face, or against their arms or hands. Jake was behind her, crushing skulls together and on the pavement. Gina saw my signal to protect the van, and then sent a skinny motherfucker flying across the street with a strong kick of her foot and a swipe of her chain belt of shanks. They took down seven niggas and left me four.

Enjoyment filled me and I chased down the remaining four who ran off deeper into Dante's code. I didn't give a fuck that they were leading me into the middle of hell; all I knew was that those niggas needed to go down, and go down they did. I had a silencer on me so I was able to take down two before they disappeared into the chaos. Turning, I trailed after the other two, climbing apartment ladders, and then managed to jump deck to deck in their towers, to take down another.

This fucker shot at me, the bullets whizzing past me, until I was able to tackle him and watch him dangle over the edge of a balcony. Fear was in his eyes, which fueled me and made me smile. I could see he was young, looked about my age and the reality of that was all in that cat's face. He started to plead, but I didn't give him a chance to finish. My own shank came out in the form of an ice pick and it slammed right between his bulking eyes. Those shocked eyes rolled into the back of his head, I pushed him off the edge watching him fall while I whistled a tune then jumped into another tower deck, climbing down the ladder.

I knew the other dude was farther way, so I picked up my speed, zigzagging through the hood, jumping down ditches and finding the quickest way to catch up with the nigga. I found a spot between a dumpster and a back door where I hid and I waited in the area I had seen him go. Like a predictable punk, he was hiding. So as I waited on him, he eventually came out and looked around pulling out a cell.

He nervously walked back and forth, looking over his shoulder. His fit seemed like it was swallowing him. Saggin' pants, a big, oversized pullover hoodie, and dirty kicks. He looked like any white kid in London who was into what some would call the urban culture, wasn't really a threat unless you saw all his piercings. One in his lip and some over his ears. As he dialed, I focused my Glock on him, pulled the trigger, then shot off his hand. His gurgling screams rent that air.

"Don't kill me, bruv, I swear down, I swear down dat I won't tell Dante a thang man. On my blood, this is for mah—"

Slicing across his face, I listened him scream again, as my blade glistened in his blood. I walked around him in a circle as he fell to his knees and I chuckled, "Yeah, I don't fucking care, homie."

The end of my shank sliced through his jugular and he fell against the dirt of the road. I studied how he fell, my Timbs kicking into his skull until I saw his cell and snatched it. Nigga had dialed someone, and I could hear them on the other end. Laughing low into the phone, I hit end then copped the number with several of the other contacts before smashing it against a wall.

Lights flickered in the alley where I stood. Coolness of the night sky cooled my body down and my back arched forward and I threw my head back yelling to the whole block that nigga Tempa T's "Swing": "'Swing that back to your face, proper. You get smashed, proper. Round your head, proper. Stamp stamp on your head, proper. Sixteen blows killer combos, bust your nose, proper. Merk you!'"

Amusement filled my chest when I heard murmurs kick start around me. Rustling made me shift out my Glock, but a blur sped by me with a familiar lopsided smirk. Nigga let out a cocky laugh, stuck his tongue out, and grabbed his nuts, then threw his hands in the air doing an Azonto dance. Something he always did when he was slicing cats.

I knew that nigga Speedy was here. Me and Jake had seen slashed up body parts as we stepped up to the community center where Ray-Ray was. I didn't think on it until I saw him now. He musta followed Gina and protected her back; now this nigga was running through the codes murking dudes and I let out a laugh as he disappeared covering us while probably using some of his own boys, like Tunez, as his backup.

My head shook and my Glocks slid back in hiding. Before anyone could see me, I ran back down the alleyway to find Jake. As I made it back to that spot, Jake pulled up in the white van. He already knew what time it was. Diamond opened the passenger side door and Gina reached to pull at me. Jumping in, I glanced at them both as Jake sped out of Dante's code.

"You snatch up the two niggas who was driving this shit?" I asked.

Perspiration spilled down Jake's face, dripping onto the shoulders of his black jersey. Both of his giant hands fisted the steering wheel and he nodded while he drove.

"Yeah, Trig, Jake put them in the back. There're some kids and teens back there," Diamond rushed out as if she were trying to catch her breath.

"And I'm untying them, Trig. Ew you got a nigga's ear on your hoodie; that's nasty," Gina hoarsely said with a frown while using the tips of her nails to pick it up and throw it over her shoulder.

Baby girl leaned over to wipe at Jake's face kissing him, then moving to kiss Diamond before sliding to the back, speaking softly to the kids.

"Yo, I thought you were staying in the flat, baby girl," I asked, holding on to my temper with her.

"Ah huh, I was, but like I changed my mind, 'cause Diamond texted me. I snuck around the back ways and beat you there. Yep, I know the codes too, and I bust some teeth out." Gina cheesed then sucked her teeth. "Speedy gunna be mad, but he'll be a'ight. I'll make him a shank and he can get me more fried Mars bars. I'm hungry."

"No, he's not and maybe he will, Baby G. That bashy nigga is covering our tracks and tying shit up. God save him." Jake gave a boastful laugh as he hyped us up on Speedy before sharply turning the van.

Having both Diamond and Gina speaking to me made me realize the dumb shit they had done and I turned to glance at Diamond as we sped down the streets of London. "Yo, you almost got put down there, shawty. What the fuck were you thinking? Naw, let me tell you, you weren't. Fuck is your problem? Do you realize what you just did? Do you realize that every time you do some stupid-ass shit I gotta come and get you?"

Jake's laughter filled the small space of the van with that of the grunts of the two men behind us. I could see out the side of my eye that Gina was working on getting the kidnapped kids and teens free. Several of the free kids moved behind Gina and they had the two snatchers held down, bound, and gagged. It made me smile but I wasn't about to show that to Diamond or Gina right now. A nigga was pissed off at them both, but mainly Diamond.

"Whatever, Trig, you fucked up my rotation. Was trying to get snatched up to get to Ghost and you just ruined that, but that's cool. We got those two in the back. That's what counts, nigga, so get out my face with that rah-rah," Diamond hollered back. She rolled her eyes, sucked her teeth, and flipped her hand in my face as we rode on.

Shawty was on some real bullshit if she really thought that being snatched up by Dante was really going to help anything. And if she put her fucking hand in my face one more time we were going to have a problem. I didn't realize that she had me so mad, that I had spit that shit out right in her face.

"So! What the hell you going to do? Huh? You going to put your hands on me? Do it! I'll gash you the fuck—"

I snatched her so fast by the bun on the top of her head, twisting her in her seat. She gave a yelp because she was tangled by the seat belt. My snatching her like that threw her off the yackin' she was doing. My lips locked down on hers hard. I fed her my tongue, found my hand on her titty, and kissed her so raw that I felt her body shake in my grasp as I held her arm with my other hand. My light brown eyes glinted with the light rise of the sun and I stared her right in her face.

Part of me was proud as fuck that the stupid shit she just did paid off, we got two goons to bleed info from, and her stupid shit with Gina had us saving some kids from being snatched. But, another other part of me was still pissed at her that she had thought of something so fucking stupid at the same time.

"You still acting on stupid. Fuck your rah-rah and think about what your actions do to others, a'ight? Pull over into the marshes, Jake. We in one of Anika's codes where Dante wouldn't even think to look here," I pressed.

"You two need to fuck, bro, and a'ight," Jake clowned.

"Ah huh. You two are slow as fuck," Gina instigated, her voice still light and hoarse.

Ignoring them both, me and Diamond just looked at each other before shifting back to where we were as he parked the ride. The sound of the seat belt signal dinging with that of the van light illuminating the small place had me moving to the back of the van. I glanced at all the kids, and opened up the doors so they could get out.

"Tell my man Jake and my girl Gina what endz you come from. We'll get you all home a'ight, and you tell them everything you saw, heard, smelled, touched, tasted when they snatched you. Tell them where you all were at, who you were with, too, a'ight?" I detailed to each teary-eyed, disheveled kid and teen.

They all nodded, some of them talking a mile a minute to me, and others reached out crying to hug me before I urged them to hit up and told them to ignore everything they were about to hear.

Closing the doors of the ride, while I climbed back in, I saw Diamond inch closer, then slap the face of a bald, slightly fat, yet muscled white guy.

"You know what this is about to be, so I'ma tell you to get to chattin' and don't play games or my nigga is about to make it worse for you," she smoothly suggested in a lethal sexiness that had me eyeballing her for a moment 'cause I swear she was throwing vibe like her aunt.

Both men grunted and I gave a slight shrug while kneeling in the back of the van. Digging in my pocket, I took out my shank and didn't say a thing. I just reached out to grab the bald one's pinky finger, sliced it off, and then threw it in the face of the other one. Both men screamed into their gags, but I wasn't done, snatching the black-haired biracial-looking guy's finger. I slowly worked the tip of my blade into his fingernail. I jiggled it, watching the blood slowly flow, and I smoothly popped that bitch off and chuckled at the sharp feminine scream he gave. Glancing up at Diamond, I nodded to her to speak for me again.

"Spill that shit. Give us names, locations, and the reason of your boss's bullshit, okay!" she shouted, slapping each one again.

I read each nigga's eyes, could see they were down for their boss, so I gave a bored sigh, then flipped to the bald guy's hand. I took his other hand, and gave him the same pinky treatment that I gave the dark-haired dude. His screams saturated the van and I shifted up to take the dark-haired guy's face in my hand and I pressed the tip of my shank into the bridge of his nose waiting.

Brown eyes widened as I twisted the tip deep. I watched him squirm then I took his gag out of his mouth. "Talk."

"We were ordered to take kids no one wanted; then we were told to just start snatching from ya codes. Any kind, just take ya," he stammered. My knife twisted again and he screeched out, "Okay okay. I just know him by S.B. I'm new here. I don't . . . I promise . . . Leave mi nose please!"

Diamond shook her head in my face and I chuckled. I had no intention of not cutting his nose off, so as I stood, my blade sliced that shit right off and I moved to turn the bald-head guy's face my way. He saw nothing but blood and a nose. Diamond waved behind me and I smiled down at the cat, as I nodded for her to address him.

"Your turn. Speak," she cooed as she held down the other, who was rocking and shaking over the shock.

Pulling down his gag, the nigga straight spit in my face; luckily I had my hoodie zipped up but the fact that he spit in my face pissed me all the way off. That was some shit I didn't do. So I kicked open the van, jumped out, then snatched that nigga by his bounded ankles and pulled him out the van. I watched him fall hard banging his head against the van and the ground. Fury had me going, and I gave Diamond the signal to off that cat she was sitting on and I took the time to drag this nigga to the front of the van.

Jake and Gina both watched me from afar wondering what I was about to do. He saw the shank I had in my hand and the anger in my body and he moved Gina and the kids away so they wouldn't see what I was about to do.

"Nigga, you don't spit on me and not expect me to piss on your grave, check it." I moved to pop open the hood of the van. I looked at the inner working of it until I saw the battery. We really didn't need this shit anymore, so I pulled it out and dropped it against his hand.

"So, you're the one who gets a hard dick off this shit, I heard you, so don't deny it. Now usually I'd cut ya tongue out but we need that, so guess what you get?" A sinister smile lit up my eyes and I popped open the car battery and pulled out a tube that held what I was looking for.

Reaching for his face, I watch that nigga buck at me, but I fed him the end of my fist before holding him down, opening his eyes, and pulling the tube over it.

Lovely acid sizzled out and landed on the whites of that nigga's eyes and the scream he gave made my day. "Drip, drip, motherfucker."

I waited until his body stopped shaking; I pressed my shank against his throat and let him spill all we needed to know. He gave us locations, numbers, IDs. I found out that both of these niggas were corrupt cops and I learned that they worked on their own dime, going code to code, pulling out kids, teens, and even women, and selling them on the black market, either for the sex trade, or for ruthless people who would do anything for a kid, or infant. This shit was crazy and the names he spilled spun my head. I memorized everything he said, even who S.B. was. The final kicker for me was that this nigga knew exactly who I was and who was taken from me.

"Where are they?" was the last thing I growled to that jiggling bastard as he pleaded for me to stop his torture. Blood, flesh, and battery acid covered my gloved hands and my mark while I kneeled over his now shirtless body.

The low, tired, raspy voice of the nigga let me know he was on his last leg and he gave me the exact code where he had last seen Ghost and Chyna. He let me know that he had seen them both locked up in a cage with S.B. and Dante in a room at his compound. He had told me he was going to take Diamond next, but of course, that wasn't going to happen. Then he gave me the icing of the main location of Dante's with that of other crews that worked with him.

Dante was a shifty motherfucker and now we had knowledge of what he was doing. I offed the pig next to me, gutting him open and carving DIRTY C AND PEE'DO in his body. Walking back to the van, I did the same to the other cop Diamond had offed and I pulled her out of the van. What was there would be left for the coppers to be witness to. We had names. Thanks to their cells, we had numbers, too. Shit wasn't going to be easy but we had two motherfuckers to take down and our fam to get back. Fuck politics; ENGA was in London now and the blocks were ours.

Chapter 12

Ghost

We were woken up at like the crack of dawn. Kids were scared 'cause we could hear other kids screaming down the hall. There was gunshots and stuff. We didn't know what was going on. The room was still dark. The only time there was light was when the door was opened and they came to snatch another kid.

"Dem chat too bloodclot much. Close uno mout. Mi shoving swords up pussiholes, yeah?"

That nigga Dante was crazy. He kept coming in staring at Chyna like he wanted to do something to her. Every time they took a kid Chyna would scream and ask what they were doing to them. I could tell the ones she was fond of. Dante seemed to only pick kids that she talked to so she told me not to talk to her no more. So I didn't. We could hear dudes talking about how some cops had been killed and how it had been found out that they was taking kids. So now since kids were missing the law had started to look for them and Dante didn't want any found alive in his house. That scared me.

I hadn't ate since I been there so I was hungry as fuck. Scared and hungry. They ain't let me out the cage so I had to pee there, too. So did all the other kids. The room stank like shit and piss. I prayed Trigga was coming for me soon. My legs were hurting and I was tired. I ain't sleep at all. I remember when they first brought Diamond to Dame's house. I would watch her from my spots in the wall and see how she ain't really sleep either. When she did them niggas tried to take her to the basement. I wasn't going to sleep. I was thinking about my family with Diamond and Trigga when Dante walked in.

"Bring them two to me," he told one of the dudes standing in there.

He was talking 'bout me and Chyna. He walked over and put his face to the cage smiling like a fool at Chyna. She ain't even look like she was scared of that nigga. When he stuck his hand in the cage to grab at her titty she grabbed a hold of his face. She was reminding me of Diamond when she clawed that nigga like a stray cat then spit in his face. He didn't even seem to care though.

"Don't put your hands on me, you bitch uphill gardener," she spat out.

I ain't even know what that meant, but that nigga Dante just laughed. I knew he was bent when he wiped the blood and her spit from his face and licked his fingers. He unlocked the cage, snatched the door open. As she kicked at him with her feet, he grabbed hold of her ankle and yanked her out. She hit the floor hard, bumping her head against the concrete floor. She moaned out loud and her eyes fluttered. I could tell the fall and hit to her head almost knocked her out. After that these big niggas snatched me out the cage I was in. They took Chyna to one room and me to another. I was trying to look around for a way out. Trigga always said if you got in, you could get out. I saw that they had a window open but I ain't know how far down the ground was.

"Put her in line with the rest of them," Dante said as he sat back at the head of the long rectangular table. "Niggas chirping like birds around this place. Fucking up my endz. Give me the muchies, eh?"

He laughed then kicked a dead body by his feet. There was a dead man there with a hole in his chest. It was a big hole like somebody had taken something out of him. Dante had guns, knives, and his cane lying on the table by him. I ain't get how he was eating with all that blood lying around. I was shivering and cold. Just like the other naked kids.

"Bring another one around," Dante said as he tore into a piece of meat.

He was eating like a dog. No shirt on. His white pants had blood all on them, too. Those fingernail scrapes down his face didn't make him look any less of a bad man. It made him look like a monster. A little naked girl stepped forward. She looked like was from like India or something. Trigga always made me read and stuff so I could spot different kinds of people like it was nothing. She had her hands in front of her privates and was crying so bad she was shaking. I was hoping he wasn't gonna do nothing like try to do bad things to her that grownups shouldn't do to kids, but when he shot her right in the head and the other kids started screaming, I ain't know what to do. I was frozen. He called another boy forward. When he pulled the sword from his cane, he cut the boy's head off. Some of the kids started screaming louder and running around the room trying to hide. I couldn't move. I ain't ever seen no nigga kill no kids like me like that. Dillenger's face flashed in my head.

"Messing up my ducats. They kill my boy. Pussiclots murder mi brudda, kill mi son."

He was talking like a crazy man one minute and then calm the next as a couple of men brought Chyna back in the room. They had put her in a white dress and took her hair down. Her hands were taped together and they ain't take the tape off 'til she was sitting down on the right of Dante.

"Bring me dat gyal," Dante said looking at me.

I started to scream and tried to run but they were stronger than me. Them niggas placed me right where they had placed the other girl and little boy. Now that I was standing closer, I could see a door cracked. In the small room I saw bodies of the other kids. My whole body almost collapsed. My head jerked when a big white dude walked in and dropped a plate that had something on that looked like a roast in front of Dante.

"Want something to eat, bitch?" he asked Chyna.

"Fuck you," was her response.

Dante only shrugged, stuck a fork down into the meat and bit into it like a rabid dog. He wiped the back of his hand across his mouth then looked down at the body lying beside him.

"Your heart is better outside ya body than innit, yeah, man?"

He was talking to the dead corpse. Both mine and Chyna's face twisted when we realized that nigga was eating a human heart. I couldn't help it; I threw up all over the floor. That made Dante look over at me. He studied me for a long time like he was trying to see if he knew me.

"You knew my boy?" Dante asked me.

I shook my head. "Naw, I ain't know no niggas you know, nigga." I was scared as shit, but that bitch nigga wasn't gone know it.

"They say they see you with my boy, gyal."

"Fuck you and fuck yo' snitches, nigga. Where I'm from snitches get ditches. Fuck the stitches."

Dante wasn't amused. "You have an American accent, yeah. I know who you are and who you with, yeah? They kill my boy, so I kill you, right, innit? Put her on the table," he told the dudes.

Chyna was looking from me to him in a panic as the dudes stretched me out on the table. Dante stood and kicked his chair back, picking up his sword. My eyes widened when he aimed it at my privates and I cried out loud from the fear of being cut. I didn't know a lot, but I knew if he cut me there, I would be hurt something serious. To show just how serious he was, he took the blade and sliced the crease on the left side of my inner thigh then he did the same to the right side. I'd never known pain like what I was experiencing. It hurt so bad that I started slobbering from the mouth as I yelled out.

I screamed and cried like the baby I was. "Owwww! Please stop, please, don't cut me no more."

Chyna jumped up and grabbed his wrist. "Stop it, Dante. You're mad, man. I'll do it," she screamed at him.

He stopped just inches away from pushing the sword inside of me and grinned at her. "You'll do what?"

She swallowed and looked like she was about to be sick. "I'll do what you want. I'll give you what you want. Just don't hurt her no more, yeah? Don't hurt no more kids, Dante. I'll do what you want," she yelled.

He didn't say nothing but I was glad when he move the sword. I ain't never had nothing in me and it hurt. Dante picked up the heart he had been eating and bit down into it again.

"Good," he said as he chewed. "Because I'm not one to make a woman do what she doesn't want, yeah?"

I didn't know what he was talking about, but was glad when he told the men to let go. Chyna grabbed me up in her arms. She sat back down at the table with me in her lap whispering to me that it was going to be all right. It was then I kinda figured that she was older than she looked. She looked like she was about twelve or thirteen. She just had a body that said otherwise.

"One other thing," Dante said as he looked outside of his window like he was deep in thought.

"What?" she spat out at him.

I couldn't see what he was about to do because I turned my head and started to hide my face in her chest. I was really still just a baby and for the first time, I missed having a mama. But when her body jerked and when Chyna's screams rented the air, my head popped up and looked at her then over to Dante. That nigga had stuck a fork clear through her hand.

"You ever put your hands in my face again, yeah, I'ma cut yours off. That's fair, innit?" he asked her as he twisted the fork then pushed it deeper before snatching it out.

Blood spilled from her hand. There was slobber hanging from Chyna's mouth and tears running down her face as she cried. I ain't know what to do, but watch as that nigga strolled from the room like he was a king.

I didn't know how much time had passed as me and Chyna sat there, but I just knew I had to get out of there. Dante had left the room and hadn't come back yet.

"We have to get out of here," I whispered to her.

"I know and we will."

After she had wrapped her hand the best way she could, Dante put me and Chyna in his room. I woulda been put back in the cage but Chyna told him that she wasn't gonna go to his room with him unless he let her clean me up. After he smacked her down to the floor for being defiant, he let her bring me in the room with them, but he threw me in his closet. I tried not to make too much noise as I looked around for anything to use as a weapon. I wasn't naked it anymore, but my thigh still hurt like hell from being cut there.

I cracked the door when I heard Chyna crying again. Dante was on top of her on the bed. I wasn't a big kid but I knew what he was doing to do to her, especially when she screamed out again. She ain't have to do that for me. I felt like I shoulda jumped from that window and killed myself or something. I couldn't take hearing that nigga's grunts or hearing her cry so I covered my ears and backed as far into the back of the closet as I could. No matter how hard I tried to cover my ears the squeaky noise of the bed came through so did Chyna's cries. It was like Dame and Diamond all over again. I thought our nightmare was over but, really, it was just beginning.

I didn't know how long I had been in that closet before I heard a loud boom like something had crashed into the house.

"What the fuck?" I heard Dante yell then he laughed. "About time you came to play, Phenom!"

The hard sound of running feet sounded against the floor as the room door opened and Dante exited. Nothing but gunshots and niggas groans could be heard but when Chyna slowly pulled the door open and held her finger to her lips for me to be quiet, I was grateful.

"It's my daddy. I knew he was going to find me. But we still have to get out of here," she said. "You afraid of heights?"

I shook my head. "I ain't afraid of nothing if it's gonna get us out of here."

"Good, because we have to jump from here into the pool to get out of here, yeah?"

She was about to say something else when Dante snatched the door open and yanked her by her hair as he dragged her from the closet.

"You want me, Phenom," he yelled while she kicked and screamed. "Got to get through ya seed to get me, bruv," he kept yelling then laughed.

That nigga was naked as a jay bird I saw when I crawled from the closet. He stood on the massive banister on the window outside his room. I looked around in a hurry for anything I could grab.

"All I want is my daughter and the little girl and I'll let you live, nigga."

That was Phenom. He kinda sounded like Trigga sometimes. I was in my own world as I crawled underneath the bed then out on the other side. I saw a shank lying on that nigga's nightstand. I quickly grabbed it and crawled back under the bed.

"I don't give a fuck about living, blood. All mi care about is how good and fine Chyna's pussihole felt against my dick."

I could see that nigga had a gun in one hand with his arm wrapped around her neck and a shank in the other that she held to her. When he dug it into her back and she screamed out, I army crawled like Trigga had showed from under the bed. Before he could stick her anymore, I stuck him right on his back on the side where Trigga had told me the kidneys be at. That made that nigga backhand me as he yelled out and turned around. It hurt like shit and I flew back into the bedpost, but that got Chyna outta his hands.

"Come on, Ghost," she screamed.

She was frantic as she ran with her uninjured hand outstretched to me. She took my hand and we rushed from the room and headed for the stairs.

"Trigga," I screamed out when I saw him.

He was in the middle of a fight with a dude who looked to be ten times bigger than Jake. I watched as he took an elbow to the face then a punch to the gut. That didn't slow him down. He ate those punches and delivered a few of his own. Only on his fist were gloves that had barbwire wrapped around them. When he threw a straight jab to the big man's face, blood started leaking.

"Run, Ghost," was all he yelled out as a big nigga tackled him to the ground.

"You know him?" Chyna asked.

I was proud so I smiled. "Yeah, that's my daddy."

Me and Chyna kept running until we got to the bottom of the stairs. Once we did we saw Anika hacking up a nigga who had Diamond pinned to the ground. When her machete came down she took out a big hunk of flesh. Looked like she had cut a slice out a piece of watermelon. I knew that nigga was dead. Diamond pushed the body off of her, but she was bleeding bad from her stomach.

"Mommy," Chyna squealed and ran into her mama's arms.

I didn't have no mama, but I had Diamond so that's who I ran to. "You hurt, Diamond," I said.

"I know. I'll be good. We gotta get outta here. Did he hurt you, Ghost? Did that nigga touch you?" She was on her knees as she hugged me then pulled back to look at my face, examining me.

"I don't want to talk about it," I said low.

We was standing in what felt like a warzone because bodies was flying and bullets. When Big Jake stood at the top of the balcony and tossed a nigga over, the body almost hit us.

"My bad," he yelled down but didn't have time to say much else as another nigga was rushing him. "Motherfucker! Where these niggas keep coming from?" he groaned out as he fought.

"You have to get out of here now," I heard Anika tell Chyna. "You know where to go. Take them there. Speedy and a girl named Gina will be waiting on you. You can trust her. Take your cousin, Diamond, and the little girl with you."

Chyna nodded. "You found me. I knew you would. I love you, Mama."

"I know. I love you too. And of course we would. Took us awhile, but always remember, we'll always come for you. No matter what."

"Daddy is—"

Anika nodded and cut her off. "I know. Just go. Go now."

Those weird police sirens were in the distance. I looked around to see if I could see Trigga again, but he was gone.

"Come on, guys," Chyna said to me in Diamond. "Bloody hell, you're bleeding bad," she said when saw Diamond. "Come on, cousin. We gotta get out of here."

Chapter 13

Ray-Ray

I didn't remember going to sleep. The last thing I remembered was lying in the back of a car. From there I blacked out because of the blood loss and the pain. One of Dante's goons had cut me good. I never saw that nigga coming. If my aunt hadn't been there, I probably would be dead. We were no longer in my flat because Anika said it wouldn't be safe. After me and Trigga had made those two cops talk, we were going to go back and tell Anika and Phenom, but Trigga said fuck it and we headed out to Dante's mansion on our own. That was when we saw Anika and Phenom had already beat us there.

Nothing but bedlam ensued afterward. All I remembered was me, Trigga, and Big Jake went in swinging.

"Diamond, watch your fucking six," Trigga had yelled at me after he'd put a bullet in a nigga's skull who was trying to sneak me when we first got there.

"Sorry," I had yelled.

I remembered jumping on the back of a big white nigga and shanking him in the throat. All I could think about was getting Ghost. My mental was eating a whole through me with images and thoughts of some grown man violating baby girl. So every nigga I came in contact with, I treated them like they had done something to Ghost. As I slid through a nigga's legs then stuck my shank in his dick, I imagined he had violated my Ghost. I was hyped on adrenaline, taking nigga's lives left and right until that one had caught me.

If you thought anything you had seen in the US was bloody and gruesome, nothing was like what we seen in London. Them niggas believed in shanks, baseball bats with barbed wires, and hand-to-hand annihilation. They used guns too, but unlike the stories you heard of in Chicago, New York, New Orleans, Atlanta, and Detroit with the gun violence, in London, niggas liked to get up close and personal when they killed you.

"How're you feeling, cousin?" Chyna asked me when she saw my eyes were open.

"Hungry. Where's Ghost?"

"She's still sleeping."

I nodded as I tried to sit up. Chyna stood to help me.

"Did she tell you what he did to her?" she asked me.

My heart almost fell out on the floor. My worst fear was that she had her little body violated sexually by a grown man.

I shook my head. "No."

"He was going to stick his sword all the way up her you know what. Was going to gut her from the inside out, but I stopped him, yeah. He still cut her bad on her thighs though. I couldn't stop him before he did it, yeah? But I tried. We're supposed to protect the lit'ul ones, innit?"

I nodded. "Thank you. That's all he did to her right? Nothing else?"

"Well he cut her pretty badly but I fixed her as best I could. She still needs to see needs to see the medics."

My eyes watered, heart was heavy. I didn't know whether to be glad she still had her innocence or sad that he had still hurt her anyway. "How did you stop him?" That had me curious because from stories I'd heard, nothing could stop Dante when he was set to kill or fuck you up. Chyna stood from the bed. I could tell by the way she looked off what she had done.

"I did whatever," she mumbled then quickly turned to look at me again. "But don't tell my dad because he wouldn't be able to handle it, yeah? Don't tell him."

She looked young in the face, but she was built just like I was. Genetics gave us breasts, hips, and ass. Even on her petite frame they stood out. Gina walked in and I smiled up at her.

"You okay now, Ray-Ray. You were cut bad, but that doctor they had fixed you up."

She said down and hugged me, then kissed me like she always did. It was always a passionate kiss with Gina, tongue and all. When she pulled away Chyna looked on with wide eyes, but didn't say anything. I knew she was probably trying to figure out what was going on but the front door opening alerted us to the rest of the family coming back in. Chyna was the first one to dash from the room. I could hear her screaming for her daddy as she raced down the hall. I couldn't move that fast because my wound wouldn't let me.

"Chasity," I heard Trigga call and wasn't surprised that was the first person he went to.

I was coming down the hall just as he was. Yeah, he was concerned about me. That was why he paused and looked at me, but his heart pulled him into the room with Ghost and I wasn't mad at that. She jumped from the bed like she was never sleeping and hopped in his arms.

"I knew you was coming, Trigga. I knew you was gonna save me," she cried. "I was scared for real, for real. Like I was really scared, but I knew you was coming."

I smiled at the sight but was crying myself because of what Chyna had told me happened to her. I didn't know what was going to happen when Trigga found out.

"Always, baby girl. I'ma always come for you no matter what."

"Sorry I got snatched up. I wasn't meaning to. Was only trying to make sure that li'l nigga didn't snitch on us. I wasn't trying to make no more trouble."

"Shhh with all the rah-rah," he joked with her. She smiled. "You did good."

"I did?"

"Yeah, you did."

I looked farther down the hall and could still see Anika, Chyna, and Phenom all hugged up. Both Anika and Phenom were still covered in blood, just like Jake and Trigga. Gina was up around Big Jake's waist as he hugged her. He always had to pick her up to her because he was so big and tall and she was so much shorter than he was.

"Did he hurt you?" Phenom asked Chyna.

I wasn't surprised when she shook her head no. "No, Daddy. No."

I didn't think that nigga would be able to handle the news that Dante had raped his daughter. Took her innocence. I dropped my eyes when Anika looked at me. In her eyes was that burning question that I would not answer for her. I turned back to Trigga who was still hugging Ghost but his eyes were on me. Although he didn't know his cousin, I could tell he was relieved to hear she hadn't been hurt either, although it was a lie. He laid Ghost back in the bed and told her he had to get clean then he would come back.

"Did he hurt you, Ghost?"

She quickly looked at me and then I turned back to Trigga. His face fell so hard and I swear all the color drained from it.

"He cut her, Trigga, on her thighs," I told him quickly. "Was going to use his sword to gut her from the inside out. Nothing else. Just cut her real bad," I told him repeating the words Chyna had told me.

He used both of his hands to roughly rub his face as he gave a guttural groan to show his pain at it all.

"I'm sorry, Chas. Swear to God, never again," he assured her.

"It wasn't your fault, Trigga."

Even though she was saying that to him, Trigga was going to take that on him.

"We have to get her to a doctor. Chyna said she did the best she could trying to fix her up."

He only nodded. Big Jake groaned like he was in pain at hearing it. Gina was crying.

"Chyna save me though," Ghost quipped.

I shook my head and held my finger to my lips. Trigga looked up at me. He had always been able to read me so he knew why I was telling her to be quiet.

Gina asked, "Well did y'all kill that nigga?"

Jake shook his head once. "He got away."

My head started to hurt in that moment. This shit was never going to be over. We wouldn't know any peace because, to be honest, we had never known real justice either. From the cradle to the grave, all we ever knew was death and street justice.

Chapter 14

The Intermission

Trigga

In this life, you got two choices: life, or death. In understanding that shit, I came to learn that no matter how hard we tried to run, wasn't nothing going to keep us from the bullshit that came with being hood misfits. Wasn't nothing to be done in it. We started from the bottom, made it to London, and shit still came and followed us. Now we were here cut up and bleeding. Bleeding from the heart, the mind, body and soul and wasn't shit going to heal it all.

I glanced around at the new spot we were at. It wasn't hard to see that Ghost and my cousin Chyna had been hurt by that nigga, but it wasn't my place to tell them that they were lying. I knew why they were and glancing at my uncle, I could see he saw the truth just like I did. Living in the streets like we both did, it wasn't shit we didn't see. Wasn't psychological scars that couldn't be read in the eyes of street survivors and today that shit was apparent as the open wounds on our body. But, one thing I learned about code was that you let it be what it is and plan for another day.

My head hurt. My body ached and I felt sick and shit. Felt as if I was back in that closet watching my fam die around me, but only thing was that we all had survived. I told Gina that that nigga Dante had gotten away, but that wasn't all the way true. I had the knowledge of knowing that he was somewhere bleeding the fuck out as he tried to heal. See, back at his mansion compound, Phenom and me had found that cat trying to ghost out. I ran past dead bodies that were piled up everywhere, some with holes in their chest, others with holes in their skulls.

Ghost had told me as I hugged her that that nigga was eating kids and other niggas' hearts and shit. I told her that nigga musta been on some old world, demonic voodoo shit 'cause he was trying to scare niggas with that loco Hannibal shit. But, it wasn't doing shit for me, it was just fucking disturbing. Anyway, because I was faster, I was able to follow him through a meat locker, where Phenom came after me.

Nigga was covered in nothing but blood and naked as fuck. It was pure insanity and pleasure that I used when I made my environment my weapon and decided to take it out on his body. Meat hooks were all around us, some with bodies swinging on them and some empty. Reaching up, while I stared that nigga down, I unhinged a hook and placed it on my belt buckle.

The sound of my heart thumping in my ears and the trickle of sweat slipping down the side of my neck had me going through all the codes I learned and the teachings of Sun Tzu. Being subtle and not a threat allows for the expert fighter to leave no trace. By being divinely mysterious, he then becomes invisible, thus making him the master of his enemy's fate. Taking my hoodie off just to get into my zone better, I adjusted my Glock while assessing my enemy from my hidden advantage point. See, I understood one last teaching in that, speed is the essence of war, especially in taking vantage of the enemy's unpreparedness. This nigga hadn't expected this type of retaliation and now he stood in front of me like a naked mole rat, covered in blood with a maniacal expression on his face.

In that moment, it had me laughing out loud, as I sneered and fisted my hands. My shoulders rolled in place and I grounded my feet, making sure to fix my gloves while playing bored. “Nigga, ain’t shit about you scary, let’s get that straight.”

I carefully kept my steps quiet and cautious, noticing how Dante erratically turned in circles trying to see where exactly I was in the dark meat locker. Nigga gave out a disjointed laughed, then spit on the floor while wiping at his soaked stern face.

“Face me, blood, or little nigga as your people say. Wut ya gwan use on mi ey? Ya hoodie?” He chuckled. This fool reeked of anxiousness, ready to kill and maim while he tried to goad me into talking again.

All I could think about was nigga had jokes.

I tapped a hanging chain then gave a menacing laugh in the darkness. “You one funny dude, my nigga.”

“I can be even proper funnier once I rip your sphincter muscle from your asshole, bruv. But again, what can a child as you do to a monster like me? Eh? Oy, bring out our toys and play with papa. Because if you were a true threat you wouldn’t stall like you are.” Dante crooned as if eager to get his hands on me.

I gave a light laugh. He was trying to trip me up but fuck the rah-rah. He was on some loco shit, thinking I was just going to use a gun or shank to get at his big ass. Clearly ain’t know shit about me. Nah, I was schooled by the best and I knew I was going to use my weapons and then some.

“A’ight then, old head, let’s do that shit, and see who comes out a victor yeah?” I threw out.

My voice traveled near him in a way that had him swinging out at air. This exposed him for me to side swipe him and with a punch then slam of a meat hook into his side. His shocked harsh scream gave me sensational pleasure. But I knew not to be blinded by it, so I moved back into the shadows of the locker, grabbing another hook and placing it on my belt.

No lie; dude was a good fight, because though he screamed from the pain, he also seemed to get a sick pleasure in it, which appeared to amp him up at the same time. While I tried to use the shadows to my advantage, he used his own knowledge of the set up to his benefit as well. As I was moving in a circle, Dante shifted into the same shadows. I listened to the pattering of his bloody wet feet. While I focused on any tiny sound from him, I soon was sideswiped by a hanging body.

The force of it sent me slamming into the cold siding of the meat locker. My locs swung in my face with a slight stinging swat and I turned to push out of the way of the fist that followed behind it. Teeth clenching, I grunted then laughed when Dante's fist hit nothing but wall. Nigga was so concerned about getting to me that he should have been protecting his nut sacs. One kick then a slap of chain from a chain I snatched up gave me the satisfaction of seeing him fall to his knees. I let his face meet my knee then I moved out of his grasp to move to the other side of the locker.

"You play dirty, you fucking cunt!" Dante roared out.

Laughter came from me, but for real, my head hurt from the sudden open hand hit then slam against the wall. This nigga rushed me like a line backer. Everything around me felt like a whirlwind, and I pulled at my knives sending them into his demonic flesh. Spit and blood went spewing everywhere as we met fist to fist. My head met his face, cracking his nose, and chipping his teeth.

I felt him lift me in the air to body slam me but I was quicker. I took another hook and sent it into his back, using a military flip, to break out of his hold. Dropping to the ground, I pushed up, pulled out my Glock, and sent several bullets into him and into the hanging chain and hooks around me. The sound of ricocheting bullets had me cursing out loud, reminding me at how small of a meat locker it was.

"Fuck!" I grunted out loud, the moment a bullet whizzed by me.

Dante gave his own laugh then rushed me again. This time he had a hook he took from his own body and waved it at me. Standing, I shifted my gloves and several shaved iron nails slide out. Ducking like Mayweather, I sent each fist into Dante's flesh, cutting and slicing.

"Nigga, you like to walk around this bitch like you're God.You ain't nothing but flesh and bone just like the rest of us," I spit out.

Blood trickled down my face, and the slash of the hook Dante wielded cut me good, hitting my arm and near my back. Though he was a big dude, he moved with purpose, but he also was slowing down from extreme blood loss. Taking another hook, I swung it upward meeting his chin and causing him to stumble backward. I dropped the hook, rushed to pick up the machete that he had dropped. I had to be quick. Just because the nigga was down didn't mean he was out. Just as he extended his hand to grab me, the long blade sliced through his flesh. I watched in amusement as his hand fell to the ground. The nigga was so stunned it took him a minute to realize what had happened before his painful yells rent the air.

Behind me in the hallways of the compound, I could hear gunplay going off. It had me determined as ever to get at Dante and take him down.

Finding an open window, I moved behind that nigga, leaped up to grab a hanging chain and I wrapped that shit around his neck. It was easier to grapple with him since he only hand one hand now. More hooks sliced into that fool. I bucked and twisted. Dante's only hand scraped and dug at me, using whatever he had to stab into me, but my hold was better. Chuckling with a grin, my fist pounded into his skull. He may have only had one hand, but the nigga was still resourceful. As I was holding his neck in a chokehold with the chain, he slowly started to stumble. I took my fist to the side of his head a few more times just to weaken him more and I smiled as that demonic fucker fell to his knees.

"Nigga, how about you play my game now? How about the hunter become the hunted, bitch-ass nigga?" I smirked, slamming my fist into his face and sending him backward into a wall.

By the time Phenom got to me, I was covered in that nigga's blood, as missing meat hooks marked where I had taken them and slammed them into that nigga's thigh, side, shoulders, and hand. Dante wasn't an easy mark, shit, that was clear because he got away. He busted me up good, but I let him know I wasn't to be fucked with and my uncle got to see that shit. In that moment, I squashed the anger and distrust in him. Was no use for it. We had an equal enemy and I got why he did what he did.

Now with knowledge of what happened to Ghost, and what I could tell happened to my cousin Chyna, wasn't nothing in this world I wouldn't do for my fam. Sacrificing my life was included. I was a renegade nigga, born from intellectuals who were formed by the streets, raised in the gutta to be a mercenary and take the law in my hands. I was Trigga, that nigga with the Glock and a bat and shank somewhere in my hoodie.

Walking out of the room, my eyes locked on my uncle. Only reason that nigga was able to escape was due to one thing alone: he had help. As I took Dante down, each meat hook digging and sticking into his body, white light washed the whole area and had me looking up. The sound of a Glock going off had me ducking down and rolling away for protection in frustration.

I watched as Phenom rushed in returning fire, several bullets hitting a body that became clear in the light. The nigga I had watched back in the Jamaican codes stood there with a callous grin on his face. A blunt hung out of his mouth as he stood in his designer suite, he held open a door for Dante to run through, and I noticed when Phenom hit that nigga and his lackey near the small of their backs before they both disappeared.

My unk and me followed as fast as we could but they were gone. Wasn't shit to do but come back here to make sure we all made it out alive. That was what it was. Once Phenom got a look at the nigga running with Dante, he told me the guy was MI5. MI5 was to London what the CIA was to the United States. Just like his twin, Dame, Dante had hands and eyes everywhere. It could never be doubted that the Orlandos didn't have power, but when you came after mine, your power meant nothing to me.

And while we walked out of that place, I picked up my souvenir: Dante's severed hand, which I wrapped up for both Ghost and Chyna. Frustration had me occasionally glancing back to where I had pinned that pussy-ass nigga down and it started pissing me of off that he got away. Check it, though both of them niggas may have gotten way, best believe both niggas were feeling death at the door. And though Dante may not fear it, he now knew me and mine would willingly hand him to that Grim Reaper.

Yeah, man, now, here we are, surrounded by this win for now. My eyes locked on my family, and I reached back to hug Ghost to me again before letting her go. I needed to clean up and we all needed to get a plan together, but for now, all the shit that had come our way, was going to have to be put on pause.

The soft tapping on the bathroom door had me turning away from my reflection in the mirror where I stood gripping the skin, lost in thought. I stood in my baggy jeans and beater. My Timbs were in the corner with my shirt and hoodie. A nigga was in his zone, didn't want any disturbances but the rapping on the door started up again and I gave a low, "Yeah."

"Trig. You okay?" came from the other side.

It was Diamond. From the way her voice softened with a hit of worry in the mix, I knew she was concerned about a nigga. I didn't feel like having her see me in my thoughts like this. I still had the rush of kills in me, still had the fresh raw emotion from Ghost being taken, with that knowledge that that nigga may have fucked her up by cutting near her private area. Shit was weighing heavy on me and I felt old as fuck. I may be eighteen, but I was starting to feel forty.

Diamond's knocking continued and I could see the fresh tears in her eyes from earlier, in my mind. I had seen the nurturing way she was with Ghost was the same way she was with Gina. She was there outside of her own pain. The thought of everything that just happened today, had me opening the door looking down at her before pulling her inside and locking it behind her. For a moment, I just held Diamond's small waist in my hand while I stared into her doe eyes. She had that bun on the top of her head again and it had me looking away for a moment, noticing the bandage around her waist where she got hurt.

"You were stupid as fuck, got hurt, but a nigga is proud of you, li'l shawty," I mumbled.

The shower ran behind us causing currents of steam to surround us. I could see she wanted to say something but I ain't have time for all of that, my mouth was on hers before she could talk. I knew she was shocked that I was kissing her like this, by the slight gasp she gave, but the moment my mouth had hers, her body melted against a nigga like an M&M in my hand. She held me down.

She did some stupid shit, but she held me down in this game. Which was what had me holding her now like I did, but it was also that she held down Ghost in this fucked-up battle. She ain't have to do that. She ain't have to stay. She could have stayed afraid but she let it go like a true soldier.

So because of that, because she somehow after everything back in ATL and everything here now in London had stepped up and learned game, she deserved proper treatment. That was why I slid my hands down over the dip in her back to have her thick ass rest in both hands. I gripped all that she had, separating each cheek, and then lifting her up around my waist. When her legs locked around my hips, I pressed her hard against the door of the bathroom, while tonguing her down.

The sensation of her nails scraping down my back then at my dirty white beater made my dick swell on hundred. I felt her pull my beater off over my head, like she was just as hungry as I was and she took my mouth in return. As we fucked by our mouths, I ran my tongue over the surface of her eager tongue sucking and scraping my teeth on her juicy lower lip. The way she moaned, was definitely something I planned to make her do again, 'cause that was raw and sexy as fuck.

When she pulled my locs out of its ponytail and yanked hard on them, a nigga pulled back. I couldn't help that shit 'cause she had me feeling myself for real. I knew I possibly was scaring her with how my jaw clenched and the vein in my temple thumped with the same beat as my dick, but I didn't fucking care. Pussy was what I wanted and Diamond was what I needed. So I sat her down, and grabbed a golden wrapper condom from the medicine cabinet.

Being careful of the bandage around her waist, I then ripped, and tugged off her leggings so my fingers could their way in to her juicy pussy. She was so silky, creamy, and hot. Reminded me of some fresh Krispy Kreme and it had me dropping to one knee then leaning forward to lick at her wet slit. I kinda wondered if she tasted like icing and she did, which was on point.

The moment she moaned, "Kwame," I forgot about finishing my tasting because my dick and nuts were so heavy with desire that there was no turning back from what we both needed. Ripping the condom packed open, I quickly put that shit on then I moved back up against her, and set her around my waist. The moment I entered her, my sacs clenched and had me almost punching a wall as we stepped into the shower. Damn, she was icing.

I guess it was about time we got here, and I wasn't about to stop for shit.

The moment she tightened around me, then bowed her head on my shoulder with her wet hair spilling over my shoulders, and then said my name, I knew she was shocked from the thickness of my dick and the way I felt against her. The way her eyes seemed to change colors and the way her lips were parted, our body's language told me she had been wanting this for a long time. So I gave it to her.

I wasn't a nigga to be rough and shit unless the mood called for it, but we both had been waiting on this, and fucking is what I gave until it softened into making her come, over and over. By that time, water was running over our bodies and her nails were scraping down my back again and gripping my ass. While my hips moved against her like a nigga was dancing, dipping in and out to where the sound of our wet bodies slapping sounded like the beat to that nigga Wale's "Bad" track, I bent my head and got me a mouthful of her plump titty.

The way she arched into my mouth had me rolling my tongue over all of her as I sucked her nipple until she came again. We stayed like that, locked up in the shower until morning came and she couldn't take anymore of my dick. Diamond, aka Ray-Ray was my ride or die and in this life, the words of my mom speaking about me one day having a jaguar for a queen had me thinking hard. Diamond and I had an empire to build with our fam and now aunt and uncle, because we all knew, that nigga Dante was going to come back gunning even harder, especially once he found out his weak spot was exposed and taken down.

As Diamond chilled with me under the shower, we spoke about how both Phenom and Anika took out Dante's secret family, his pregnant wife, and other sons who were living in Hampshire.

Diamond gazed into my hooded eyes, her legs wrapped around my waist. I was going to have to change my condom soon, but shit it was what it was.

"So what are we going to do now? We did some crazy shit," she half moaned and whispered.

Turning, I held her caged against the shower wall, my locs dripping with the water that rained on us and I kissed her lips. "With reason. We all had behaved how that nigga Dante acted, erratic in madness and chaos."

Working my hips to make her gasp how I realized I liked it, I gave her slick smile and explained game. "Check it, a nigga who thinks he's an untouchable king always gotta be put in his place, because when his back is exposed, there ain't no coming back from being got."

Baby girl arched her back in a way that let know what I was doing felt good to her, and she dug into my shoulder while working her lips to speak. "So that's why Dante's codes are now ours, and his legacy was only left with him and that cop nigga S.B. lying in their own blood."

I smiled at how she was getting it and I gave her nod while my voice drawled out in silky sex, "Yeah, so as he lay healing, planning up, me, you, and our misfit family are gonna sit back and do the same thing. We're gonna be waiting in the cut to bring that blood vengeance to the end as we head back to the A. So you gamed?"

Diamond's heated cookie tightened around my dick, making me slide in and out of her again as I listened to her pretty ass slap against the slick wetness of the wall.

Her sharp, "Yes!" made my dick harder and I kissed her lips as my mind thought about our next move. ENGA to the fullest.

Chapter 15

Phenom

Six months after the showdown in London town

The harsh sound of metal locking into place echoes in the distance with the loud clamor of a steel door behind me.

"Cell lock fifteen, inmates all within!" blasted in apathy.

The worst thing for a man is to be locked up away from the ability to move in freedom. You take for granted the ability to move in fluidity, where the life, the air, even the light that fuels and moves you in your destiny and actions are no longer yours to control. When that is taken away, when all your power is pulled from you, dropping you into a cave that has you descending into the true meaning of being an animal; that is when everything changes for a man. When walls meant to hold you in start to choke you and snatch the breath from you. When that animal you thought you were turns into something deeper, more sinister, beyond a monster and a caveman. When you turn into the essence of primal, that's when shit gets real.

There is nothing that can prepare a man, thug, or nigga on the street for that reality in this shit called prison. It turns the hardest of hard men into either pussy, newfound saints, or something ungodly. Me? I was beyond ungodly. My journey here was for ven-

geance and to safe guard the new generation. I knew this nigga's seeds were already monsters, but I knew that, too, would correct itself as it always does when chaos runs its course.

"What'chu looking at, nigga? You that nu-nu huh? They sent me a nice sweet piece of fresh pussy to play with?"

I watched the oversized monkey, who looked dipped in ink because of all the tattoos covering his body, quirk a thick eyebrow that was too maintained for my taste. He sized me up. His hand gripped and squeezed his dick inside his jumper while a wide perfectly straight-teeth sneer appeared on his sinister face.

Internal laughter had me stoic.

See, this nigga was what I called a monster queen or a prison wolf, a nigga who used his dick as a weapon to get him some hairy pussy with nuts, but who also tried to play it off as if his fucking ass wasn't a lowdown glittering thug, just to exert his power. Regardless, that wasn't my concern. I could protect myself without issue.

Walking into the cell, I pulled my then waist length jet-black locs back into a knotted ponytail, while keeping my eyes on the goon in front of me. Both of my hands dropped to my sides then fisted in my stride. I rounded that small closet deep area that was our shared cell and locked my eyes on the acronym DOA branded against the side of his neck.

"Nigga, you dumb or some shit? You can't speak to a man in his own piece? Nigga, you a guest in my house! Respect the door!" he growled at me, leaning forward onto his wide-legged thighs.

Every syllable he spit at me had me cracking my knuckles as that nigga kept popping off at the mouth.

"Bitch, ya 'bout to be my new ass; the other didn't make it, dog. That's why this part of the ghetto penthouse is

called hell and for you to be in here with a nigga, you musta done some fucked-up shit or pissed the big dogs off fresh meat. So guess what, give me some pussy," he commanded, as if he was king.

"Give you some pussy? Nigga, you gay," chortled from me just to antagonize him.

Like my homie Biggie said, "Fuck all that planning shit. Run up in they cribs and make them cats abandon shit. Revenge I'm tasting at the tip of my lips I can't wait to feel my clip in his hips."

Grounding my feet, I watched that nigga only slightly tower over me the moment he pushed up from the bunk. A smile played across my lips while I stared into his white beater-covered chest. The power of two alphas stuck in a room together had the cell feeling thick with power, which fueled me for the game. Two tatted-covered knuckles, one inked with DOA, the other inked with 4-LIFE came at me in a flash. I let this cat I knew as Lu on the streets reach for me, as my fist snuck past him to connect to his rib cage.

Instinctual follow through made me duck quickly under his arm as the shock threw him for a loop. I swiftly moved to the bunks that were to be our beds and I pulled hard to shake them off their hinge. Laughter came out when I heard his shock at how easily the beds ripped partially from the wall. If he hadn't become so cocky and had paid attention to his surroundings, he would have noticed a different guard loosening the bed a few inches every other day.

"Ey, yo what's this shit!" he bellowed out.

"My juice card, nigga," was all I said as he rushed me again.

Arms wrapped around me and tried to squeeze the life from me. I felt his hand yank on my locs as I strained to get free. I knew he liked a fight, studied his ways on the streets before he got locked up. Heard a lot of shit on the so-called DOA King, but right now, he was none of that, right now, without him even knowing it, he was about to be my bitch.

"Ah yeah, you can't run now. After I fuck you, def know I'm gonna murk ya, then eat ya flesh later," he growled against my ear.

The sewage-hot stench of his breath hit me hard like the whiff of a cow's shitty ass, and had my face connecting with the base of his nose, mouth, and then chin.

Adrenaline pleasurably flowed through me with the feel of his blood coating my face. I held the handmade massai dagger I had hidden in my locs in my hand, and then inserted into the side of his neck before slicing down until it hit his clavicle bone. Blood painted the small cell. Its ruddy thick and sticky essence showered over the side of my hand then hit the floor in a splat. Lu's yells became sharp then guttural in that moment. His grip tightened then loosened, allowing me to break free. Several fist shots from me connected to his face. My arm curved under to land under his jaw as a means to send his head back to hit nothing but the concrete wall.

The way he fell made me smirk. I moved forward quickly. My footsteps were simple as I grabbed for him. Heat had us baking like roasting chickens. Sweat ran down the both of our faces, with that of his blood. I licked my lips, tasting the salty sweat from me and I tilted my chin up and bit my lower lip in a laughing scowl.

"Yeah, nigga, you was sayin'?" came from me in my New York accent.

My kicks then squeaked against the slick floor as I walked forward and wound the metal wire that had held the bunk beds together around my fists as I spoke, "Check it. Never been one to play with my meat, but, nigga, you beefy, you feel me? So let me play and explain. You ordered a hit on my blood. My fam. Took them out and sat back and reaped the benefits until all of that crumbled beneath you and it left you here while your weak-ass sons stayed in the streets scraping up the pieces. You fucked up big time. Got lost in this prison life and thought there was no one who would come for you. No bueno. A red eye from London was nothing for me. Getting in here was like pissing in the wind, my nigga, and all of this to say, rest in peace, nigga."

He let out a quick roar then sent a hard shoulder slam that sent me flying in the air, and then landing against the concrete wall near the ceiling. His muscled arm scooped me up as he tried to power drive me, which worked. I fell to the floor hard but used the momentum to roll as he stood over me akimbo style, his hands on his hips and a smile across his insidious face.

Blood pooled in my mouth. The sweet unique taste of it spilled down my throat and made me spit. Dizziness controlled my actions. I slowly rolled to my side while he pulled on my body as he spoke.

"I live this shit every day, homie. Your British ass, or whatever the fuck you are, ain't shit to me. So I killed your people. Yeah? Too bad none of them here to watch how I flay you alive and feed you dick. Ain't none of the niggas or guards you ride with gonna help ya now. You don't fuck wit' what you ain't ready for, patna."

His laughter sickened me. But see all of this was nothing but a game, an act to get him right where I wanted. Watching him work his dick out as I played as if I was struggling brought me time to angle myself just right. I pushed up then landed my foot upward into his face. A hard swift blow from my knee followed to put him on his back. That wire I had wound around my hands wrapped around his neck and I bit down on my lower lip as I pulled. See, when a nigga is built for killing, he never let time tick away. This was his art and right now, I was painting my canvas with him.

The sound of flesh tearing, his bloodied gurgles, and flopping thick body became music to my ears. His twitching body became my next target as I took the broken leg of the bed and spread his legs wide and laughed.

His no's became erratic. His once golden skin went from red to ashen like Michael Jackson. The way he clawed at my hands and then the wire around this throat made me even more hyper in my madness in the chaos. As his head bowed backward, his bulging eyes black as coal locked on me in intense hatred as I removed one hand from the wire and slammed that metal broken bed leg into his wide mouth, breaking teeth.

"Slob on that shit," I cooed.

I let him throat that shit as the rusted piece of metal scraped into his airway stopping so I could have room for my next move. Patting the top of his wave lined head; I tsked at his gagging and whispered, "Beg for it like you tried to make my sister beg for it when your seed attacked her."

Slobber ran down his mouth. Mucus coated his top lip and a vindictive glimmer lit my eyes the moment I snatched at that wire, pulled, and then severed his trachea. It was then in that moment when I stood, wiped my hands off, and pulled on the other leg of the bed that seal the rest of the deal. I knew he was still alive. Knew he could see what else I had for him, which for me, I knew the rest would be the last he would remember.

Stomping on his flaccid dick, as I crouched low between his legs, I tapped the metal post on the floor in rhythm while I spoke, "Your seeds are next, now make that pussy pop."

The end of that post ripped into his asshole with a forceful thrust. His shrill and muffled scream had me furiously standing then stomping my foot repeatedly over his head. The satisfying sound of his bone and brain matter crushed under my foot.

No one took from me, ever. This life was mine, and mine alone, and everyone in it that was solely connected to me were mine to protect. Wasn't nothing I wouldn't do for my blood and this nigga was the testament of it. Knocking in rhythm on my cell bars, the doors of my prison opened. I sat positioned over my kill. The side of his neck that held the branding DOA now rested in my hand; an almond brown flesh patch, my trophy of reminder of this day.

My actions caused a heat wave through the prison. Officers kept their distance. Those who were on my payroll, and those who petitioned to be on my payroll after that day, let me out of the small cell and led me to my freedom.

That day my name became synonymous with street legend. The rest of D.O.A in that prison were wiped out by my hand, through my soldiers, and the ones on the street were quickly handled except for his seeds. His seeds, I left for the future to handle, the beginnings of that next phase of the game already buzzing in my ear. That was also the day I cut my locs in remembrance of my baby sister Fatima, her husband, Jamir, who had always been the blood of my heart, my little niece Assata and then her brother Kwame, who was lost in the streets.

"Phenom!" roared around me as inmates, some banging on the doors of their cells and others giving me props down below, gave me respect.

"Phenom!" made my body shake before the name, "Ahmir!" shook me awake.

Licking my lips, my hand ran down my face, the waves of my close-cropped hair and over my goatee as I sat back in my oversized chair in our penthouse in Atlanta. My lids blinked a couple of times before my light brown eyes focused on the only piece of perfection and harmony I have ever known outside of my own blood. We went through hell and heaven together. I did my dirt in growing up as a youth in the streets, and she did hers, but we always came together.

As the wisdom of the lotus sutra states, a sense of being part of the great all-inclusive life prompts us to reflect on our own place and on how we ought to live. Guarding others' lives, the ecology and the earth is the same as protecting one's own life. She was that for me and so was my family. I vowed to protect my brother-in-law and sister's son and I intended to keep doing that.

In my weakness, I'd failed him, but since then, he has seen the lengths a father will go, a man will go, for his own soul and his own family. My nephew has that now with my enemy's seed, a little girl who felt like she should have been born to our blood long ago, Ghost. He had her as his child now and I could only continue giving him those lessons and let him see me for who I am, in order for him to trust in me still. That was my mantra in life as it was to keep my world protected.

"Mm mm, my queen, tell me what you need and I'll give that which you want," I sultry yet groggily groaned as Anika smoothly slipped between my legs to sit on my lap and place her arms around my shoulder.

She felt like silk. Her sexy weight along with her thick shiny naked thighs rested against my manhood had me slowly becoming hard. She smelled like Shea butter and sweet almond oil and was dressed in only my open button-down shirt.

"You speak in your sleep, my king, so your queen has come to give you some balm. She wants her lion. So come fill her up, like she needs," she commanded in the seductive, enduring commanding way that only she could give me. Her gold-painted fingernails sensually stroked my jaw then chin.

My fingers found their way to her hair to stroke through her Havana twisted braids as my eyes soaked up the beauty of her flawless cocoa skin. Her belly was flat right now, but I knew soon that a child would be there if the look in her eyes that spoke its secret desires were true. It was time we created new life and it was going to go down but for right now, that was not the objective.

"I'll give you whatever you want," I murmured low.

I was rewarded with her smile and the feel of her legs parting to straddle my waist. "Remember you pick up the family from the airport and our eyes are watching the ones who watch us. For now, we do not have to worry about the heat that Diablo's vengeance has set off for us all. For now, they get to settle in, see what their actions have created these past six months and they get to settle into their new world, like we once had to."

My lips skimmed the side of her neck, as my fingertips found their way around her raised nipple. She knew I did not want to speak that motherfucker's name in our house, nor as we shared this intimate moment. "No doubt, my queen. London gave them a new foundation, but now it is time to take those lessons learned and get back to business but with a fresh outlook."

Pulling her hair back, I leaned forward to scrap my teeth against her neck while I spoke low against her thumping pulse. "They are legends in the streets now, and are being gunned for hard because of our common enemy, as well as others who feel that they can weaken them and us. Theirs, and his death is going to come, because we all have unfinished business, especially with his side handler. Let's see if our misfits can handle that shit, like I believe they can."

Reflecting back, we had all spent the last six months living in London after that battle with Dante, where we hunted down everyone connected to him. Gathering all we needed to plan our revenge and ready ourselves for his retaliation. My global circuit kept me hipped up to any glimpses from him and his handler S.B. who had also disappeared, until I was told they had both hit the grid in Cali then back in the A, a month back.

The moment that happened, the plan we all involved each other in kicked started and both Anika and I went back to the States to prep for battle while my nephew and the others built their names in the codes. As they say, there is no time like today to take out some motherfuckers, and that was what we all intended to do.

My queen, my wife Anika, slipped down my body, her smile causing my dick to thump in my pants as she released me. Her soft sweet moan was all I heard with that of a "yes" before she swallowed me whole with a smooth slurp. She had her needs and so did I.

Though I was schooled by true OGs back in NYC, I was still young, a product of the '80s but a kid from the streets of the late '90s. Maturity came only from my experience in survival and it also had me learning a lot from my nephew and his makeshift family. It even had me taking on the mantel they proudly sported in fondness and pride.

ENGA versus the last of DOA. It was a long-overdue battle and one that definitely was about to be ended with our enemy's death, or ours. Chaos was power that only me and my family controlled and we planned to paint the streets with our enemy's blood; ENGA and nothing more.

Episode 4:

The Showdown in A-Town

Victorious warriors win first and then go to war, while defeated warriors go to war first and then seek to win.

—Sun Tzu

Chapter 16

Trigga

"Virgin UK flight 218 has now landed. Welcome to Atlanta."

Damn it was good to be back. By back, I meant in the A. London wasn't all the way good to me, but it schooled me. The past six months there was spent dealing with niggas and broads coming left and right at us since we had chopped down that nigga Dante's kingdom and his little imp sidekick. After that, wasn't nothing peaceful about London for me, but I survived it. I swallowed my pride two months after everything and stepped to my uncle.

Watching Ghost heal, seeing the small changes in her after coming from Dante's hands was what made me do it. Shit wasn't math for a brotha. She'd been hurt and that shit burned in my body like acid. Wasn't nothing I was used to at all, but watching how my unk watched us all, I saw in his eyes what I was feeling. So I squashed my beef and sat with him, learned, and told him I'd open his throat from ear to ear like the Joker if he played me and mine again. Blood ain't supposed to do what he did, but I got it, and that was his one time with me, feel me?

He hipped me to how he and my pops grew up. Dirty in the streets of the BK. Surviving however they could just to keep fresh, but also to get dough before they were snatched up by his great-grandpops and schooled on real OG knowledge. They learned knowledge that was mixed with religious and Nigerian principles, which changed everything for them.

I sat and soaked it all up. Everything that was in both my pop's and mom's journals came to light and synched up through the words spilling from my uncle. As he schooled me, I watched my fam. Big Jake would sit and learn, as would Ghost, just to be near me. Gina and Diamond would sit with Anika as Diamond began her lessons too.

When we weren't sitting and learning game, and dodging the dietary lessons my unk wanted us to favor, I'd train Ghost, Chyna, Ray-Ray, and Baby G some of my moves. Speedy would teach them ways to hide weapons and craft them, Big Jake would teach them how to box and shoot, while I made them all repeat the principles I learned in my books. Every day we'd all shift off, where I would train with my boys, and vice versa and every day we'd all get stronger.

How I trained, the shit wasn't easy. I made all the women cry in some way but I had to. The streets weren't going to be gentle because they were chicks and they needed to never forget that.

"Pay attention, Ghost," I said firmly as I clapped my bandaged hands twice.

The frustration on Ghost's baby face had her features contorted as I gained her attention. We were in a secluded padded basement back in Hackney. It looked more like a boxing gym without the ring if you asked me. A sheen of sweat covered my arms, shoulders, and face giving it a glowing reddish tint as I looked down at the little girl I called my own.

Ghost was tired, almost about to pass out from exhaustion, but she was determined to prove to me, who she thought of as her father, that she was a fighter and would never be taken without a fight again.

Her hair was braided in six long cornrows on her head. The tips flapped against her back as she did a spin kick and tried to slide between my legs. She was too slow and I think that annoyed her more than it did me in that moment. As she rushed by, I caught her quickly and lifted her into a sleeper hold. Even on my knees, I towered over my baby girl. The hold wasn't as tight as I would put on a nigga in the street, but it was tight enough for her to have to fight her way out of it.

Diamond stood off to the side watching. Stress had her eyes watering as she stepped forward. She wore black workout pants that showed off her curves and a pink sports bra that matched Gina's. Her hand moved up to her mouth and she bit her lower lip before waving her hand in trying to get my attention.

"Trigga, stop," she called out to me. "That's enough!" she pleaded.

I looked up in her direction, but I wasn't even checkin' for her. Too much shit was playing on rewind in my head. From intel hitting us back about sightings of Dante in the boroughs of New York, Miami, Washington, North Carolina, Texas, Cali, and even New Mexico. To people from the Trap hitting our secret circuit talking about how scared they were because they thought they just saw Dame's lame pussy ass walking the streets again. Stress was running through me and had me ready to go to war.

It didn't take my unk to let us know that he was building up his army. Ready to hit us OG style and try to start a turf war. That shit was elementary and simple to gather. What had me pissed off was that he now was using his power to try to get us tied into some deep-ass dirt. He was trying to get the feds to connect us to pushing the drugs in the streets and trafficking kids and shit. Luckily, the feds only knew us by our street names and because Jake and me always kept our shit covered, facial shots wasn't even possibly. This was why my unk and Anika went back to the States to set up our return, and I was here training the other misfits.

"You think she'll be able to make another nigga stop because she's had enough?" I asked Diamond, raising an eyebrow tripping off of her in the moment.

"Trigga, baby girl has had enough for the day. She's tired. She needs to rest," she pleaded with me as Ghost was still doing her best to get out of the hold.

I snapped my eyes away from her and back down at the little girl I knew we all would protect with our lives. "Stop struggling. Shit's useless," I barked at her. "It's just going to tire you out, Chas. Think smart and move swiftly, but never make unnecessary moves, depleting useful energy," I continued in trying to school her.

"I'm . . . trying," she whined.

"Bruv, I think she's done for the day, yeah?" Speedy asked his lights eyes reminiscent of me and Phenom's.

"Yeah, Trig. She's needs rest now," Gina added on.

Chyna was still sitting in the corner. She had yet to recover from the beating her body took in one of my famous training sessions before I'd turned my attention to Ghost. Chyna's black tights and sports bra were drenched in her sweat. She looked as if she was about to vomit. Speedy had his hands wrapped in black boxing tape as his blue gym shorts hung low on his slender hips. His toned yet slim tatted chest heaved up and down as he fought to catch his breath finally. He too was still drenched in sweat.

"Kwame," Jake called out to me as he approached the black mat. "You need to ease up."

Annoyance had me narrowing my eyes. I opened my mouth to go off but whatever both Jake and me was about to say was cut short. Ghost held my pinky finger in her clasp and put all the strength left into bending it back. I had told her a week earlier that it was a weak point on a man's hand if done the right way.

Baby girl took my technique to heart and did what I had taught her well. I loosened my hold and when I did, she managed to free herself. She jerked her head back, hitting me in the nose. My right arm still had her in my grasp as I stood, but she used the heel of her foot and swung back at my dick. This had me dropping her instantly on her ass with a grunt.

She rolled over, grabbed a pencil some dumbass had lying idly by, and when I rushed to pick her up again she'd aimed the sharpened end of the pencil right near my carotid artery. My baby girl was breathing like she was about to have an asthma attack and tears were rolling down her face, but she'd done what I had trained her to do and it had me smiling on the inside. Why? Because of how I had taught her, and how she had just done the damn thing, I had no choice but to hold my hands up in surrender.

"Good," I calmly praised her.

My hands ran down my sweaty face. At that moment, she was outright crying. I hadn't noticed until she dropped the pencil, wrapped her arms around herself and looked away, speaking to me a small voice, "Can I go lie down now?"

Her voice was shaky and I could see she was beyond fatigued. Even though she was crying, Ghost was still a pretty little girl and it had me shutting down, because I wasn't prepared to see her crying. So I gave her a curt nod that she could go, and she quickly made her way from the room.

"Can I go too?" Chyna asked, causing me to turn her way.

The amped zone I was in was slowly fading away at the sight of seeing that Ghost was hurting, so I threw my towel over my shoulder in a shrug and nodded. "Yeah, go."

Gina also decided to jump in and stress me. "Me too, Trig? A bitch is tired and hungry and shit. You got us down here like we 'bout to go to war or summin'," she complained.

Her voice had come back, but she would forever have to sometimes clear her throat to speak clearly. Locked in the stress of knowing that we needed to do better, that we needed to be ready for Dante had slight annoyance tingeing my voice. All of it over the fact that no one was getting what we were going to have to face and I shook my head at a chick I always felt was like my baby sister. "We are."

London was hard shit then. So many emotions, so much time spent getting ready and my fam couldn't get peace because we had to be ready. Diamond always found some way to be the voice to pull me back as with everyone else, but I couldn't help that sometimes they just wasn't getting it. Speaking on her, shit. I was not even sure where to start.

Standing in this airport, my mind was open like never before. Dressed in black Timbs, gray slacks, a white button-down shirt with a black vest, my locs were pulled back. The fitted cap I wore hid my face. Lessons were learned in London. Lessons we all, me and my fam of misfits, were still learning. Even while I checked the eyes of those who watched us mixed in with the crowd of people who bustled around us in the airport, I knew that we were being observed and that it was not like it was before.

We were in a new level of power and what we learned was going to definitely test us in our survival. Check it though, I say all of that because Diamond and me, shit. I don't even know.

My hooded eyes drifted her way as she stood next to Gina holding her hand as Jake stood off on the side shifting on his feet as if he were their bodyguard. Baby G was scared to be back. All the shit we went through, running from the A, only to go through more shit in London, really ain't give her time to mentally heal. Same shit I believe with Diamond, which was why I ain't even know where we stood right now. Shit, it ain't like a brotha was really trying to wife her or be one-on-one with her.

I mean, ain't nothing against her but, on some truth shit, we all got thrown together 'cause of the streets and the violence. She wasn't made for this world. I was born into it, she wasn't. Now that we were back in the A, like, damn, would she really want to stay in this? Stay with me? Nah, I wasn't even sure, even though she held me down through all of this. But wasn't that something different then really wanting to stay in this, stay with me? Shit. I don't think it would even be fair for her if she did because she had a future before being snatched up and dropped into the bowels of hell better known as the Trap. Yeah, her fam was part of the Trap and my world, but she wasn't.

She was just another girlie on the block, going to school and not worrying about nothing but living, until her fam fucked up and we took her. I had a hand in that. Shawty might start to resent me if she doesn't get that shit back. I mean, I was a part of her being snatched away from her world of security. Another thing, Dame fucked up her mental and body, and dealing with Dante kick started that shit all over again. Why am I saying that?

'Cause two months in, after her and me hooked up, I caught her playing in dust again. I almost lost my mind when I snapped on her. Shit had me fucked up and pissed at her for stepping backward into that shit. Things were supposed to be different but it felt like everything was the same. I mean, shit, look. I got why she was doing it, 'cause the ghosts of that place never can heal right, when we haven't had the time to. But it just felt like, damn, a nigga can't even substitute that poison and bring you a little peace?

That's when I knew wasn't shit I could do for her but protect her and help her find her destiny again. So yeah. I don't know where we are, even though we still kickin' it. I'm a young dude. I don't even know what settling down even looks like. Don't even know how it operates. I mean, yeah, I see my unk doing it, but that's him and I'm me. I'm gonna do me to the fullest and keep my game intact. Ain't shit change but the survival tactics, feel me?

So standing here watching her, she had me wanting to get that again, but also had me on guard. This world wasn't meant for her. She deserved better.

Anyway, like I was relearning from my pop's and mom's journals and even Phenom's and Anika's lessons, one must separate the true self from the personality. Which ultimately reflects the mask of personality. I've been schooled on that since birth and that's the power that flowed through my veins.

Knowledge of self without trying to be something one is not is priority.

The feel of a small hand in mine had me staring down. A smirk played on my face before disappearing as I stared down at the little girl with several chucky twists in her hair. She was dressed like any nine-year-old would be: bright colors and a pair of kicks I got her while in London with her book bag full of books and weapons hidden as toys. This girl right here was my weakness and it fucked me up every night I went to bed 'cause I knew she would be used against me.

Which was why she and I continued our training together. Chasity was sugar and spice. Things I used to do when I was her age as a kid were lessons I schooled her in and she molded it into perfection. I knew if she ever got fucked up again, what I taught her from my mom's and pop's journals, and what Anika taught her as a young female warrior of the streets was going to keep her protected as best as we all can do for now.

"Wayment, bruv, this is ATL? Ya didn't tell how many fine sistas there are here," sounded to the left of me.

When I turned to check its source, I saw Speedy walking back and forth with a goofy look on his face as he eyed the many females who walked past his way. I knew the moment his teeth flashed and he turned my way smirking then sticking his tongue out with a thumbs-up that someone needed to snatch him. Laughter had me stepping forward but I stopped when Speedy was snatched up and prevented from walking up on some bad chick's ass.

"No time for that, Moseif. You have a party to set up for. All of you remember what we spoke on so let's be out, my family," Phenom simply stated, before turning around and walking between two special services–looking cats on each side of him.

The tense squeeze from Ghost's hand had me looking down at her. I pulled her to me and locked eyes on Diamond, as she moved to fall into step with me and we headed out.

Hours later, we stood in an opulent mansion in Buckhead. This place was a cover spot just for the party, our welcome home banger. Everything around us was lit in cool tones, blue, green, and purple as Speedy spun tunes. All around us was people in our age group, and I stood against a pillar in a walkway with my arms crossed watching everyone. Dressed in leather blue jean hoodie, dark jeans that matched, a white shirt under the jacket, and my infamous Timbs, I nodded to the music and watched as everyone moved as one like the sea, with their hands in the air.

The plan was going down. Now that we were back, Phenom explained that the five-o would be looking for people associated with Dame. That meant Jake, Baby G, and Trigga, as well as his newfound chick Ray-Ray. But who they wouldn't be looking for was Kwame Kweli, Jackson Hawks, Gina Lewis, Diamond Jenkins, and little Chasity Kweli. Yeah, we'd legally changed her last name. Honestly, they wouldn't even know to look for Ghost; she didn't exist in their world, which was good.

Five-o only knew about a kid in a hoodie, another big-ass dude always sporting shades, and the many tricks Dame owned, which worked in our favor. We knew if the law started hunting for us by our looks, then Dante's hands were all on it. But that nigga knew nothing about our real names except for Diamond. That nigga didn't know her last name at all.

The game was on and this party was about checking out our old enemies and getting our names in the streets. Everyone here was after my goods i.e. ecstasy and fresh product I could lace them up with. No, I wasn't really about lacing my people with drugs, but sometimes being in the jungle meant you had to adapt. This was a warzone and I had to put pride and principle to the side for a minute just so I could get the job I'd set out to do done. This time I was only here to go after one nigga, wanted to get him before he got me. So, this shit was all a game. Trigga was back, and shit was about to get buck.

My smile widened even more as a sexy almond-butter shawty with an ass asking to be grabbed came up to me and pressed her lips against mine. My hands rested on her curvy waist and I pulled back to drop a pill on the tip of her pink tongue. All around us smoke blazed in the air causing a fog while people danced on tables or in the pool, swung from light fixtures, and got hyped as London grime flipped to dancehall music. A smirk played over my face as the heat of the party felt like everyone was fucking.

Groups of people melted together started parting like the Red Sea and that was when Diamond stepped through the large crowd. Ma was dressed in black and white zigzag leggings, with a tight black cutoff top that showed off her stomach but fell in the back like a dress. On her feet were wedged black kicks that tied up around her calves and her plump lips were dipped in red as her hair sat on her left shoulder in a French braid. I watched her tap the chick in front of me, who was grinding on my dick, on her shoulder, then snatch the broad by her weave.

The music seemed to go on pause, as I heard Speedy shout with a laugh, "Oi! Pussy on pussy! Tuneeeee!"

Horns blazed around the room and the party got super hyped. My blood, Speedy, swayed with the music. He had one hand on one broad's tit and his other hand on another's tits. Beats headphones were on his ears. His long hair braided in designs that looked woven, swayed against his shoulders. I noticed that he tilted his head to the side to whisper in a dolly's ear before growling at the girl and pretending like he was going to bite her as he pulled both chicks around him and they giggled. Nigga was a straight clown and real with it. But back to the fight in front of me though.

My dick thumped instantly against my thigh in my jeans as Diamond caused the broad who kissed me to bend backward while exposing her neck and her titties from out under her mesh top, before falling on her ass. Fists went flying with the rhythm of the beat. Cat growls, and grunts sounded off and Diamond kicked the chick so hard, that the broad rolled on her side holding her scratched up face.

Jake held Gina back from joining in on the fight, whispering in her ear, as her eyes reflected back and, "Oh yeah," and she turned in his hold to dance back on him, while leaning her face up to brush her lips against his.

Everything was all right in my world as I studied both chicks go at it Worldstar style. Rolling a lighter against my fingers, I tossed it in the air then crossed my arms over my chest before the broad who kissed me scrapped at the floor where Diamond dragged her then ran off into the dancing crowd holding her face and covering her tits.

"Trick-ass bitch. I collect hair like bag of weaves. Keep yackin'," Diamond spat out, jumping stupid like she was about to go after that broad again.

She turned with one hand on her hips, looking at her nails as if filing them while smacking her lips as she chewed on her gum. "Trigga, don't make me cut you, nigga," she snapped.

I smirked. Yo, shawty was on some hoodrat shit for real. I wasn't expecting none of that to get as sexy as it did. But betcha it got the attention of those we wanted it to. My hand reached out to pull Diamond to me from behind. When her plump ass fit against my dick just how I liked it, and she looked over her bare shoulder at me, with narrowed cocoa black-lined eyes, I knew we were going to be fucking as soon as we found the time to slip away from the game. Shawty was a bad bitch, regardless of how confused she got me.

She turned in my grasp, reached out to grip my jaw then wiped my mouth before giving me her tongue to taste while she dutty winded with my hand on that ass. Shawty smelled damn good. She felt like butta too and all I could do was chuckle at the bullshit and mutter, "ENGA."

Chapter 17

Dante

I stood over my brother's and my father's graves. Nothing in me made me want to pay honor to either one of these niggas. Weak motherfuckers. Both fell because of pussy. Pussy set my father up. Some white bitch undercover cop fucked him, got in his head. The nigga ended up in prison, then dead. Damien dug into some young underage pussy who threw him off his game. Fucked him up. Now he sleeping six feet under right next to pops. Weak niggas, I loathed them. Still, my brother was my family and family had to be avenged. Blood was thicker than mud any day and I knew Dame would be gunning at a nigga for me if the roles had been reversed.

The fact that Phenom and Anika had taken out my wife, unborn child, and sons did something to me on the inside. I'd kept that part of my life hidden from the underworld I lived. I'd underestimated my enemy just as he had done me. Only thing was, I never got to see my family again. Most people said I didn't have a soul. After seeing my wife sprawled out underneath the balcony of our bedroom window and my two eldest sons with their brains panting the pavement, I knew I didn't have one either. Phenom and Anika would pay for what they had done to me.

"Any particular reason you called this meeting of the minds in a graveyard, my man?"

The sun was shining but the day was cool and windy. Twelve men surrounded me like the Twelve Tribes of Israel. Of the twelve, only six had had found me before I had to come looking for them: Armando, the head of the Latin Kings; Nicola, the head of the Russian Mafia in the south; Valentino, head of the Italian Cartel; Prodigy, head of the Jamaican Lords in Georgia; Kim, head of the Asian Clan; and Stiff, head of the Black Sicilians stood closest to me. He and Valentino had beef, but that was to be discussed at a later date. Those six men hadn't answered my call to arms when I'd put it out and required me strong-arming some of their shipment and money to get their attention and since the death of my brother had already damn near bankrupted the underworld of the A, they got my message and came quickly.

After S.B. had checked them all for weapons and one of Kim's men checked me, I sent S.B back to the car as did Kim his man. I turned to look at the men who'd all been under my brother's rule during his time on this earth as the head of state. It was nothing for me to find out that out of the twelve families, my brother had wronged these six men in some way. That explained why they all looked at his mirror image with a scowl.

"You know why you're here," I responded. "I think we have a common enemy."

"We?" Prodigy repeated as if what I said had been comical. "Mi brudda, me and yuh got no common enemy."

"I think we do. His name is Trigga. His uncle is Phenom."

My eyes narrowed as I studied six men in question. I paid close attention to their reaction at the mention of that little nigga's name. Armando's jaw ticked but he remained quiet. Word around the way was that him and Trigga had beef because of some shit that happened between him and my brother. Nicola puffed on a Cuban cigar but remained silent as well.

"That little black motherfucker who fucked up my way of life for the last nine months?" Valentino asked.

The way he spit the word "black" out like it offended him wasn't lost on Stiff. While Valentino looked like the classic Italian gangsta in a suit and tie with the long black trench coat blowing in the wind, Stiff was a dark Sicilian with more black features than white Italian. The tension was thick, just the way I wanted it to be.

"Ah, di young boy dat tek down yuh brudda?" Prodigy commented.

For some reason, the way that nigga was smirking like he got a kick out of my brother being dead made the scar on my upper lip itch.

"Please, tell me why he is my problem," Kim finally spoke up. His chinky eyes never wavered as he gazed at me.

"Is it me?" Valentino cut in. "Or did that little black piece of soot not fuck up all our money when he popped Damien?"

My eyes cut at Stiff when he slowly turned his attention to Valentino. They called him Stiff for a reason. That motherfucker barely moved and when he did, it was like he was a fucking statue.

"One more time, Valentino, and I'm going to leave your body in this fucking grave field," Stiff warned.

Valentino's eyes narrowed as he stepped forward. "You threatening me, you sunbaked motherfucker?"

"Cut the shit, you two. Measure your dicks later in private. This man here is talking important business," Kim countered and squashed the rising tension. He may have been the shortest motherfucker out of the six, but no doubt he was one of the deadliest. He was quick and could kill before you knew you were dead.

While Valentino and Stiff stared one another down, Kim turned to me. "How will me going along with your agenda suit me? Will it get me my money and product back?" he asked.

His expression was serious. I simply smirked and nodded.

"What's my return on investment?" Stiff asked.

"Before my brother died he ran most of these zones. I'm willing to give them to those who show me allegiance in this turf war. I want that little nigga and everybody associated with him dead. No body parts found. That includes that little girl they have with them, too."

"Mi no fi tink yuh 'ave the right fi do that, eh?" Prodigy spoke up.

I could tell by the way his lips turned up that he was going to be a problem. "Why not?"

"Nigga, do yuh know who Phenom is? Yuh really trying fi rumble wit dis nigga over his blood?"

"He did take out DOA," Stiff mentioned.

"It's one of him and how many of us?" Valentino interjected.

Stiff grunted. Kim rolled his shoulders. Prodigy laughed. Nicola and Armando remained silent.

"What's so funny?" The chill in my voice when I asked the question had the rest of the men in the graveyard turning their attention on him as well.

He threw his hands in the air, grinning. "Mi dun know. Maybe shits funny because one man tek your whole dynasty and him blood come buk fi finish di job, eh? Or maybe tis shit is funny because these here ma'fuckers is trusting of a man who has nothing fi lose, yuh? But everyting fi gain. Mi no fi go fi battle wit dis nigga for you."

As he continued to speak, spittle flew from his mouth and his grin turned into a scowl. I rolled my shoulders and stepped front and center so that it looked as if me and Prodigy were in the middle of the ring about to square off. The thumb on my right hand clicked around the hook of my cane.

"So, you saying you don't want fi do business, eh? Saying you no trust me?" I switched my accent from the American one to match his Caribbean one. Prodigy shook his thick, matted locs and matched my stance.

"Would you trust a man wit' one hand?" he sarcastically responded.

He wasn't afraid of me. That was good. I liked that shit. It made my dick hard. After he asked that last question the rest of the men looked down at my hands. My heart blackened with ice thinking about how I'd lost my hand. The nub that remained twitched underneath the artificial limb that now resided where my hand used to be. Since I had both hands gloved, none of the men had noticed. The fact that he knew this told me where his allegiance lay. I didn't have time for bullshit and I didn't have time to play games. All these motherfuckers were expendable to me, but none of them needed to know it until the endgame was near. The fact that Prodigy was standing in a graveyard challenging my agenda made my nuts coil.

Before his next breath was taken, my sword was released from my cane. The end of it connected to his abdomen. His grunts and groans serenaded me as he bent forward with blood spilling from his mouth. I shoved the knife clear through his back.

"Yuh don't motherfucking look a gift horse in di mout, pussiclot," I growled and snatched the weapon back toward me as I twisted it.

When he dropped to his knees, I cut that nigga's head clean from his body. My dick pulsated with the need to release in that moment. I could feel my pre-cum leaking from the tip as I watched his head roll near Armando's and Nicola's feet. There was a look of disgust on their faces.

"You two are quiet, why?" I asked without breaking a sweat.

"Nothing to talk about. That little motherfucker ran his mouth. Got me put on blast in front of the people," Armando stated.

"If you about to put my sources back in line, then my loyalty lies with you," Nicola added in a thick Russian accent. "Nothing else to talk about."

"Good. Then this meeting is over. We'll meet again in two days. Until then, I need volunteers to go meet with Phenom."

"Wait a minute," Stiff said looking at me.

"What?"

"Anika. Where's the African queen?"

I looked around at the men and saw that they were none the wiser about the connection between Anika and Phenom. I chuckled inwardly. I'd just keep that tidbit of info for leverage later.

"What about her?"

"Why isn't she here?"

All eyes were on me.

"That is what we need to find out, gentlemen."

Deep inside I wanted to kill every nigga in my presence, but I needed these pawns to get me inside and have their people tell me what I needed to know. I needed their little runners and street imps to be eyes and ears. Phenom and his little pussy-ass nephew had to pay for their sins. Once and for all DOA would have its vengeance. We ended that meeting after setting all the plans in motion for their people to get close to that little makeshift crew of wannabe hoodlums. I had one ace in the hole already. I chuckled at the thought. They would never see that one coming.

"How'd it go?" a thick British-accented voice asked me as I slid into the back of the limo.

I looked over at S.B. and grunted. I really didn't want to talk. "We can talk later," I told him.

My dick needed to be sucked. The dead body of Prodigy still lay in the graveyard over my brother's grave. The hard on I had from that needed to be handled. I pulled my dick out, leaned back with my arms stretched wide. That nigga knew what to do. For as hard as he was in the street, he sucked a mean dick in the back of that limo.

Chapter 18

Ray-Ray

That party set everything in motion. We'd already had a plan before we stepped feet back in the A. I couldn't lie and say it wasn't different being back home, because everything was different. I was no longer the Diamond I was when this whole thing had started. I was wiser and more cunning. I saw everybody as the enemy who wasn't a part of our misfits' crew. Me and Trigga's relationship had been rocky. I didn't know what the fuck love was but I knew I felt something when I looked at Kwame Kweli. That was why it was nothing for me to whoop that girl's ass. It was supposed to all be for show, but when I saw her put her mouth on Trigga, something fragile in me snapped and it was nothing for me to lay hands on that ho.

In the past six months, between watching our backs for Dante's retaliation, I'd gotten my high school diploma. Anika had made sure of that. Trigga and I walked a thin line between wanting to be together and really not know how to get there. We did the best we could with what we had.

"Prodigy is dead," my aunt said as she walked into the house, breaking my train of thought.

She dropped the backpack that was on her shoulders. She didn't stop until she kissed her husband on the lips. Army boots covered the bottom of royal blue tights giving her more of a high school teenager than and street queen, which she was in ATL. Her Havana twists lay on her head in two goddess braids just like her daughter.

"What do you mean?" I asked.

"Dante gathered all of the bosses here and word is that Prodigy didn't make it out. He was one of the bosses that aligned with me when Dame was on his bullshit," she explained.

We were all gathered in the front room waiting for Phenom to give us the daily scoop. Trigga, Speedy, and Big Jake had been on the block doing what they did. Me, Chyna, and Gina had done a walkthrough of the old neighborhoods just to show our faces and to get the hood talking. Talked to a few old associates and acquaintances just to show that we were the new "kings and queens" of the streets. Believe it or not, most people had known it was us who took down Dame simply because of the cops he'd had on his team. They'd been asking questions nonstop. Word was they had even put a bounty on our heads.

That didn't stop us. We wouldn't stop until everything that resembled DOA was good and dead. Everything was a ploy. Chyna was pretty in her own right, but you added me, her, and Gina together strutting our asses around the neighborhood and you better believe every nigga, bum, and bitch wanted to holla, as was the plan. Gums were bumping. Niggas was jawing and it was all about the ENGA clique.

"I didn't see that coming," Phenom admitted.

"Me either. Was hoping he was smart enough to contain his anger. Word is Dante beheaded him right in front of the other bosses."

"So this nigga on some scare you into submission type shit," Trigga asked.

I looked at him while he leaned forward rubbing his big hands together as he kept his eyes on the window in the kitchen. I knew what he was waiting for as he glanced at the Movado watch on his arms then back at the kitchen window.

"I don't know really," Anika spoke.

"And we really don't care," Phenom added. "Need you and the gang to get ready for tonight. The bosses are requesting a meeting with you. They don't know that we know they've met with Dante. So they think the meeting is about us coming back to claim our reign and hold on the A. I've been telling our eyes and ears to put word out that you came to take the seat Dame vacated since he was your kill, nephew. Think you can handle that?"

Trigga gave a curt nod and jumped up when he heard a loud thump from the kitchen. Phenom smirked and shook his head. Even when Trigga wasn't training us, he was training us. We all waited in silence as Ghost rounded the corner. A dark purple hoodie covered her face. Black baggy jeans and wheat-colored kiddie Timbs were on her. She stopped when she saw us all standing looking at her. She slowly pushed the hoodie back revealing freshly done braids and bright eyes.

"Why didn't you come through the kitchen window?" Trigga asked her. The bass in his voice let us all know he wasn't pleased that she didn't do exactly as he'd told her.

But what surprised us all was when she looked up at him and answered, "Because you expected me to."

I looked at Trigga and for a while he just stared her. Then a slow, easy smirk adorned his features. "Good girl. Never do what a nigga is expecting you to do, not even me. Good girl."

My heart warmed when Ghost only smiled, pulled out her iPod, turned her volume up, then placed her headphones on as she took a seat on the couch.

"Hey, hey," Trigga snapped her fingers to get her attention.

"Yeah."

"Did you get that information I told you to?"

"Yeah."

"Well?"

"Well, dang, daddy, you said not to speak on it if you wasn't alone so I ain't speaking on it 'cause you ain't alone." She lightly sighed, rolled her eyes playfully, then tossed her book bag to him. Obviously none of us knew what the two of them were talking about. Trigga looked in the book bag and grinned before zipping it back up and tossing it over his shoulders. I tried to reach for the bag to see what was in it but he smacked my hand away.

He turned his attention back to his uncle. "Now, you were saying something about a meeting?"

"Yeah, you and your crew of misfits here are going to make a grand entrance at this here meeting tonight," Phenom explained.

"You know most of these men, Kwame. Men who used to break bread with Dame so plenty of them want your head on a platter for killing their money and product supplier," Anika added.

"Yeah, and most of them niggas was shady as fuck then too," Big Jake added folding his beefy arms as he stood wide legged.

Trigga nodded in agreement. "True deal, and since we ain't got Prodigy on the inside anymore, we're pretty much fucked on what goes on with them behind closed doors now, huh?"

Phenom gave a curt smirk. "We never get fucked, nephew. We do the fucking, feel me? Get'cha game face on and be ready to roll in an hour. Me and my woman gotta make a run. This here is your show, nephew. Your crew. Make these niggas bow even though they don't want to, feel me?"

Five minutes later, Anika and Phenom were gone and Trigga turned to me. "A'ight, this is what it is: I'ma walk into this meeting on time as a fake show of respect for these nigga's gangsta. You know make them think I respect them as old head OGs from the street. That will be my act of respect."

I had to ask, "Then what?"

He nodded, keeping that backpack Ghost had given him close. "This is where y'all come in as my act of defiance. Y'all come in twenty minutes later. No sooner, no later. Twenty minutes. That's to let them niggas know they don't scare me, don't run me, and never will. You feel me?"

We all nodded in agreement.

"And what about Ghost?" Gina asked.

"She knows what her agenda is. She'll be safe."

"Then let's get a motherfucking move on," Big Jakes booming voice thundered.

I could only shake my head with a smile. Finally, we were the niggas with an agenda, only we intended to be smart in carrying out ours.

Chapter 19

Trigga

"All warfare is based on deception. Hence, when we are able to attack, we must seem unable; when using our forces, we must appear inactive; when we are near, we must make the enemy believe we are far away; when far away, we must make him believe we are near."

The minute hand on my watch kept my attention as I gave a mental countdown for the show and repeated the words of Sun Tzu in my mind. Ghost and Chyna were back at the main house taking care of business that they couldn't handle with us here. Ghost was too young to go to the meeting and the fact that Chyna was here, we wanted to keep her hidden from Dante for a bit while teaching her about ATL. My mind stayed thinking on those two's safety while both of my hands fisted on my thighs, making the chains I had inked on my forearms with different words of teachings pop out. Jake sat next to me in the driver's seat of our silver and black Bugatti, with Speedy parked behind us with Baby G and Ray-Ray in the blacked-out military-grade luxury SUV. Jake and I were both dressed like businessmen.

Me, I had on a black fitted suit jacket, with a hoodie designed in it. Underneath was a crisp white tailor shirt that was open at the collar and rolled up on my arms. I stuck with dark denim fitted jeans and leather black military-style Timbs that looked unlaced at my ankles.

Jake, was dressed in a similar fit, but without a jacket, opting for a simple vest. His low-cropped waves were perfect in their circular style and we both had on shades.

Bling sparkled at our ears. My locs were carefully braided into a knotted ponytail, done by Baby G. We were swagged up and decked out. Smelling tight and ready for war. We hid our weapons London style. That meant that even though we were dressed like money, we kept things all the way street, with weapons hidden on us since we knew we would get a pat down. If London had taught us nothing else, it taught us how to adapt.

In the SUV, Speedy was hooked up like us, except he had on a jacket with no hoodie and his braids were gone and replaced with a bushy ponytail. Baby G and Diamond decided to put on deep purple matching bandage dresses that pushed up their tits and made their asses fatter. Diamond explained that the kings of the past would wear either gold or purple, and since they didn't want to put on all gold, they decided for the purple with gold accents and bling. They let Ghost and Chyna pick out the accessories and bling.

The points of our looks were to deceive and distract. The goal was to piss people off. To make all the bosses, who we all knew hated that we even were alive, think that we had taken the money they lost and used it to build our empire. Like a lion hunting in the middle of a storm, lightning exposes the prey and anger always reveals knowledge.

Thinking on that, my clock kept ticking. Time was of the essence. I sat rubbing my hands together, working on my thoughts. Kendrick Lamar blasted and Jake's booming voice had me breaking out of thought to check what the homie was saying.

"Yo, you think after everything, we can finally get some peace?" Jake seemed to asked me but I could tell he was on some mind shit.

"Maybe; you know how this life is," I simply responded. Shit, I knew not to put all my money on one thing. After London, a nigga knew we'd never have peace, even in the grave.

Jake gave a sigh and ran a hand over his waves, glancing at me. "Yeah, you're right. Just saying, think we can get made like Phenom and Anika. Feeling like all we been doing was running. Life wasn't perfect with that nigga Dame, but we had chill days. Just need some chill days feel me?"

My homie was on some heavy deep shit right now and I could get why. "What up, man?"

"Naw, nothing really, just thinking," Jake said.

When a nigga who ain't used to thinking starts thinking that's when you know you need to get your nigga right. Had to make sure he wasn't on some other shit that may get us killed. He did that shit before and had me acting out of character, but he was my blood now, my brother; had to look out for a nigga who always was looking out for me.

"Check it, what up. Don't get pussy because we going inside this joint. Everything is everything. Once this shit is handled, we'll get to just chill set and keep our backs protected feel me?" I tried to encourage.

"Yeah, I know, man; trust I know. Just thinking on Gina is all. Baby girl needs that peace. After everything, all the shit, we gotta look out for her; I gotta look out for her."

I eyed my homie and knew he was on some heart shit. Wasn't nothing I could do about it though I understood it on some level, because Baby G was like my sister. So he was right on that, she needed to be protected.

"Yeah, I hear you, man—" I was saying until Jake cut me off.

"I mean, me and baby girl just gotta you know, chill for a bit, maybe just I don't know, get out the game all the way so she can have something normal like?"

"Normal like what, motherfucka? Told you, no matter what we do, we can go be doctors in Egypt or some shit, niggas will always gun for us feel me?" I cut back in, almost getting heated 'cause the nigga was pissing me off.

"Yeah, man, I know, but shit, she deserves it. I learned in the church that it's a season for everything; come on, brah, just get on my level and understand where I'm coming from," he pleaded, watching me with a stern look like something I had seen in my uncle's eyes with Anika.

All I could do was nod my head, because I had promised to protect and be down for everyone in my crew. If that was what he and Gina needed, wasn't shit I can do but try to give them jewels and gold, so they could have privacy and peace once this was over. A part of me quickly echoed that I was tired. Tired of all the shit.

So, I held my fist out to give my nigga dap, a homie I'd always hold down in this life and next and he gave me dap back.

"It's icing, man. Whateva y'all need I'll work to get it. Especially for Baby G," I reassured him.

Jake turned back in his seat, his huge, muscled, and bulky form rising with each quiet breath he took and I knew he was going back into his killa mode. "Guess it's time, brah."

Checking how Jake held the familiar cross that his grams gave him, I gave a slight nod. We all understood that this shit was on a whole new level, the big times. Which is why Jake covered us all in prayer before we headed to Buckhead. Code stated in a boss meeting that we couldn't touch each other, but with Prodigy being taken down for popping off at the mouth like he did, we knew anything could happen.

"Yeah, bro, down for whatever. Pull up and let's be about this shit because my fingers are itchin'."

Pumping his breaks to signal Speedy, we watched the SUV turn down a street way near the St. Regis Hotel and we pulled up in the back of the hotel. The sound of Future sounding like a wet cat in a pool from Jake's cell had him connecting it though our speakers as Speedy hit us up.

"Ay, bruv. Watch ya circuit a'ight? And don't get your ass kicked to fast before we can get in there, ah ha!"

Both Jake and I laughed as Speedy clowned us. Gina's soft, raspy voice cut through and commanded both of our attention because it was still so light.

"Jakey and Triggy! Bring that magic but don't knock some heads off too fast, and don't take so long 'cause I get bored 'n' shit den lose ma focus," Gina softly whined.

How she said it made me laugh. I was about to tell her that my name had an "a" on the end and not a "y" as I usually do, but right now, I didn't feel like it. So, I leaned forward, giving Jake dap then took off my seat belt ready to bring the show. "A'ight, Baby G, I got you too. Let's handle shit."

I moved to open the door but stopped when Diamond spoke up. "Still though, be careful."

It was kinda strange how she said that, though I knew she was talking to the both of us, something more was there like, like li'l shawty was saying something more specific to me.

"We will. Just do what you two . . ." Laughing, I adjusted my shades and continued, "You three do. Let's ride out, BJ."

Coming to St. Regis was something I wasn't expecting. I thought these goons would be at Magic City or some shit, with asses shaking, money raining, and pussy in our laps. But, nah, that wasn't the case. Jake and I were some black kids standing in an old world moniker of the South hotel. The fact that we were in the back had me feeling some type of way.

One, I knew this was because all of us were on some illegal shit, but two, I could feel my skin color was the reason as well, if you get what I'm saying. We were led by two burly guards. Each cat was the same hulking height and build as Jake, but he had an inch or two on them. One looked like the Rock; the other looked like Booker T from WWE.

We let them pat us down, and Jake returned the favor. We were then led from the back of the lobby on through a bustling, hot kitchen. That led us to a back room in the basement of the hotel that revealed a gambling hall, no, more like a casino with broads sliding down poles and offering us drinks while hostesses of every shade and hue came by us and took us to the back of a private room, where the various twelve street dons sat around a huge dark oak meeting table. The surface was so shiny that I could see the ugly faces of several demons reflected within the niggas before me.

Armando, the head of the Latin Kings, Nicola, the head of the Russian Cartel in the south, Valentino, head of the Italian Cartel, Kim, head of the Dragons a.k.a Asian Clan, and Stiff, head of the Black Sicilians sat smoking cigars with a familiar gold imprint around the base with the other dons. One I had seen that crooked cop, fed, whatever the fuck he was portraying his ass as, S.B. smoking when he took down some Jamaicans back in London. A smirk flashed on my face as I took that little note to head. Niggas were choking down Dante's dick, I saw.

With Prodigy having been axed, I knew everyone here was confused as to why his seat was now filled by a pretty, feminine Jamaican queen. Word on the street was that after Rasta J stepped down to let Prodigy take over, it was his daughter who now stepped in her rightful place, and supposedly, she was a wild card. But I knew it was only a replacement chosen specifically by Anika. But no one ever would know that link.

So my eyes gazed over her caramel skin, where her locs fell over swollen breast then her cushy, plump lips as she puffed from her cigar and leaned back like a queen. Legend was her name and lethal with arsenal was her MO. While I sized up the room, the massive double doors behind us almost closed, but I glanced at Jake. Jake nodded and I primped the arms of my jacket then dropped my hoodie back. Jake stopped the doors from closing all of the way and stood between them watching us and watching the other people in the hall behind us.

Silence filled the large room and I stood stoic, saying not one damn thing as I waited on them to address me. I may not be that nigga who was rising up the ladder of Dame's world anymore, but I was still that silent killa. Niggas addressed me first and not the other way around. So I listened to pins drop, scoping the only open chair left. Not fazed at all by the disrespect in the room, I walked to it then rested my hand on the back of it, refusing to sit.

"This moolie is gonna sit down one day," cut through the silence and had me eying the source. Valentino.

Stiff, who called himself having beef with that nigga because Valentino didn't like his ass either regardless of them both having Italian blood, gave a nasally snort. Anika had told me about the beef between those two when she and Phenom gave me the rundown of each street king. But as Stiff tapped the ashes off his cigar and leaned in close to whisper something to Valentio, it was clear that regardless of their beef, I was their common enemy.

Power was everything, so I continued doing me and playing the game of the new kid on the block. A smirk played around my face in that moment. "Lords, I would have brought gifts but we all remembered how that turned out before right?" I joked, making reference to the poison Dame had fed many of them before to get to the number of Lords we had sitting today.

Eyes cut me like daggers, and each one of them became targets for me as I sat.

"What can I not do for you all today? I guess you all wondering if it's true? That I'm now king of Dame's world?" I leisurely asked. I noticed the cigar in front of me in amusement. I wasn't about to put that shit anywhere near my lips which is why it stayed exactly where it was.

"So you're Phenom's blood?" a don asked.

I knew my unk's representative was in the mix so it amused me that they would ask that. Slick move.

"Is he really serious here? Why is that kid so cocky?" I heard another one of the twelve dons ask.

This was a female, who I turned, gave a wink to, and looked down at my dick. "Because of that and am I? And Phenom? Shieet, nigga nothing but a legend, a ghost to me, so if he is, he is. If he ain't he ain't but that nigga got mad power and I respect it," I calmly said and turned back to address the whole room.

The sound of Jake moving to the side to allow a waitress in with a bottle of Conjure and a glass for me had me waving her off. A clear mind was needed with these motherfuckers so I was good. By the way, I liked how they played me. No disrespect to Conjure, but these motherfuckers were sipping Dom, while they offered me a different type of drink? Yeah, the fuck right on that shit. Come at me another time.

Motioning with my hand, I waved for the waitress to come to me. Mami was dressed in blinged-up pussy imprint showing boy shorts and a bra. Her red hair spilled down her shoulders like crinkled waves and I noticed how Valentino was copping her. Nigga was known for hating black men, but loved him that black puss.

My fingers drifted in her hair as I spoke low to her. I watched her honey and bourbon skin flush slightly red, the moment my voice dipped into a drawl for her. I knew everyone at the table was pissed at how I was playing them, but I really couldn't give two shits and a handshake. What I was doing, was telling her to bring in extra chairs for my crew. As she sashayed away, I tilted my head to the side to watch how her left and right ass cheek seemed to play soccer with each other and jiggle just right. Shit was sexy but I really wasn't copping her.

"So!" I boomed, clapping my hands together. I leaned back and rested my finger against my temple as I spoke, "What it do? I ask again."

"Nigga, you really think you about some shit don't you? Fuck this right here; this is what's going to happen. You have no power here, bitch. None. That's what this shit is about. And by the time you get out of here, know that you won't make it. Feel me? Like you niggas say in your zone."

I studied that nigga for about a good minute or so, just stared at that nigga to make him uncomfortable. My fingers tended at my lips and my eyes narrowed staying on his Flava Flav with Bubba Gump lips–looking ass, until I could see a slight change in that nigga's breathing. He didn't know what that fuck I was going to do and I liked it that way.

"Stiff! Wow. Sorry, Stiff is your name right? Black Sicilians right? Same niggas who stole about fifty kilos of hard dust from the Dragons? Kilos that I helped acquire for Dame to sell transport to the Dragons from the warehouse you and your mafia took it from? Remember? Yeah, that was you, right?"

My eyes flashed in the smoky cave of the room we all resided. Heat pulsated from Stiff. No movement came from him, but all emotion showed in the goon's eyes. He knew what I had just said was truth and it made me laugh out loud at how he really thought he was going to play me.

"You lying—" Stiff barked but the Dragon Kim's slight movement toward him had me quickly cutting in.

I wanted to save that shit for later. "Forgive me, that's my fault right? Each and every one of you are mad why? Because I lost you money and product right? Yeah, I can see it in your eyes. But check it, every last single one of you owe me for what went down. I put more money in your pockets than what you even think you lost. You don't believe me? Check your accounts."

Rustling started at the table. I sat back and watched. Buzzing from their cells went off, and as they pulled out their cells, my crew walked in with the waitress who looked wide-eyed and slightly scared. Gina gave her a wink and placed a finger against her pink bubble gum–tinted lips, motioning for her to keep silent while she walked in. Diamond wiggled her fingers in a flighty wave then gave a sexy smile at many of the men and women she had last seen in Dame's kingdom. Speedy stood grinning like the Joker while rubbing his goatee on the opposite side of the door with Jake. Ray-Ray and Gina both sat at the left and my right with flourish showing of silky shiny legs as every don at the table gawked.

But it was a low grumble of disrespect from Valentino that had my finger's itching when he said, "Ragtag cunt misfits. Fucking bingo-bongos always late, which shows they aren't about shit."

Sliding back in my chair with my arms folded over my chest, I narrowed my eyes and sucked my teeth as a nerve in my jaw ticked. I knew to igg that shit right then and there, but in my mind, he was sporting a pretty sizzling bullet hole, signed and delivered by my own hand. But, see, I was used to motherfuckers showing their power with an ass kicking or cut throat, but shit, I really wanted to kill that nigga. Wanted to so bad that I could taste it, but instead, I stood up, walked slowly around the table, and spoke.

“As you see, each of you have fresh product.The money you have is what was figured and owed you plus interest from when my former boss played each every one of you. The only wrong I’ve done is meet up with you all here today, because you all clearly ain’t got shit to offer me but death and that’s cool. But we got more business to handle before it gets down to that. Second . . .” I glanced at Diamond and Ray-Ray. They both stood and dropped several silver suitcases down using their leather gloved hands to open the cases, before sitting back down.

“Inside is a new product called indigo. The hottest thing on the streets right now and been tested at various locations in the A. Think of this shit as molly and ecstasy all in one, but with the proper chemical balance not to kill mafuckers if they OD on the shit. Each of you have a claim to market it, and not every packet of indigo is the same. So know that this shit is all on equal footing and the rest is up to how you all distribute it. You all only can get indigo through me because it’s created by me. Now, cutting and distribution, I’ll repeat, is up to you all. If you down then get in it, but if you can’t handle that I am a better businessman than a nigga none of y’all were loyal to, then, that’s cool, I’ll meet cha later in a back alley.”

Every don in the room cautiously reached for the case and looked the product over; several jars of liquid indigo were within, next to a small clear box of indigo powder. I kept walking, with my hands behind my back. My eyes never left Stiff or Valentino.

Diamond’s calm voice reminded me of her aunt as she took over. “The moment any of you close the cases and pull it to you, you then become a partner. The moment you don’t, it was nice doing business with you. By the way, Valentino? Fuck your life.”

Gina’s raspy light voice cleared up interjecting, she stood, then walked near Valentino and sat on his lap, running her nails over his scalp then harshly tugging on his ears. "Daddy was neva good to any of ya and it was Trigga who always made the moves to get ya your product. Remember Daddy was the hand that fed ya but also tried to kill you and word is you all looking to do that same shit again? Tsk, tsk. Fool me once . . ."

"Fool me twice and you end up strung up with your dick cut off," Diamond finished for Gina.

Both cut their eyes at Valentino and Stiff and both gave a sexy, lethal giggle of hate.

"Or leave with a lost limb," I growled low.

Gina smoothly slid off Valentino's lap. My anger flashed quickly across my face. I pulled what looked to be a cigar holder out. It had been hidden in the inside pocket of my jacket. All the men at the table watched me, wondering what my next move was about to be. I liked this part of the game. Toying with the dons gave me power absolute. They had no idea just what was about to happen until it did. I pressed the little button on the side of the cigar holder and watched in glee as a long thin sharp blade appeared. Before Stiff could blink, two of his fingers went flying in the air. In the commotion, I flipped on the table, stood up, and kicked Valentino directly in his face before cutting off his left ear before he could react. Blood spewed and covered the walls.

Shouts picked back up and I turned to glare at Stiff as he cradled his hand. I jetted across the table again, letting my Timbs mark his face and making him fall backward. Dons tried to grab me. But it was Gina and Diamond who gave them the warning not to even move when they flashed their hidden Glocks.

Once I was done breaking that nigga's ribcage then moving to Valentino, who was now being held back by both Gina and Diamond who had a blade pressed against his bobbing Adam's apple. I strolled back over him doing the MJ prance and gifted him with the same pain. Once my moment of anger died down, I stood up, slapped Valentino against his face with a blank stare then I brushed off his jacket just to be a prick.

Shock and quiet filled the room. Several dons nodded in respect including the new Jamaican Lord. Everyone hesitantly moved to sit back down. Other dons helped both Stiff and Valentino to their chairs while they bandaged their wounds with napkins and handkerchiefs.

Me, I strolled back to my chair, wiping blood from my hands before turning to sit back in my chair with my leg thrown over the arm of my chair while watching everyone's faces. I already knew who was with me and who was against me. Already knew they were scared of that nigga Dante and already knew how the dons were going to play this: up the middle on both of us. Which was why I loved the art of revenge.

When being the instrument that brings chaos and forges revenge, I could always see the weaklings in the game who were trying to do me one better. Everyone at the table was feeding me information without even knowing it. So in a sense this meeting was won by us; on another level, I knew though he wasn't here, Dante was pulling mad power.

Was I scared about it? Naw, but I for damn sure was feeding from it.

The slam of a fist on a table tried to intimidate me. But I was really bored as I leaned in my chair yawning and looking at my watch. Each don began to fight with each other. Barking like dogs. Each one of them suckers were foaming at the mouths. Lips curled, eyes dark in chaos and I just sat back watching it all until I got bored with it. Both Valentino and Stiff were eying me in hate. But what the fuck did they expect? They bring disrespect then they have to deal with the consequence.

Standing with a bored expression, I reached behind me to pull the hoodie I had back over my face and held my hand out to Diamond. Several dons noticed my movements and quickly got quiet, shifting in their seats then pushing their chairs back. The weight of what I was holding my hand out for, settled against my palm and with a loud bang, Dante's severed hand landed on the table before me. Although it was slowly decomposing, it still looked intact. Call me psycho, but I kept the shit in formaldehyde as a trophy. The strong and pungent smell caused several people in the room to frown and jump back.

"Oh shit!" came from both Armando and Nicola, two niggas who were observers just like me and knew not to open their mouths through the whole process.

"The last nigga who thought we weren't about business lost his hand," I bellowed in authority. "See, you all seem to think that just because we're some kids that we don't deserve respect and that we don't know what the fuck we're doing. Me and mine have claim to the throne and motherfuckers like each and every one of you is what has bred us to be exactly what we are: killas. Continue underestimating us. We feed off of that. But what you won't do is fuck up our money. All funds have been cleared and this meeting is over. I leave you with a round of applause from a nigga that you all think we don't know is in league with you all. Let him know whaddaup and I'm ready whenever he is. Shawties, grab our shit, time to go."

I turned my back and headed to the door while grabbing the severed hand of the nigga they all were linking up with, as well as Valentino's left ear and Stiff's pinky and ring finger from his right hand. As Gina and Diamond also grabbed the suitcases, I saw out the corner of my eye, several of the dons sitting at the massive table leaving calling cards in their cases.

A smile played across my face. I waited for the doors to open as Diamond and Gina walked at my side.

"By the way, what was that shit you said Stiff and Valentino? Oh yeah, by the time these ragtag cunt mooglie motherfuckers walk freely from this room, not only will five of you monkey-ass cunts not make it out but, as the rest of you survivors will see, every last one of your goons and bitches in this casino hall who you were going to use to take us out are already sleeping with death."

Nodding at Jake and Speedy, I chucked the deuces in the air. "Enjoy your cocksuckers and Dom. One."

"Buh-bye!" Gina cooed, waving at each and every person in the room with a giggle.

While we walked out, my hands rested against both Diamond's and Gina's backs, giving show. Jake and Speedy closed the doors behind us, locking themselves in the room we just left with the twelve dons.

The pretty waitress who had served us earlier came out of her hiding space in the gaming area and grinned at Gina. Her name on the block was Smiley and ma didn't have to say nothing, which she didn't just in case ears were listening. See; never fuck with street kids who've grown up with a hood mentality. We all knew our shit and we all have access where others don't.

Niggas wanted to play us? Well get played at the same time.

The sound of incessant muffled shouts and a distinct Joker-like laugh from Speedy in the room with that of house music suddenly bumping from his cell let me know the numbers of our kills had just rose. Check it, we always have a plan. Drinks were laced to slow down the dons as gas pumped into that room to make those we didn't want to kill fall asleep. So as my boys had their fun, me and the dimes surrounding me stepped over the dead bodies that lay around us in the basement gaming area. Each one of them had been taken out by my crew thanks to a lot of the skills we learned in London.

"Trigga, can we come back and visit the St. Regis and stay in the hotel? It was real pretty upstairs," Gina linked her arm through mine while we walked up the stairway.

A chuckle escaped from me and I nodded. "Yeah, just gotta make sure they clean this shit up thoroughly."

My eyes locked on Diamond. She had slight cuts on her arms and top of her breasts from struggling with Valentino. She had held her own and came up looking a winner in a room of niggas who used to look at her as nothing but property. Shawty glanced her big, pretty doe eyes up at me, which reflected the smile on her face and she used her thumb to wipe blood from my face from under my hoodie. Li'l shawty was sexy powerful with it in that room and I hoped she held that power close to her always, especially later tonight.

"On to phase three," Diamond said with a light giggle.

I gave a rare true smile and nodded in agreement; everything now was in motion and ENGA was about to spread around on the streets.

Chapter 20

Dante

I had S.B. drop me off at the entrance of the food court of the mall then told him to park near the rear emergency exit and wait for me. I had business to take care of. As beautiful of a day as it was outside, my mood was foul as fuck. I didn't want to be here. The place was too crowded and being around a lot of people annoyed me. Yet, I had to handle some business that needed to be addressed with urgency. I tripped a little kid who bumped into me as he was running past. Ignored the obvious stares coming from women and men. The smell of the greasy food made me turn my lips down into a scowl.

As soon as the female in my line of vision saw me coming she decided to try to run. While my brother may have allowed pussy to cloud his judgment in his last days, he always knew how to use his dick to get what he wanted from a bitch. That was how I'd found the little gem. I'd made the girl so frightful of me in the last few months that I was sure she had pissed herself when she saw me coming. The younger the bitch, the more stupid they were. One thing my pops had taught me that I lived by, you had to catch a broad while she was young to get into her mind. When a plum turned red it was ready to pluck, when a girl turned twelve, my pops said she was ready to fuck. While the chick I had my eyes on was older than twelve, same rules applied. All you had to do was step into where their fathers were supposed to be.

That was what I had done to the chick who was trying to run from me. I'd asked her, coached her into doing a simple thing and she had yet to do it for me. When I'd touched down in my brother's old codes, she was one of the first females to run to me.

"OMG, you look just like him," she'd crooned.

"But I'm not him," I'd told her.

"I can be for you what I was to him," she'd said as she eased closer to me and laid a hand on my arm.

I hadn't ever been a nigga who liked to be touched without my inviting you to touch me, but I saw how eager she was to be next to me. I smirked, gave a lopsided smile and then nodded for her to get in the back of the car with me. That would be her mistake. Now, as I stood in the middle of the food court, she wanted to act as if she didn't remember what I could and would do to her for failing me. I knew she remembered, hence the reason she tried to run, but I felt as if I needed to remind her anyway.

I didn't have time for the chase. So, I pulled out my Sig and fired aimlessly into the air. The food court in Southlake Mall cleared out so fast you wouldn't have thought it was crowded beyond elbow room just moments before.

Amid the screams and yells of the public, I spoke out. "Please do not fucking run from me," I belted out. "Now, I've tried to be nice about this here thing, but you won't let me be. Why the fuck is that? Huh?"

She'd stopped with a look of fright so real in her eyes that it made me roll my neck and shoulders just to get a handle on the predatory way her fear fed me. I walked up to the female and snatched her by the back of her neck. Her neck sunk into her shoulders as my hand gripped her. It didn't matter to me that people had seen my face. They would simply think I was a dead man walking. This young pretty bitch I had my hand on was moving too slow for what I wanted her to do. She was supposed to infiltrate the party the other night to get details on some things and somehow, she managed to not do that. That angered me, pissed me off because I didn't have time to play games.

"I'm . . . I'm sorry. I wasn't running," she lied.

"Oh yeah. What would you call it then?" I bent down so my lips would brush against her ear as I spoke to her. She was shaking, trembling so much that I could feel the vibrations in my arm.

When she didn't answer me, I yanked her around in a tight grip to make her look into my face. "Are we going to have to take a trip back to my place? Do you want to revisit the chamber, my pretty?"

Her eyes widened and she started to cry. "No, no, God, please no. I'm sorry. I'll do what you want. I swear. I just need some time is all. I promise."

The bitch was close to one of the people in that little rag and tag crew of Phenom's and that little fucking runt Trigga. She was a feisty li'l bitch until I snatched her up and took her to my chambers. Fucked her like the nothing she was. Then, I passed her to S.B. and allowed him to do the same. I was a man that didn't believe in leaving any hole untouched and she had a virgin ass, until I tore into that motherfucker.

The sirens in the distance forced me to shove her toward the exit down the hall near the restrooms. I kicked the emergency door open and pushed her into the back seat of the stretch Hummer S. B. had waiting for me. It was a no holds barred kind of fight for me. Everybody was a pawn in my game. I slid into the car after the woman and watched as she cowered away from me.

"Have you made contact yet?" I asked the young girl.

She reluctantly shook her head.

"Is there a reason why you haven't?"

"I don't know where she is." Her voice was shaky. She was crying like she knew she was about to get her ass whooped. She had her purse covering half of her face while her eyes stayed locked on the cane on my hand. Her body was very familiar with this cane.

"You're lying to me. I know you're lying to me. Do you need more time or do you not know where she is. Which one is it?"

She didn't answer quick enough. Her eyes widened when she saw my fist coming toward her face. She threw her hands up and her purse went flying across the car as she screamed bloody murder. Since she thought I was going for her face, she covered with her arms leaving her stomach open. My fist connected to her soft flesh and blood mixed with spit flew from her mouth.

"Fucking lie to me, bitch," I growled as I repeated the strikes to her gut. "I'ma put you in the vicinity of where she's been spotted daily again and this time"—I snatched her up by her hair with one hand and then forced her face down into the leather seat with the other—"this time, bitch, you better make contact."

I knew she couldn't breathe by the way she was flailing her arms about. The whimpers and muffled screams only served to make my dick harder and to make me angrier. The blows to the stomach had even made her piss her pants. However, her fat ass in the air like that made my dick hard and if bloody pussy didn't stop me from fucking, neither would pissy pussy.

Chapter 21

Ray-Ray

"Would you forgive Dame if he came back and asked you for forgiveness?"

My head jerked to the side as I look at my friend, sometimes lover, Gina. Chyna's eyebrow raised on the right side. She looked just as confused as I did.

"Um, where did that come from?" I asked her.

She ran a hand slowly down her stomach and with the way she stopped and cupped the bottom let me know she was thinking about the son or daughter she would never have. "Just asking," she murmured.

Her eyes had watered as we walked. I stopped and turned to her so she could have my full attention. "No, you're not. What's going on, Gina?"

Traffic zoomed past us as we stood on Upper Riverdale Road across the street from a BP gas station. I studied Gina's chocolate features as horns blared at us because of our attire. It was our duty to stroll these streets and turn heads. The tattoos, or tramp stamps as people in the hood called them, read ENGA just below the dip in our backs. It showed that we were a clique. There was another tattoo that sat just over my heart with the word TRIGGA'S etched inside of a heart. I'd just gotten it day before. He'd yet to see it, but even if me and him never got together, he would always have that place in my heart.

We all rocked the same side ponytail and had on shorts that rode almost too far up our asses with black tights underneath them. No matter what we set out to do each day I had to always remember it was only for show. That was what kept me going strong. To know that we were so close to killing that nigga Dante kept me on my game.

Chyna stopped walking and stood on the other side of Gina so we could both see her clearly. She was going through something and I wanted to know what.

She looked up me quickly then her eyes darted from side to side like she was trying to formulate her thoughts. "Me and Jake saw my mama the other day," she finally said.

My eyes widened. Chyna looked on confused not knowing why my reaction was as such. Nobody knew that Jake and Gina snuck away and stole time together. Gina told me that she and Jake had just wanted to steal a few hours away too be a normal couple. I ain't never tell Trigga because I figured Jake would since they were close like me and Gina.

"Say what now?" I asked.

"Yeah, me and him was sneaking out the movies. 'Cause like, we just trying to have some normal girlfriend/boyfriend type stuff. We ain't ever really had that," she said then looked down at the ground. A sad, dark expression washed over her face as she glanced back up at me. I felt a chill come over me. "But anyway, she called my name all loud and shit. She was there with some new nigga she fucking. She was always fucking some nigga. And he was married 'cause I seen the ring. She ain't shit, but always wanna call me a ho and shit."

"Damn, did you answer her?"

Gina nodded. "I ain't really want to, but she had seen me then. I was kinda embarrassed 'cause I ain't really want her to meet Jake and all you know? This bitch come running up to me hugging me and shit. I almost shanked her ass."

"Bloody hell, Gina. Why yuh want fi shank your mum?" Chyna asked. She had a frown on her face that showed she would never understand Gina on that, but that was only because she didn't know Gina's mama. Gina's mama had put her out on the street when she was just sixteen. That was when her life was put into Dame's control.

"Because that bitch is fake. She ain't right, Chyna doll. She ain't right. She ain't right!"

I grabbed Gina's hands because I knew she was seconds away from pounding her closed fists on the sides of her head. By now, Gina had started to yell and the couple who had passed us started to look over their shoulders. I took Gina's hand and started to walk again. I didn't want to be in one place for too long because we were on a time frame.

"She hugged me, Ray-Ray, and I swear it felt like my flesh was moving, like worms under my skin. I don't know why I felt like she was the reason that nigga stomped my baby outta me."

Chyna stopped and raised both her hands as she shook her head. "Swear down! Who stomped a baby out of you, blood?"

I briefly explained to Chyna what Dame had done to me and Gina after we got set up by some people in his crew. Told her how they had made it look like me and Gina was trying to run away. After meeting Gina's mama, I couldn't be mad at Gina for feeling the way she did. Maybe if she had been a good mother, Gina would have had a better life. But I was more shocked at her hugging Gina. Last time we ran into the woman she acted like both Gina and I had Black Plague or something. I found that strange.

"Why she hugging you?" I asked. "That shit is suspect."

"Same thing my teddy bear was saying because he know what I told him about her. Then this bitch gone talk about how she has always loved me and made a mistake and shit. Bitch, you ain't made no damn mistake. For as long as I can remember she been a bitch to me, Ray-Ray. Jake was telling me you know not to snap and shit, but I felt funny 'bout her too, Ray. Thank ya for not making me feel stupid."

"Naw, you ain't stupid, Gina. I don't trust that at all."

Gina stopped again. Juicy J's "Show Out" blasted from the speakers of a Cutlass Supreme with a candy red paint job and the logo for Skittles. Dirty niggas and bum bitches strolled about the hood as we walked through. Even though it was a little cold, bitches were still dressed like it was summertime. The smell of weed, alcohol, piss, and sour trash assaulted my nose and I knew we had made it to our destination.

"And you right too," Gina said to me. "You know why? Bitch gon' tell me when she found out she had cancer her way of thinking changed. So she only trying to get right with God so He won't send her to hell where she belong."

The three of us had been walking down Mt. Zion Road in Jonesboro. We'd parked our car near Arrowhead. After we walked through Highland Vista apartments, we made our way down Tara and jumped across to Mt. Zion. We were just about to walk back into the apartment complex when Dominique spotted me.

Highland Vista used to be called the Seasons before some other property management had bought it out, and now it was more hood than hood could get. Gang signs decorated the sides of buildings. Niggas stood outside with gold grills, souped-up whips, and loud rap music blasting. Pants sagged off asses showing dingy drawz and colorful boxers. Gold chains, some fake, hung around necks and swung low.

I was about to say something else when a voice behind me called my name.

"Oh my God! Ray-Ray, is that you?"

I turned my head toward the direction of the familiar voice. It was a voice I hadn't heard in months but would recognize anywhere. Gina and Chyna both turned to look with me. The combat boots on our feet made crunching noises as we all looked at the girl I'd once called a best friend.

"Who that bitch?" Gina asked loud enough for Dominique to hear.

Gina wasn't trusting of nobody that wasn't a part of our immediate family. She was always on alert and so was I for that manner. Dom was a mocha-hued girl with shoulder-length hair and green eyes. A light sprinkling of freckles were on her face just underneath her eyes and cheeks. While she had never been as thick as me, she could still wear her clothes to make it look as if she had curves. She had on a pair of skinny jeans and a midriff. She stopped her stride midway to me when she heard Gina call her a bitch and put her hands on her hips.

"Girl, who you calling a bitch?" she snapped. "I don't know you and you damn sho don't wanna know me, bitch, so you better calm all that hot shit down. Ray-Ray, who this girl and why she all hype and don't even know me?" Dom had a look on her face that said something stunk.

"Yo, cuzzin, who dis bloodclaat gyal, eh? I swear down she can get got," Chyna spoke up.

Dom turned her attention to Chyna and scowled harder. "Bitch, I don't even know what'chu just said. Speak English, ho."

I had no idea what Dom's ass had even been doing around these parts. She was in Clay Co, short for Clayton County, and had no reason to be. She lived out in Henry County with well-to-do folks. The only reason she and I were friends was because my parents sent me to private school when they were alive.

But that had always been Dom. She wanted to hang in the hood. Loved to speak our language until she got back home around her parents. And she had always had the loudest mouth, talked the most shit, but could fight about as well as a seasoned crackhead could tell the truth. There had been plenty of fights I'd had to jump in because she'd written a check her ass couldn't cash.

"Hey, Dom," I spoke back to her. I couldn't even lie and say I was happy to see her because I wasn't. Not because I didn't love her anymore, but because I wasn't the same Ray-Ray she knew before. When she hugged me, I tensed up but returned her hug. I almost got teary-eyed because I barely remembered what it was to be that innocent sixteen-year-old I used to be.

She pulled back from the hug and looked at me. "Damn, bitch, rumor had it ya ass was dead. You know they found yo' mama and daddy dead in the back of the Woods? What the fuck happen to you?"

Bringing up my parents took my already nonexistent excitement to see her down a few more notches. The Woods was another set of apartments in the hood, but I had already known that tidbit of information because Trigga had told me. He told me a lot of stuff in our time together.

"The cops put me in a safe house until they could get my mama and daddy's killers," I lied.

She looked skeptical. "That ain't the shit I heard. Niggas was saying that nigga Dame had you hoing after he popped ya folks and before niggas bodied his ass."

My jaw twitched in annoyance as I tried to keep my cool. "Oh, yeah? Who said that shit?"

"Girl, that shit was all over the hood."

"What the fuck you know about the hood wit'cho white bread ass?" Gina asked out the blue.

I didn't know what it was, but Gina and Chyna were not feeling Dom. Maybe it was because they could see how uncomfortable I was. Or maybe Gina was still tripping hard off running into her mama. I didn't know. Part of me wanted to be happy to see her, but that other part of me, that new me, knew that she and I could never be as close as we used to be. I could never bring her into the world I was a part of. She had a chance to live life. Even though she was always hanging in the hood where her ass shouldn't have been, she still had a very good chance of a normal life. I remembered when she and I used to hang around these hood niggas thinking that was life we wanted.

We would flirt around with the idea of being a made hood bitch, then sneak back in our perfect worlds. Dom didn't ever know about how my mama and daddy did drugs. She never knew the way they fought one another because they knew how to keep on a good game face and because they tried their fucking hardest to keep me as far away from the streets as they could. I never wanted Dom to experience what I had been through.

"Bitch, I'm a li'l sick of you coming at me sideways, ho. I'ma give you a scar across yo' fucking face to match yo' neck," Dom popped off at the mouth.

I knew before Dom even finished popping off it was a bad move. Gina reached in her back pocket and made a move toward Dom so quick that I didn't even have time to stop her. Chyna simply stood back and smirked. Gina had slapped Dom so hard she flew back against a car and was laid out flat. I moved to stop Gina, but Chyna grabbed me.

"Li'l girl, I don't know who the fuck you talking to, but let me hip your bony ass to something. If I sliced my own fucking throat, imagine what I'ma 'bout to do to yo' fake

Ciara wannabe ass," Gina threatened as she squatted over Dom with a blade to her throat. I didn't even realize that Gina had literally smacked the blood from Dom's nose.

I struggled against Chyna's hold. "Baby G, she's cool people. Let her up, baby."

"I don't give no fuck if she cool people or not. Nobody 'bout to ever be talking down to me again." She held the blade close to Dom's throat. Ol' girl's eyes widened in honest terror as she looked up at Gina, but she wasn't about to look like a punk in front of the whole hood.

"Bitch, you better get the fuck up off me or kill me. Otherwise when I get up you better be running," Dom bluffed.

"Damn, shawty smacked the brown off baby girl," one nigga said from the gathering crowd.

"Worldstar," somebody else yelled out garnering a few loud laughs and low snickers.

"Oh hell naw, bitch. I know you don't think you just 'bout to roll up in my set and be smacking bitches," I heard a female call out.

We were drawing a crowd which was exactly what Trigga told us not to do. He'd said to make people notice us without them noticing us. You know, make ourselves seen around the way without making a scene around the way. But Dom didn't know Gina and her mistake was thinking she could talk to her any kind of way. Gina and I talked about a lot and the one thing she was always afraid of was being back in a time when she allowed people to talk to and treat her any kind of way.

While Gina went to work smacking Dom around, I looked up to see who was talking and it was the same girl from our party a few nights ago. She still carried the scars of our battle from the party. As soon as she saw my face, she smirked. "Bitch, you bold," was all she said before she came swinging for me.

I saw one of her friends grab Gina by her ponytail and start pulling her off Dom. Nothing else was said. All I saw was Chyna's boot connecting to a girl's leg. The sound of her knee cracking would forever be heard around the hood as niggas yelled oohs and ahhs. I took a fighter's pose and swung on that big-titty bitch from the party. These hood bitches in the A would never be ready for a fight with the three of us, especially not Chyna. She'd grown up in London where they fought to kill not just for bragging rights. So even with two bitches on her she had the upper hand because they couldn't handle her. Her mother's and father's teaching was in every punch, kick, and swing. When I saw Gina covered in blood, my heart started racing. I didn't know if she had done the cutting or had gotten cut.

Either way, I had three bitches on me and they were tagging my ass, but I wasn't going down without a fight. As I long as I saw Chyna and Gina was still standing, I was good. My adrenaline was on a hundred as my hair got pulled from left to right. Shirt got ripped from my body. But my fist kept connecting to faces and throats. See, I wasn't about no jumping shit. My mama always said in a one on one if you got your ass beat then it just wasn't your day. But daddy said soon as niggas and bitches decided to jump, it was all bets off. Out came my blade and the brass knuckles. Yeah, those bitches ate my face up while I reached my weapons, but once my knuckles were on and my blade was in my hand, it was over. I sliced one bitch clear across her face. She screamed out and fell back, hitting her head on the ground.

All around me all I heard were yells of "Worldstar" and niggas geeked over titties popping out like they had never seen them before. Once it was down to me on two, I swung my fists and knocked one of those bitches' head back. I could tell the brass knuckles had rattled her brains. She stumbled dazed but I didn't have time to focus on her. My left hand came around and sliced the chick from the party chest. I wasn't playing no fucking games with these hoes. I didn't know who they were working for. Shit, I didn't even know if Dom hadn't set this whole thing up, but this shit was feeling suspect as fuck to me. Once I'd made the three hood monkeys back up off me I grabbed a bitch from behind who was helping to jump Gina. I hit that bitch so hard, I saw teeth fly from her mouth. Gina grabbed the other girl by her hair and slammed her down to the ground so hard I knew her skull cracked in a good three places.

I turned to see Chyna's face had been sliced, but she was stomping a mud hole in a bitch on the ground. She had stomped her all the way under the car. We were so busy fighting that we didn't even see that the cops had rolled up on us. When I went to try to kick one of the bitches that had jumped me, I felt my world tilt and I was slammed to the ground.

"Police! Get on the ground! Get on the ground," rang out around me.

Walkie-talkies blared with calls for back up for gang-related activity and all I could think about was Trigga being pissed at us for getting locked up. The officer's knee was in my back and he had my arms twisted so awkwardly behind my back that I felt like my shoulder was about to snap. Once he had me handcuffed me and searched my pockets, he snatched me up. He was a white man, looked to be only a few years older than me.

"Yeah, I got a black female, no ID," he spoke into the walkie-talkie on his shoulder after he'd roughly searched my pockets.

I looked around frantically and saw that Gina was giving the female officer trying to cuff her a hard time.

She looked at me. “I ain’t going to jail, Ray-Ray. Nobody will take care of my teddy bear if I go to jail,” she said with tears in her eyes.

I knew she was talking about Big Jake. The female cop tried to cuff Gina but Gina was always one step ahead of her and too strong for the thin woman.

“Somebody get over there and help her get that perp under control,” the officer holding me ordered.

When I saw that Gina was really scared of going to jail, I yelled her name to get her attention. I made sure to call her by her street name.

“G! G!” She finally looked at me. “Stop struggling. Listen to me.”

“Yeah, it’s best you listen to your homegirl here otherwise I’ma have to come over there put my foot in your black ass, female or not. Stop resisting,” the cop holding me yelled at her.

“G,” I called again because she was swinging on the officer.

When I saw three male officers running toward her, my flight or fight instincts kicked in. “Run, G! Go,” I screamed.

Gina kicked the female officer in her pussy, forcing her to releasing her hold on the one arm she did have and Gina took off toward Tara Boulevard. They’d never catch that bitch. She could run a full five miles at top speed. Trigga had trained her that way. I was thrown to the ground again, harder than before. I felt when the concrete tore my skin away from my chin. I looked over to see that they had Chyna sitting on the ground. She wasn’t cuffed and an EMT was looking at the wound of her face. I remembered that Clayton County PD was filled with cops on Dame’s payroll. I’d take the fall but no way I subjecting Gina or Chyna to the system.

“Cuzzo, run!” I yelled at her. “Run!”

She wasted no time. She rolled over her head, did a quick ankle breaking move to get around the two officers who tried to grabbed her and she took off full speed ahead in the opposite direction Gina had run. It would have been stupid for them to run in the same direction. And she didn't have no weapons, so if they shot her in the back, going to jail or getting fired would be the least of their worries. Phenom would skin them alive. I knew, even as I saw officers take off after her, that they would never catch her either as they carted me off to jail.

I didn't know how long they had kept me in that isolated holding cell. I'd refused to tell them my name and even if they ran my prints, I had no record. The more I sat and thought about the shit that had happened, the more I was feeling like Dom had to know that we would be walking back through that set. I could have been wrong. I mean Dom was smart but she wasn't hood smart. So, I pushed the idea that she had set me up out of my mind.

The only phone call I made was to Trigga's burner phone. I put in the code 911 and waited. When the phone beeped three times I knew my message had gotten through. All there was left to do was wait.

I didn't even know I'd fallen asleep until the doors of the holding cell were snatched open. I didn't put up a fuss as the female correctional officers roughed me up while taking me to a room that read interrogation on the door. The fuck were they about to interrogate me about a fight for? I thought. My body ached from the fight. Face burned from the scratches on my face and chin. My question was answered when I looked at the two plainclothes detectives in the room.

"Shit," I mumbled.

I knew those two, had seen them with Dame plenty of times to know that they were as crooked as the letter S.

"Shit is correct, Ray-Ray," the female cop said to me. She was a dark-skinned bitch who had one blue eye and one brown one. The hair on her head was white like she was that bitch Storm from the X-Men. The man was white and looked like all he did was like to swing to niggas from trees by ropes.

"Have a seat," the man ordered me.

I slowly sat down in the brown folding chair and looked at them both. They were both smiling and chewing gum with a look on their faces that said they'd hit the jackpot.

"We've been looking for you for about a good nine or so months. Where you been hiding?"

I didn't answer the woman, just scowled at her.

"Oh she's a tough one, Detective Cunningham," the male detective quipped.

"I see. Let's see how tough she is when we send her ass up for murder."

I tried to play calm, pretend as if I was in control of my emotions, but I wasn't. I wasn't trying to go down for anybody's murder. "I didn't kill anybody," I said, a bit worried that what they were saying had any merit.

"Oh, but you did," Detective Cunningham groaned. "She did, didn't she, Detective Oxford?"

"Yes, she did. The name Damien Orlando ring a bell to you?" he asked.

My jaw ticked, eye flinched, but I didn't say anything.

"Do you know who Trigga, Big Jake, and Baby G are? We know you do. At first we thought all you niggas got caught in that fire that burned Dame's mansion to the ground, but then we got word that you four motherfuckers had mysteriously made it out alive. How's that possible, Ray-Ray?" Detective Cunningham asked me.

I shrugged nonchalantly. "I don't know what you're talking about."

She laughed and sat back in her chair as she squinted her eyes at me. Detective Oxford opened a folder and slid four pictures in front of me.

"We've been watching your little shit faced crew since you got back to town." I looked at him. "Oh what? You thought we didn't know you were back? Of course we did," he said then howled out in laughter along with his partner.

I looked down into the faces of Trigga, Gina, Big Jake, and Chyna. I grunted with a smirk when I saw Chyna. They really didn't want to bark up that tree.

"What's so fucking funny, little girl? You think this nigga loves you don't chu?" she asked pointing at Trigga.

I cut my eyes up at her.

"We know all about that little public display of an ass kicking you put on another girl at a party because she came at your drug-dealing little bastard man all wrong. You think if you take a case for this little nigga that you'll be that main bitch, huh? You'll be 'wifey' and all that, huh?" she asked using air quotes around the word "wifey."

This time I laughed. They were so fucking far off in their thinking. That was what would hinder them. They were thinking we were just your average street thugs. They thought we were on that typical hood shit. That was never our fucking genetic makeup. We were hood, but we were misfits. That meant that while we may have had to some illegal shit to get by, we were smarter than even your most skilled hoodlum.

I was still handcuffed so there was no way I could prepare for when Detective Cunningham jumped up to walk around the table. She slammed my head against the wall and pressed my face there.

"You think this shit is a joke?" she asked breathing hard in my face. "You think I won't put a bullet in your fucking head right now and call it a day. Nobody will care. Nobody will give a shit about your little black ass just like nobody gave a shit when Dame popped your parents. Did anybody look for your little black ass then? No."

I was gritting my teeth because the pressure she had on my head hurt like shit, no lie. If I didn't have those cuffs on me we would have been scrapping, cops or not. Thinking about my mama and daddy made me emotional. Neither one of them had talked to me in months. Yeah, they were dead but I'd gotten used to having them come to me and guide me in some way or the other. It sounded crazy to some but shit made perfect sense to me. I turned my head just enough to spit in that bitch's face.

"Now, that's just disrespectful and nasty," Detective Oxford commented as he stood.

He walked around to join his partner, only his hands started touching my titties and ass. I screamed out until he put his hand over my mouth then gun to my head.

"Shhh," he whispered.

My eyes looked up at the cameras in the corners of the room.

Detective Cunningham saw where my eyes were trained and laughed. Her hand grabbed my pussy. "None of those are on. We can do whatever the fuck we want to do to you in this room, you little disrespectful bitch."

"We sure can," Detective Oxford agreed. Tears fell down my face. "Ooohhh, now she cries."

"Now she cries!"

"Save those tears, you're going to need them where you're going." Detective Oxford moved his hands then tapped his partner's shoulder. "Did she ask for her attorney?" he asked looking down at his phone that had vibrated. "I think she asked for an attorney."

"I remember her asking for him." Detective Cunningham smiled wickedly as she roughly stroked my pussy through the green jailhouse jumper they had dressed me in because my shorts showed too much skin.

Just then a knock on the door got their attention. Detective Cunningham moved her hand and slung me back down in my chair by my hair. My head hurt like I had been kicked in it. I could still feel their hands all over me and wanted to vomit.

"Ahh, your attorney is here, Ray-Ray." Detective Oxford grinned. "And look, he's got your release papers!"

I was hoping that Trigga had sent somebody to bail me out of this fucking place. When I caught Oxford and Cunningham on the streets I was going to show them better than I could tell them about fucking with me. But to my horror, in walked Dante. My whole world started to crumble when I realized they were about to let me walk out of that damn jail with him. I quickly jumped up from my chair and kicked it at them. Dante reminded me so much of Dame that I couldn't put two and two together and realize it wasn't Dame I was looking at. He was dressed to perfection just as his brother used to dress. Beside him stood two men dressed in black. One I knew as S.B. from London. The other one looked familiar but I couldn't place him. Dante's eyes never left mine and when he gave a lopsided smirk, I knew there was no way in hell I was leaving with him.

"No, that is not my attorney," I yelled.

The door was open so other correctional officers came running to see what was going on. S.B. and the other unnamed nigga grabbed my arms and pulled me from the room.

I screamed, "No! Somebody help me. This man is not my fucking attorney." I kicked and bucked against their hold as much as I could.

"Detective Oxford, you sure this is her attorney?" a correctional officer asked. The look of concern on her face was real.

"Yeah, she's a nutcase," he told the woman. "You see what she had done when we brought her in here."

"Yeah, it's best she's released to him so he can put her back in a safe place. She's a danger to everyone around her," Detective Cunningham added with a grin on her face.

No matter how much I screamed and yelled, nobody did anything. It was then I knew that nigga Dante had a power play just like Dame did. Everybody just stood back and watched me being dragged onto the elevator against my will and did nothing. When the elevator doors closed, I kicked S.B. in the nuts and backed against the other side of the wall. I couldn't even bring myself not to look at Dante. My chest heaved up and down heavily. I felt like a sheep in a lion's den with my hands cuffed.

"So we finally meet, Diamond," Dante spoke to me.

"Fuck you, nigga," I responded.

"If you insist," he replied coolly.

He made a move toward me and I kicked my leg out almost kicking him in his dick. He side stepped it easily and lifted me from the floor by my neck.

"You'll be a nice little piece of bait to dangle in front of the two I want. Tell me where they are," he demanded.

"I ain't telling you shit."

"Suit yourself," he said then dropped me to the floor just as the elevator dinged.

S.B. and the other cat yanked me from the floor and forced me to walk out the station. All I could think about was what that man would do to me once he got me back on his turf. All the shit that had happened to me when I was controlled by Dame started to replay for me in 3D as they led me down the long concrete walkway outside. There was no way I would subject myself to that shit again, but didn't know what I could do without a weapon and with my hands cuffed.

"Yo, my main motherfucker Dante," a voice rang out.

My head jerked up and my heart could have jumped out of my chest at the sight of Trigga. Both S.B. and the other crony stopped ready to draw their weapons but Dante stopped them.

I couldn't really see Trigga's face under the hoodie but I knew it was him. The stance, the voice, and the way he had his hands behind him told me it was him.

"You didn't really think I was about to let you walk up out this piece with her did you, my nigga?" Trigga asked him.

"Let me?" Dante repeated. "Good thing you meet me here, bruv. That way, when I kill you, you can go down the way your father did. You know it was a dick-hardening moment when I slid that bullet in the back of that nigga's skull, eh?"

Dante laughed. I saw Trigga's arm twitch and knew what was coming next. We were still on federal property and I'd come to learn that Trigga was a nigga who gave no fucks. I finally understood what Phenom meant when he said you had to wake up wanting to die more than the next man. Trigga woke up every morning wanting to die more than the next man. That was what made him more dangerous than your average street urchin. I elbowed S.B. in his face then ran toward the grass and hit the ground. As soon as I did, Trigga's hammer let go and started to sing a pretty song of death. I saw Dante make a quick jump to the other side of a parked van. S.B. did a football move and fell behind a car. That other nigga wasn't so lucky. A bullet caught him square in the eye. I kept my head down as I army crawled from the grass to the parking lot after I grabbed the dead cat's guns. Three more men jumped from a van and started raining bullets down. A siren went off. I could see guards running to the door then ducking back inside as bullets came their direction.

I rolled onto my back and aimed the gun at one of Dante's henchman, hitting him directly in the spine. When he fell to his knees, I gave him a hole in the back of the head to match the one in his back. I saw Speedy run past me in a blur. Next thing I knew, another body dropped with its neck damn severed from his head. Big Jake had a nigga in a death lock from behind. I swear when he snapped his neck, Jake grinned and licked his lips. A big white van pulled in. Phenom jumped from the back, picked me up and tossed me in. Last I saw was Trigga capping two niggas who looked like guards but because they were shielding Dante, they were the enemy.

"Anika, baby, we have to get out of here. They have two much firepower coming and they're going to try to barricade us in here."

I looked up and saw my aunt in the driver's seat of the van. She had been leaning out the window shooting, but quickly nodded knowing her husband was right. While she pulled out like a maniac, Phenom let his chopper spray from the back of the van.

Chapter 22

Trigga

See, I knew it was time for me to ride the fuck up outta this joint, but how my bank account with my fucks were set up? Yeah, I didn't give a fuck. Stepping from behind the cop car I was squatting near, using my peripheral, I counted how many cops were around me versus the ones Big Jake and Speedy were handling. In the melee of the drama, back in the hallway, I had listened to the whole conversation going on between Dante and Ray-Ray. Had even seen the two motherfuckas who had hemmed up Ray-Ray leaving the interrogation room and burned their faces to memory. It always paid to learn how to be invisible.

When Ray-Ray hit my burner with the code, I had already been heading that way to get her because of my eyes in the street hitting me up about the fight that went down. I can't sit and act like I wasn't pissed and still am, but shit happens and now I was getting some kills in. Back to the battle.

I moved from my spot, Glocks raised, jaw clenched tight, and scanning my area. Dirty Cs covered Dante, but how I angled shit, I made sure bullets hit them and that pussy-ass bitch at the same time. Shouts sounded around me and had me turning full circle in a run and duck. My unk's ride, a big unmarked white van, was blocking whatever came out that way as he signaled for us to move on.

Part of me thought it was stupid as fuck for both him and Anika to be out here, because they had people to handle business for them but, the fact that fam was getting gritty with us was what had me giving them respect. Squeezing the clip, bullets sizzled in the air. Some grazed me; others, from my own hand, hit two specific motherfuckas who had brought bullshit to Ray-Ray. First one to go down was the white-hair bitch with the strange eyes. A grin came up on my face when I watched her fall. I made my way to her, reached out to snatch her hair then shoved my Glock in her mouth. Her dazed eyes looked up at me. She tried to punch me in the face, but my grip got harder and I gave a her smile.

"Suck the dick, bitch." Pulling the trigger, I watched a perfect hole form in the back of her skull with the fading of her scream covered me.

Several cops shouted in protest having watched that trick go down. Me, I shot at them out of spite. Rising up, I ran forward toward Dante's speeding car. Rage had me intent on catching them, even as my sprinting slowed due to being sideswiped by several cops and the car disappearing out of the lot.

That nigga Dante was getting away. And the look of his beady eyes lit up in humor as he lit up a cigar and grinned at me from the back of his ride only pissed me off even more. I struggled when I made contact with concrete and grunted with the force. My hoodie kept my face shielded as the punches and kicks of the officers assaulted me.

Using my Glock, my hand swung upward to leave the side of my pistol with some of their faces. "Get the fuck off me!"

My foot connected to whatever vulnerable part I could get to on the cops. My body became their release for aggression, even as I fought. They could do whatever the fuck they wanted but there was no doubt that a nigga was going to fight back. The sound of Big Jake's feet thumping on concrete let me know that he was taking down dirty cops left and right.

Bone and cartilage snapping and Big Jake's low voice booming, "Nigga, the more you move, the harder I grip, keep moving, because ya still gonna die."

Jake's presence had distracted the cops allowing me to roll over slightly and grab screwdriver-like shank from my back pocket to take the eye out of one of the dirty cops on Dante's payroll who was standing over me, sending him backwards in a high pitched scream.

Pussy-ass nigga.

Speedy snatched me up by my shoulder and told me that we all needed to roll out. Cuts lined both of our faces, and we ducked from bullets that kept whizzing by. As we broke camp, I saw Jake drop cops over the side of the cop garage wall, then flipping another to slam him down on his neck. Once Jake checked us ducking out, he turned and rushed to our waiting ride. Before I could get to the car, I squeezed off one last round, emptying my barrel watching the bitch I took down prior partner slam backward into a car. That crossed that bitch off my list.

Sliding in the car, we sped off as cops attempted to trail us through the streets. I could already tell that Phenom had called in and flexed his power with his set of cops, because some of the cops following us in their cars eventually made opposite turns and we never saw them again. We sped through the streets of the A, maneuvering and finding ways to lose them in the street. A text on my cell let me know that my unk and everyone had switched out the truck and were now doing a heatwave out of the hidden zone they were located.

Upset, tired, and frustrated, I kicked my foot against the door of the car, as Speedy maneuvered it, turned on a 360 spiral then backed up slowly into an empty house garage. Jake clicked an app on his cell and the garage door quietly closed as we waited it out. Moving out the car we were in, covering it up, we switched to a simple all-black Honda with tinted windows.

"Yo, man, I saw you hit that dude; it's all good, Trig, trust me on that," Jake tried to encourage me. That was cool and all of him but I really wasn't trying to hear all that.

"Naw, my nigga, see, we're 'bout to be most wanted in this fucking place. All eyes on us and you know that's what Dante wanted, man, do you see that?" I objected. Shit was unreal to me. Shit had me feel messy, had me feeling exposed, but also had me amped.

Speedy jumped in, changing out of his hoodie and letting his long braids drop behind his back. "Aye, bruv, but check it, we couldn't leave Ray-Ray in his hands. You know how he do. The chav is a sick bastard, you know that."

"No shit, cuz. Yeah, I know that. I'm just pissed at how this got played. Fuck it, we need to go and we need to do some snatching of our own," I said climbing in our flip ride, starting up the engine.

"What you have in mind?" Jake asked quirking an eyebrow with a grin on his face.

Speedy gave a slight laugh and rubbed his hands together. "More blood?"

"Yeah, more blood and death; we're 'bout to string us up an international rat. That S.B. nigga. Our checkpoints spotted Dante's ride in the streets. We may not get that nigga Dante but let's get at his driver feel me?"

Both Big Jake and Speedy laughed. They climbed in the ride with me and we headed to our old garage, where we switched out the Honda for a faster ride. Checking our trackers, we sped out as fast as we could taking backstreets in the A, just to catch up. We knew we had lost valuable time, but we were banking on Dante and his people not checking that we'd be following them.

The cool Atlanta air flowed through the car as we rolled down our window. Dante's ride was at a stoplight, and I could see the nigga popping off cigars in the back seat with some young broad. I couldn't make out her face, but I could see her swinging on him then disappearing from view. Ghosting the ride up to him, I turned in my seat and glanced at the driver. S.B. was laughing, yacking up, not even caring about another ride next to him. This fool was damn carefree, which worked for me.

The moment I leaned out the car, I knew by the loud shouting going on that Dante or one of his crew caught wind. I gave a smile, tugged on my hoodie then let off several rounds on the driver. S.B.'s eyes widened before smirking and ducking down. I knew I hit that nigga, a bullet snaked into his neck, but still he ducked, and the rest of my bullets hit the goon who sat next to him. I turned my Glocks to get at Dante, but his car door was open and I saw no one in the back.

"BJ! Speedy! You see that nigga rush into the brush?" I yelled.

Smoke was around us, and Speedy's crazy ass had hopped out the car and lit up whoever was still in the back seat. Hopping on one foot, he shook his head, and pointed down the street. "Flashing lights, bruv! Let's be out!"

Pissed off, I dropped back in my seat, and Speedy got back in; just as we were pulling off, bullets hit the side of our ride. Big Jake rode out cussing, "Bitch-ass shit! Next time I'm bringing my grenades. Nigga's surviving like roaches!"

"You ain't lied, blood, next time we got that Raid, ain't that right, Trig?" Speedy laughed.

I clutched my side blood seeping through my fingers and nodded before blacking out. "Yeah, next time it's a done deal."

I woke up later, lying in a huge bed. Found out I had been out for hours. All the bullshit we went through, my ass got clipped but I survived it. Pushing up where I lay, I touched the bandage on my side and hissed at the tenderness. My teeth clenched, my shoulders jerked up, and my locs spilled down my face while I sat there annoyed.

"Damn," I murmured.

"Say it again, because you'd be correct, nephew, damn. Lie back down."

I jumped at the sound of Anika's soft sensual voice and looked her way. I hadn't expected her to be here while I was laid up looking fucked up. I looked down over the sheet that only covered my dick partially, and I quickly covered my waist as I slid back.

Her light laughter surrounded me and I noticed that she held a bowl in her hand with some gauze.

"How're my boys? Where's Diamond? She good?" I asked quickly, looking around the room and ready to get up and get back in the streets.

"I'm okay, Kwame. Speedy and Jake got banged up too and Gina is pissed at you three. So are Chasity and Chyna," Diamond said while entering the room with some food. A plate of fried plantains, beans with rice, a grilled steak, and a tall glass of ice water waited for me, and my stomach grumbled in need.

"Yo, what was up with you and that damn fight, li'l shawty? You know the deal." I frowned, trying to keep my voice level and not blast the fuck up like I really wanted to.

Diamond glanced my way, rolled her eyes, and dropped the tray down that she held with the food. "What's up with you playing God and going after that sick-ass nigga, huh? You lying in bed fucked up, so whaddup with that?"

Giving a slight sigh, I looked up at the ceiling and flinched when Anika changed my bandage. "Here we go," I griped.

"Yeah, here we go! You don't get to come at me sideways and think that I'm not going to get you back. Come on, Trigga, you should have come back and we all could have got him later," she said.

Her hands were on her shapely hips. Her lower lip wobbled and I swear her big doe eyes were moist. I would have felt like shit in the moment, but shit, she had pissed me off.

"Ey! You don't know how I got this wound. Coulda been when I was getting your ass. A fight, Diamond, for real? Damn and you know better."

Anika's grabbing of her bowl and walking to the door stopped us from going in. She gave a light laugh and shook her head while resting a hand on the door. "Use the condoms that are in the drawer and when you two are rested and he's fed, come seek out Phenom and me. We all have some logistics to work out with this whole ordeal."

Confusion had me looking at her stupid, where Diamond quickly turned her back and scoffed, "Ain't no one trying to be with him like that right now."

Her words seemed to annoy me even more, and when I moved to sit on the side of the bed and tell her about her stupid ass, the sound of Ghost running into the room stopped that argument in midair too.

All I heard was teeth sucking and a huff and I knew Ghost was on one too.

"Dang, daddy."

"You know I don't like that shit. Come correct," I quickly stopped her. My voice bumping in annoyance, not meant for her, but meant for the chick holding my food hostage.

"Damn, pops."

"Better keep thinking of a good word for me," I interrupted her again, just to watch her huff and hide her smile.

"Dad! Let me say what I was gonna say dang! How come you let that asshole hurt you like that huh? When do I get my turn at him and I don't like that you got shot again. That ain't cool," she said, while climbing in the bed with me then stopping when I held my hand up and pointed for her to get down.

A nigga didn't want her in the bed with him while all he had was a sheet covering his meat. Wasn't down for that. I saw the disappointment in her eyes and I hocked a pillow at Diamond just to get her attention.

"What? Damn, Trigga, you play too much," Diamond said with a frown.

I pointed at my junk and she got what I was saying. Moving around the room, she went into the closet and came out with some drawstring pants.

"Chas, turn around," she simply stated.

I watched as Ghost crossed her arms and poked her lip out. I knew then I should have named her Sassy because she was on one and was getting ready to pop off before I interrupted her thoughts with a pillow upside her head. "Turn around, brat; damn, baby girl. Just do it for me."

Taking the pants from Diamond, I threw back the sheets, struggled to put them on thanks to my wound, then lay back down as shawty laughed at me for all the noise I was making while putting on my pants.

"So you just going to laugh and not help a nigga, a'ight. Still got words for you."

Diamond rolled her eyes again, pulled the sheet around me, and then told Ghost to turn around.

Cutting my eyes at Diamond, I motioned for Chas to get in the bed and she happily obliged. Kicking her feet up, she pulled out her iPod and a book and looked at me.

"Don't get killed, 'cause I need you and so does Diamond, even though she actin' like she don't, and everyone else."

My head shook and all I could think about in that moment was the kills I made and the ones I missed. A twinge of annoyance hit me again, but it was Chasity's eyes that keep me from going into the realm of darkness again.

"I do what I do. You know I ain't scared to die, but I promise to be around for however I'm allowed to be, baby girl, a'ight? Remember what I taught you."

"If I fall, I will rise, and in my last, chaos will restore what I gave," we said together.

I smirked, and reached over to tug on her braid. "You got my teachings so I'll always be there."

Diamond moved to sit down the tray over me with attitude. She really wanted to fight and I really wanted to fight her too.

She stepped back with her hands on her hips and then looked me dead in my eyes as if challenging me. "So did you kill him?"

Annoyed yet again, I glanced at my plate and picked up my knife and fork. "My bullet went into S.B. but that nigga Dante ran. He had some broad with him, don't know who she is, but you need to watch your back. Anyone step to you weird today?"

My eyes watched how Diamond scrunched her nose in thought before her teeth scraped over her bottom lip nibbling. "Yeah, that trashy bitch from the party and my old homegirl Dominique."

"Yeah? Shit, she suspect to you?" I asked while casually cutting into my food. The moment she gave me those two names, I already didn't trust that shit, but Diamond needed to think this out so I was letting her.

"I mean, Gina and Chyna weren't feeling her, and I get it. But they didn't know her, so that's whatever. That nasty ho got hers again, so I'm not tripping off of her."

I tasted my food and knew Diamond had cooked it. She had it set up in a way I liked that Anika didn't do. As I chewed, I saw Ghost laughing at how Diamond called that chick out her name, and I gave a shrug locking eyes on her.

"Check it, if you don't remember anything, remember this shit. Ain't nothing more dangerous than an intelligent hoodrat with an agenda. Remember who's for you and who ain't for you. Anyway. Food is good. We all need to hit up the heads and next time you see that broad, keep your wits about you, shawty."

Enlightening Diamond and giving her a plan on what I needed and wanted, Ghost chimed in from time to time, and we all decided we'd use her in the plan, too. Since Dante wanted to continue to try to get the upper hand, it was time to do another move on his ass. The art of war was definitely in motion.

Chapter 23

Ray-Ray

"Come 'ere," Trigga said once I'd come back upstairs.

He and I had a few more words with each other moments earlier. He was mad at me about the fight and I was mad at him for getting shot, not that it was his fault. I went to take his empty plate and Ghost back downstairs. I had to respect the way he went about handling Ghost. Their relationship was a real daddy-daughter one. He didn't like for Ghost to call him daddy though. Nigga said that Dame had ruined that for him because he used to make me, Gina, and the girls who used to work for him call him that. So, Trigga hated to hear the word "daddy" come from Ghost's mouth.

I walked over to the bed where he lay. I couldn't front like him being shot didn't scare the fuck out of me because it did. In my eyes, I saw him as an invincible kind of nigga and I knew that was my fault. I held him like to this higher standard than I held everybody else. I looked at the way his locs lay around his head like little snakes. His eyes were giving me that look he always did.

"What?" I tried to put as much attitude in my voice as I could. "I didn't go out there and start no fight you know?"

"Don't matter."

"Why not?"

"Because you were still in one. A big one that left bitches cut up all over the streets, lil'shawty, and you in jail and inches away from that nigga's grasp."

"I tried to get Gina to calm the fuck down but you know once she's turned up, that's it. I don't think Dom meant no harm. She be fake thuggin'. She ain't really about this life, Trig," I tried to explain.

"You gone have to check your homegirl then. May have to cut her all the way off. We don't need this shit. Wasn't supposed to be getting this kind of attention."

I smacked my lips, but I knew he was right. "So you gon' stay mad at me?" I asked him gazing into his light-colored eyes.

"Depends," he answered.

"On what?"

"Promise me you gone stay out of trouble."

I chuckled softly. "If you do."

"Trouble finds me, lil shawty. You know this."

"It finds me too."

He turned his lips down and shook his head once. "Nah, you find it, Diamond. You been finding it since the day I met you."

I stood up and folded my arms across my chest. "The day you met me you was supposed to kill a bitch."

"Shawty, you didn't have to come out that bathroom."

"I wanted to see if my mama and daddy was really dead."

"But if you had stayed the fuck put, your life would be much easier right now."

He was right and I often thought about that, but I also thought about the fact that my mama and daddy's lifestyle would have eventually caught up to them anyway. I thought about how no matter how they tried to leave the drugs alone, they never could. So even if they had gotten away with taking the money, their habits would have still followed them. But the one thing that made me frown on thinking what would have happened if I'd stayed in that bathroom was looking up at me.

"But then, I wouldn't have met you, and Gina, Big Jake, Speedy, Ghost; all you niggas," I said softly. I dropped my arms when he sighed and glanced off into the distance.

"Li'l shawty, do you realize you could have gone off to college somewhere and did all the shit normal kids do? You ain't have to be no misfits like us. Me, Gina, Big Jake, and even Ghost, we were born into this bullshit," he explained.

"So was I."

"Naw, shawty, your folks kept your head in school and in books and shit."

"From what you told me, so did your parents."

He gave a guttural groan and then grunted. "Shawty, you ain't listening to me."

"And you ain't listening to me. We're cut from the same cloth if you look at it."

"You weren't born a killer."

"Neither were you. You were made into one."

"Diamond, I was born a killer. My moms and pops had been training me all my life how to use a weapon, any weapon, my specialty guns. My training started in the womb. My moms and pops used to show me videos of them with head phones on her stomach, reading to me and training me from the jump. They knew what was going to be my birthright. They bred me this way. If a nigga didn't know how to aim a gun, I would'na been able to kill none of them niggas who raped my moms. Would'na been able to make it in the streets. I was born into this shit. You wasn't. You was tossed into this motherfucking jungle head first and yeah, yo ass adapted, but . . ." He struggled to sit up.

I moved to help him but he stopped me. His locs fell down his shoulders to the center of his back. His chest and back fanned out like a cobra with muscles straining underneath his skin.

"It really don't matter," I said to him.

"What don't matter?"

"Whether I was born into this or not. I'm in it now and no way I'ma be able to just go back to a normal life, Kwame. You know too much has happened to me for that and I've done too much shit. Basically, through all the shit I been through, I'm still glad that I came out that bathroom."

He frowned and shook his head like he didn't understand and I knew he didn't because I wasn't explaining myself to him good enough. While he was still knocked out from his wound me and my auntie had a talk. I asked her how did she know when she was in love. She smirked and asked me why. I ain't really want to say because Phenom was in the room. I think he knew that so he left out. I was as honest as I could be and told her I wanted to know because I was feeling something for Trigga. She thought for a moment, then she kept it simple.

"If you had to choose between your life and Kwame's, whose would you choose?" she asked me.

I thought for a moment as she moved around the room, cleaning his blood and bloodied clothes from the floor. I looked at him breathing softly as he slept.

"I know the way I'm supposed to answer this is to say I would choose his, but, he's been through enough. He's been fighting since he was just a kid, saw shit happen to his mama, found out he had been working for the nigga who had been a part of his mama and daddy getting killed. And now he's in another battle for the fight of his life. So, if I had to choose my life or his, I'd choose my life, only because he needs peace, Auntie. He just needs to rest and be at peace. It's been hell on earth for him for a long-ass time and I'd risk my life just to bring him peace. Still, this earthly shit for his life ain't been no gotdamned crystal stair so I'd choose to stay here and suffer and

send him to heaven. Even Jesus had a murderer in his clique and a nigga with a agenda."

For a while, she just sat there and stared at me. I thought she didn't get what I was saying, but when she stood and smiled, I knew she did.

"That's how you know you're in love," was all she said before she walked out of the room.

I looked at the boy who was really a man. I'd been infatuated with that nigga a long time. Then infatuation turned into admiration, and now I was in love with him. My insides started trembling as I chewed down on my bottom lip.

"Shawty, do you even know what'chu saying?" he asked me, breaking my train of thought.

"Yes, I know what I'm saying, Kwame, because I'm saying that if I hadn't come out of that bathroom I would have never met you. I would have never known what the fuck it felt like to be touched the way you touch me, or to be looked at the way you look at me, or to be protected the way you protect me. I'm saying if I didn't come out of that bathroom then I wouldn't know what it feels like to be in love."

There, I'd said that shit; and right after, I wished I hadn't. Trigga just looked at me with a blank stare. Any emotion that had been on his face drained away. That light and passion that had been his eyes just moments before, flipped off like someone had turned off the lights.

"Naw, Diamond, we ain't about to do this shit, li'l shawty," he said as he threw his legs over the bed and slowly stood up.

My heart fell to my stomach like it was attached to an anvil. "Do what?"

"This love shit. I ain't sign up for this."

I was more hurt than shocked but shocked nonetheless. My throat swelled up and mouth felt like cotton was in it. I foolishly asked, "So why you having sex with me?"

He frowned. "What?"

"Why we act like we do with one another? Why you touch me like you do? Why you do what you do to me?" It wasn't until I slapped the tears away from my face that I realized I was crying.

"Diamond. Ray-Ray. Shawty . . ." He flinched and growled low when he moved the wrong way and his injury made him pay for it.

"So, I'm good enough for everything else, just no good enough to love you?" I asked trying to keep calm.

"I ain't saying that."

"So, what'chu saying?"

"I'm saying a nigga like me ain't built for no kind of love shit like this, not that shit you talking. I mean I got love for you, yeah, but naw, Diamond, I ain't sign up for this shit." He kept frowning like he was agitated. He would look at me then glance away like my presence was annoying him or something.

"So you just signed up to fuck?" I asked.

Trigga cut his eyes hard at me, but didn't say anything. He moved around the room, kicking stuff out of his way then paying for it when pain would shoot up his side. I couldn't help but feel sorry for him when he went to reach up for a secret compartment he had hidden on the top of his bookshelf but was forced to bring his arm back down quickly because it hurt him to reach. I walked over to where he was set to help him get whatever he was reaching for. I pulled a chair over, stood in it, and grabbed the small but heavy black safe lock box.

I held it hostage until he answered my question. "You gon' answer my question?"

He looked up at me, probably annoyed because I hadn't handed him the box. "What question?"

"You know what question, Kwame."

"Don't ask questions you don't wanna know the answer to, li'l shawty," was all he said as he tried to reach for the box.

I jerked back and kept it out of his reach. For a long time I just stared down at him. I didn't know what I was feeling but it was something between rejection and anger. Somewhere between embarrassment for being stupid enough to think, even for a second, that he would love me. After all, I was still Ray-Ray, the girl who Dame made suck his dick then nut on my face in front of him. It was months later and that nigga Dame still had control of my life. I hated it. But more so, in that moment, I hated myself for catching feelings for Trigga.

When he reached for the box again, I slapped the shit out of him then shoved him hard so he would fall over the stool behind. He stumbled back, but probably wouldn't have fallen if that stool wasn't there. I stepped down from the chair feeling like I'd done something to make him hurt physically like I was doing emotionally and mentally. But when that nigga scowled and his eyes locked on mine, I backed away. And when he leapt from that floor like he just wasn't flinching in pain moments before, my black ass turned into Flo-Jo. I had been afraid of Dame, too, but there was something different in the look that Trigga was giving me. I knew when Dame got mad he was going to harm me simply because his ass was evil. The look in Trigga's eyes read something I wasn't used to.

I made a quick dash for the door, dropping the safe on his bed on the way out. I still felt that nigga moving a little too fast to be injured behind me. I looked over my shoulder and saw he was right there. I screamed running from the room and ran smack into Phenom, falling on my ass in the process.

If I ain't know no better, I would have thought he did that shit on purpose with the way he looked down at me with an amused expression on his face. I ain't have time to think about that though. Trigga had grabbed my bun and was yanking me off the floor. I screamed as I rolled over on my knees and grabbed at his hand on my hair.

Phenom moved around me to get his nephew. "No deal, Kwame. Let her go," he said to him, but that nigga still had my hair.

"Naw, I done told her about putting her damn hands in my face," Trigga spit out.

"Kwame, let her go, nephew."

"I ain't saying I'ma choke the shit out her motherfucking ass, but I'm saying I'm about to hug the fuck out of her neck passionately."

I couldn't see Trigga's face, but I knew by the grip he had on my hair and by the tone in his voice that he was serious.

From somewhere, Anika appeared and I felt her grab my waist, and Phenom took Trigga's hand from my hair finally. I wasn't gone lie like I wasn't scared, but I was just too embarrassed to let Trigga know it.

When I was a safe distance behind my aunt and Phenom had Trigga safely accosted I yelled, "Fuck you, nigga."

That bravado was short-lived when Trigga broke Phenom's hold. I didn't even waste time to see if Phenom grabbed him again. I was gone down those damn stairs so fast I almost knocked Big Jake's big, beefy ass down in the process. When my aunt finally found me I was hiding in her study because I knew Trigga wouldn't go in there without her permission. When she walked in, I jumped just in case that crazy nigga threw caution to the wind anyway.

"Sit down, Diamond," she told me. The tone in her voice wasn't really friendly, but it didn't sound as if she was mad at me either. She pulled her Havana braids back into a ponytail and sighed as she looked at me. She took her time pouring herself a glass of Jamaican rum before she sat down in front of me.

"Don't be that girl," she finally said.

I was confused, didn't understand what she meant by that. "Huh?"

"Don't be that girl who can't handle the truth and then turn to violence or hate because the man didn't have the response she wanted him to. Don't be that chick who screams they want honesty but can't handle it. So then a nigga feels like he has to start lying just to get what he want or just to keep the peace."

I glanced down at my fingers then back up at her as tears burned my eyelids. She must have known what happened between me and Trigga. "I don't understand why he—"

She waved her hand to cut me off. "Just because a man has sex with you and fuck you like he's never fucked another doesn't mean he loves you. He loves the way sex feels with you, but that doesn't mean a damn thing else. You're still young and one day all this will make sense to you, but right now, in the situation, I'm telling you to be mature enough to respect that fact that he told you the truth. He could have been like every other nigga and just told you what you wanted to hear then stuck his dick in your mouth and pussy afterward just to get a nut, but he didn't."

I really didn't want to hear her taking his side. Really didn't want to accept the fact that he didn't or wouldn't love me. I really wanted to think that I was good enough for more than sex with him, but I wasn't.

"You got ten minutes to cry, be in your feelings, and be all emotional. Then I'm going to need you to suck that shit up. We got work to do."

I looked back up at my aunt and saw that while she was looking at me, her eyes telling me the untold story of her and Phenom and I was too young to pick up on it.

"So, I'm supposed to not feel some type of way about this or him either?"

"Oh, yeah, you can feel whatever way you want for the next ten minutes. Then for the remainder of your time here on this earth and as a part of this team, you can't and won't. We don't need emotions going into the field with us. You'll be a live wire otherwise. You love him. That's your problem, not his. That's for you to deal with, not him. You never make a man pay for telling you the truth."

"He could have just said so from the jump," I defended myself.

"Did you ask him from the jump?"

"No, but if he knew—"

"If he knew what? He's not a mind reader. He's a young man who is physically attracted to a young woman. Both of you acted and still act on those same attractions, only you got caught in your feelings. Accept that, own it, and move on."

I watched as she stood and downed the amber-colored liquid in the glass in one swallow. "You got ten minutes, Diamond. That's it. Phenom has two people downstairs he wants us to meet with. They're allies and we're strategizing a game plan. Get it together. You and Trigga are important players on this team and we need both of you level-headed enough to get back in the game. Ten minutes, no more, no less. You understand me?"

Even though I didn't want to, I nodded. She walked toward the door then turned to look back at me after opening it. "Another thing."

"Yeah?"

"Never put your hands on a man and think he's just going to take it because he is a man, understand? If you're big and bad enough to pass a hit, you'd better be big and bad enough to take one. You owe him an apology. I expect you to give him one."

Chapter 24

Trigga

"You do know you're dipping all on my floor, nephew?" amusingly sounded behind me.

My face was twisted up in anger. My body felt like it was tensed and heated up all at the same time and while I was ready to go in on Diamond, my eyes wouldn't stop watching her ass. Damn, I was all kinds of fucking up mentally right now and wasn't digging it at all.

"Yo, why she have to jump stupid like that huh? Cluckin' and shit. I was honest and you mad now? Fuck outta here," I shouted and clutched my side angrily walked back into my room

Jake's laughter could be heard behind me. "I'll clean it up, fam; cool him down."

"Oh shit, bruv! Why am I missing the good shit?" Speedy sounded off as he walked past us. Everyone in this bitch was a comedian I saw.

"Chill out and assess the situation, nephew," Phenom calmly said behind me as he closed the door.

Kicking my shoes that had fallen out the closet while I had chased Diamond out the room, I scowled and pushed my locs out my face. "I am damn. She play too much. Why she even have to go there, I don't even know. Broads get too hung up and shit."

"Get dressed. I won't be at this meeting in the flesh but I'll be at it . . ." he explained walking around me to pick up whatever had fallen in the scuffle.

There was a seriousness mixed with amusement in his voice that had me watching him as I got dressed.. I'd seen his fall guy and right hand, Mirror, another cousin who always played like Phenom whenever meetings went down, exit out of my unk's office. Glancing around my room, I snatched up my shirt and crossed my arms over my chest.

"What?"

My uncle sat on the edge of my dresser with his ankles crossed mirroring how I looked. Wisdom seemed to spark in his eyes while watching me; it reminded me of how my pops would look at me as a kid and something about it had my raging spirit calming down.

"When dealing with mamis you do know you need to rephrase how you spit at them right, nephew? Honesty can be helpful but that shit can be a knife, too. You cut her," he explained.

"Man, look. I wasn't even trying to. Wasn't malice in my heart, man, she just came at me sideways and shit. We ain't got time for that rah-rah. You know that nigga would use whatever he can against me . . . us," I fussed, my hands moving in front of me in agitation.

Phenom gave a slight smile. He really was like looking at my pops in how he moved and he had my mom's eyes. Their presence mixed with my unk's was all in the room suddenly and it slowly made me feel uncomfortable. A sensation in my heart had me rubbing my chest and I look down at my feet to settle it.

"No doubt, nephew, but you already know he's going to use it anyway. Her loving you ain't shit to the mixture—"

Cutting him off, I shrugged. "Yeah, I mean it's whateva. Set her straight, we got other shit to worry about. I ain't trying to settle down or nothin' anyway; don't know why I gotta be the one she gettin' at like that anyway."

"Because your mind is turning it into a weakness, nephew. Now that shit ain't acceptable and can get you fucked up. But it ain't my place to tell you who you love, but I'm just telling you, nephew, my blood, nigga, wake up." Phenom let out a deep-set laughter that had my mind going back to the past in my family.

Everything I saw between my parents and grew up on contradicted how my street life made me feel about a man and woman. A nigga didn't have to go soft just to hold down his woman. It didn't happen with my pops and mom and it wasn't going down with my unk and Anika.

"A man chooses how he makes his bed and a grown man knows how to keep it made. Love ain't a weakness; it's power, and you can use that shit in the chaos of the madness because it can heal you and make you stronger nephew. Regardless of how you maintain that shit. Know the moment you disrespect the love that shit can turn on you and become death; know that, acknowledge that, and see that."

"But see, look it ain't even all of that."

Waving a hand in the air, the man I called Phenom stood in front of me as my uncle Ahmir. My shoulders slumped for a moment before I stood straight content that I knew my shit and I wasn't wrong.

"I hear you, see you, and know you, little dude, because I was you. Hear me when I say, you deserve the kingdom you have been born into. That means even that future queen at your side. The One Power knows what it is down and doesn't make no mistakes. Who is made for you is made for you. And in the chaos right now, she was made for you."

Thumbing his nose, Phenom tilted his head and ran a hand over his waves as if remembering something before resting it on my shoulder. "Feel me on this, and check it my blood. Later, you might learn she was eventually bred for you. Until then, you take the gifts and let it be your power. That is your right as a prince of this kingdom and a young king of the streets. Don't be that nigga in the streets who got a girl loving him and he doesn't stand by her because he doesn't know his own heart, his own self, his own feelings, a'ight? Been there done that and take that shit from me, I had pussy, still have pussy. Had to learn what worked for me as a man in love with a woman like Anika and she had to do the same."

It was strange getting schooled like this from him, only because now we were talking not about street shit, how to survive our enemies and build our empire, naw. Right now, his Brooklyn accent was flowing over me. He was teaching me how to survive being a man and wanting pussy and keeping pussy happy. The words of my mom's came back to me, and it made me rub my heart again. If Diamond was a Jaguar then pissing her off would crumble me, my empire; and on some real shit, I think I was starting to care, more than I've ever experienced with any broad or chick. Pussy used to be disposable, still kinda was, but Diamond wasn't like that. She was better than that and Dame tried to make her that, but it wasn't in her natural progression as a chick. Naw, shawty was definitely a jaguar and then, I guess, that made her a queen.

My unk's low chuckle hit me back into reality and checked back in, to hear what he was saying. "I see you thinking and that's a good thing, nephew. Listen, Anika and I went through our shit. Fucked up but always came back together. Cut the bullshit at the pass and get on the right course, 'cause if you stay on that right course, you and her can fuck up however you want, but as long as you got a understanding and unity, ain't nothing going to keep what you know in your heart as a man and what you know in her heart from causing division. Anyway, the rest you got to learn on your own and I'll guide you only a little, so don't be that nigga. Let's go."

Glancing up at a man who just basically schooled me without really saying too much, I shook my head and thought on Diamond and his words. For the first time in my life, a nigga was confused as shit, and his chest hurt all in that moment. The sound of our boots on the maple floor was my only solace until he stepped off and paused before going into his office. "Hey, tell her sorry before she does. Go handle business."

I swore I heard him laughing as he closed the door. I didn't understand why and I sure as fuck wasn't about to say sorry to Diamond. She jumped stupid at me first. She just needed to chill with all the other stuff. I mean, shit, I don't even know.

Heading downstairs Anika sat with her legs crossed in her favorite chair eating grapes from a bowl, while eying two men in front of her. Ma was dressed in jeans that were so tight, they looked painted on. Her feet were bare and her Nigerian print shirt was cut down the middle, where it showed nothing but flesh and the rounds of the breasts, but held together by a simple leather belt. Her aura shouted that she was in her home, relaxed and both of the men in front of her better respect that.

"I see he's finally made it. You two may sit as my guest finds his place near his crew," Anika coolly responded.

Her eyes never left the two men in front of her and it made me smirk to see one of them sweating as the other was attempting not to adjust his hard dick in front of her.

Making my way to the area, I saw Jake, Speedy, Diamond, Gina, and Chyna sitting waiting on me. I had seen Ghost's little feet in my uncle's study, so I knew they were watching on a monitor. Mirror walked up to me and clapped his hand on my shoulder with a nod. "You remember these two eh?"

Nodding, I made my way to them both and flashed a smirk. "Armando, my dude, *hola, gracias por su hospitalidad previa*. Thank you for your previous hospitality."

Armando's discomfort, with that of keeping his dick in order while eyeing the African queen, was evident in his posture. Smoothing a golden hand through is wavy pulled back hair, his smile was genuine when he reached out and clasped my shoulders. "Mi lucky street hood. Couldn't say this at the grand meeting, but doing business with you has still been nothing but good for me."

I said nothing at his words, just gave him dap and glanced at Nicola. Nicola stood a towering six feet eight inches and looked every bit the tyrant he was. A cigar rested between two fingers as he coolly leaned to the side watching me. I gave him the same look back, saying nothing, because if this nigga wanted to play stupid I was game any damn time. People can turn on you in the drop, if they so needed it. Both of these motherfucka were expendable at any damn time.

So I waited and watched Nicola crack a rare smile and boom out, "It's is good to see this indestructible punk's face again. Nothing but good has come for my business, too."

His slight, thick accent had me inwardly chuckling and I clasped hands with him and bumped shoulders before stepping back. "Talk to me, what's up? Nigga's still hating and gunning? I already know but enlighten me."

Both men sat down after Mirror and I sat down at the same time. They glanced at each other then back to us. "We were just telling Phenom and Anika about that whole thing, mira. Stiff and Valentino are still pissed about how you did them in the meeting. They are also pissed about how much your new product indigo is bringing in the ducats."

Nicola's booming voice stepped in and continued for Armando as we all listened. "They have fucked around and missed out big on the product, so of course they are gunning hard against you with Dante. We got word about the shoot out today and Dante is calling for us to handle you. He's done with the game and wants a full war now. That's why we're here."

Anika's calmly set her bowl down, slipped her small feet into the shoes that were near her seat, and rolled her shoulders; each of her braids fell down her face and that subtle movement registered something was about to go down. When the girls stood and the sound of a slamming door upstairs echoed in the room, my eyes closed in silent prayer and annoyance and I slid out my chair.

"Dante is here isn't he?" was all I said.

"Yes, he is," Anika quietly said.

My emotionless eyes darted to both Armando and Nicola, hatred resonating from the very core of me. Two clicks of my guns had both men standing up and stumbling backward with their hands up.

I took two strides forward ready to kill as they shouted, "We didn't do it!"

"Nephew. They are legit; let them play this shit out," echoed at my side.

I glanced at Mirror and knew he was speaking for my uncle. I chilled out and took a step back.

"We came to cover you all. Our men are surrounding the villa, we support who supports us, amigo," Armando spat out standing and tugging on his blazer.

Nicola's movements were similar and I gave him a nod, which he returned. We both weren't men to speak a lot, so that was enough of a truce for us. They pulled the Glocks hidden on them out, ready to fight beside us, and I turned around to look at the family.

"Ready?"

They all nodded, showing me their weapons. Anika motioned for us all to sit down, and the sound of my uncle coming downstairs had both men glancing in curiosity.

Anika's smile brightened the room. She walked past Armando, brushing her fingers against the side of his face with a wink before heading to Phenom. Something in how Armando watched her let me know that they had to have been fucking at one time or another. Shit was kind of comical.

"Gentleman, meet Phenom. Your loyalty has been consistent in the many, many years I've been indirectly working with you two. It was beyond time you both met the real man, since death is approaching."

The shock in the room was ever visble. Phenom had a slick smirk on his face and I could tell there was a story behind why each man was glancing at him, as if they had already met him before, just as someone else. Damn, I was curious because it was dope if that was the case.

"We've had the pleasure of meeting many times only you had no idea who I really was. Today, I greet you both as brothers in the new street council. We have many people on our agenda to handle but today, we have but one to focus on. The enemy approaches. Don't be alarmed, family, I've already been alerted to what is about to happen and I assure you, it has been handled. I'm a man with friends in high places and that includes law enforcement. It was honorable of you two to hold us down this time. Your silence has been golden. Please know that the rewards will be plentiful if we all make it out of this today. My thanks," eloquently flowed from my uncle's accented voice.

He took the seat that Mirror was once sitting in and Mirror stood at his back with his hand on his nine. Anika sat in her chair, with Chyna, Diamond, and Gina moving to her side. I glanced at my boys Jake and Speedy, then upstairs at Ghost who I knew was doing what she did best: playing invisible. I moved to stand at my uncle's right, once he motioned for me to, and my boys followed. We all played the game of talking with Armando and Nicola. It was all a waiting game. We had to make Dante think that he was catching us off guard, that he had the upper hand and the element of surprise. The sound of the front doors of the house busting open let us know that extra motherfuckas was here.

Men came pouring in as the front and back doors flew off the hinges. With a loud bang. All we saw were bulletproof vests and riot gear as guns were trained on us. This nigga had played the game differently and came at us from a different angle. Whom we thought would be Dante and his crew were really a SWAT team and judging by the cool demeanor Phenom carried I knew something foul was afoot. I glanced at my uncle, my eye twitching in anger. He just sat back and pressed his hands together.

"Don't even trip. We're protected and if any of us go missing, know that I will find you," was all Phenom said as he held his hands up. "Dante is being sloppy and showing his hand."

"Get down on the ground now," shouted around us.

I didn't have time to respond to what he'd said. I already knew no one here was going to kill us because if Dante had sent them it was only to bring us to him and he'd want the pleasure of killing us himself. So we all complied, lay flat on our bellies, and waited it out. Well, all of us except for Phenom, Anika, Chyna, and Speedy.

Confusion had me glancing up at the four of them as they stayed where they sat. The next words out of my uncle's mouth had me somewhat perplexed and amazed.

"Gentlemen and ladies, I'm confused as to why you have breached private residential property. As guests of the Black Moorish Nation, none of you have jurisdiction in this household or on this land. My lawyers will be happy to assist you all with any documentation that you need for proof as to what I've just stated. That's just in case there is any lack of understanding among you," Phenom calmly stated. He peered over the rims of his wireless glasses and folded both hands in front of his mouth then waited.

"We will not say this again. Get on the ground now," an officer's voice boomed as he aimed his gun right at my uncle's face.

Again, Phenom sat where he was, making minimal movement as he addressed them again. "I know you fellas aren't hard of hearing," Phenom stated. "It would behoove you to get that gun out of my face," he spat through clenched teeth as he eyed the cop with a deadly glare.

"They should have never given you niggas money," the cop quipped as he pulled his ski mask over his head revealing his identity. He was brown skinned with beady eyes and thin lips. Scarring on the right side of his face showed he had been burned at one point in his life. "Give a nigga some money and he starts to think he can run some shit."

The cops behind him chuckled as one dug his knee into my back. I didn't care about the pain and discomfort. I looked around to make sure the rest of my fam was okay. I'd kill any nigga, cop or not, who harmed them. If I didn't give a fuck about having a shootout at a jail, I for damn sure didn't give a shit about killing a dirty cop.

"You're worried about the wrong thing," Phenom said. "What you should be worried about is the man who has you on his payroll. There is no honor among thieves and I can assure you, you'll come to regret your decision to be in cahoots with Dante Orlando."

The cop jerked forward like he was going to hit my uncle with the butt of his gun. Mirror made a move and the cop quickly turned his gun on him.

"You feeling froggy then leap," the cop taunted Mirror.

My uncle held his hand up to stop the man who was his protector. Mirror's grimace showed that he was seconds away from stepping in and having a hail of bullets have to stop him. I knew if he moved the wrong way the dirty cops wouldn't hesitate to take him down. The tension had me anxious. I was also annoyed, but I stayed where I was watching, because knew if I moved, one of those bastards would come funny and cock off in the house. So I watched, learned, and waited.

It wasn't until a walkie-talkie squawked in the background that the cop calmed down. "It's the captain," one of the cops shouted.

It seemed like forever that we sat there and listened to the cop try to explain to his captain why he was on the premises.

"Sir, we do have the right house. Well the warrant is valid. What do you mean it's not? Wait, sir. Sir!"

Silence filled the room and the cop that blasted in our face, sneered, and then spit on the floor. Phenom quirked an eyebrow then smirked coolly.

"Don't get too cocky. This isn't over."

"Anytime," my uncle stated. "Come better prepared next time though. And you're right, they should have never given us niggas money, especially those of us who know what to do with it. Now get the fuck off my property."

For a second it looked as if the cop wanted to retaliate, but he only grunted, smiled devilishly then backed up. "Next time . . . next time I can assure you, after today there won't be a next time. You would have been safer coming with us. Back out, everyone. Let's go," he said solemnly.

Phenom just sat back with no emotion on his face as the SWAT team retreated. Jake and I watched on in silence and somewhat in awe as to what was taking place in front of us. But at the end of the day, all I wanted to know was, "What the fuck was that?"

Both my uncle and Anika stood. He bent his head down to kiss her lips and she rose up to accept them before glancing our way.

"That there, was ignorance on their part, nephew. When people are ignorant, they'll believe anything you tell them as long as you state it in a way that makes them question all they thought they knew," Phenom said. "This land is nothing more than private property and we have no claims to the Black Moorish Nation, but what we do have are friends in high places. And using those words were nothing more than code to see if anyone of the cops in the midst were friendlies."

"And that was also our eviction notice. He's gunning hard; sadly, he really doesn't know shit about how we play or who we really are. Smoke and mirrors is all he knows and today, we learned more about him than ever," Anika explained.

She glanced at her daughter, kissed the top of her head, and repeated the motion with Diamond, and Gina. I watched her head upstairs, where she did the same with Ghost, who stepped out from her hiding spot with wide eyes. Still, I had more questions. Needed to get a better understanding of what had just happened.

"That's all well and good, but—"

My uncle cut me off. "Let me break it down quickly. I see your face and I understand it." I watched the OG who was my uncle move around in thought; he rolled his shoulders and began to break it all down while casually pacing back and forth. "I've had eyes on Dante, just as he's had eyes on me and mine. What just happened was mutual reciprocity. The majority of it was an anger move that shows me that we were able to anger Dante to the point where we're throwing off his game plan. Nevertheless, back to the rest. What I did was a power play. I used a code to indicate my syndicate."

An amused smirk appeared on Phenom's face and he continued, "In doing so, I was able to pinpoint those in the force who, for all intents and purposes, work for me. All that means is my dick is bigger than Dante's and I'm one step ahead of him. The end. Now pack up. I figured Dante would find this spot, which is what I wanted, just to test him and see how deep his power goes in the States. He's messy like his father and will likely go down like his father. Now we know and it's time to go to our real home. Let's be out."

I blinked for a moment watching my uncle exit the room with Mirror and Speedy. I tilted my head mind blown, and Jake stood by my side shaking his head with me.

"Damn," was all we both said.

Chapter 25

Dante

I'd underestimated the little bastard. I'd brought the fight to many a niggas and none had been this motherfucking hard to kill. This nigga Trigga was like a fucking German cockroach. You could end the whole damn world and him and his little ragtag misfits would still somehow fucking survive. I was done. Done with the game play. My first mistake had been going after the people he held closest to him. That little girl had him coming after me like she was his kid. I chuckled at the thought of it all although I found nothing about it comical. And something golden must have been between that little bitch's Ray-Ray legs for that crazy little nigga to have a shootout on federal property. I called it a mistake because I thought he'd fold under pressure. Shit just made him come harder. I would no longer treat him as a wayward child trying to fit into a man's world. This little bastard was smart and it was time I took him out.

"Hmph," I grunted as I waited for notice to be served that I knew where they were holed up. I knew Phenom was a smart one. He was a great adversary, and so was his nephew obviously.

I looked in my review mirror and saw that all was set in motion on the private highway leading to Phenom's mansion. American gangsters were fucking stupid. How none of these niggas knew that biggest underworld king between the UK and the States was married to one of the baddest female queen pins? That was why these niggas were pawns in my game. They were too fucking stupid to be anything more.

"Bloody idiots," I snapped and I punched the steering wheel.

Time was of the essence and I had been in the States too fucking long as it was. I sat up in my seat when I saw the black vans coming down the road. Two black vans that were armored I'd bet, but it was the black Honda Civic that I wanted.

I made the signal to my men and watched as they came running from the woods like a black ops mission. Tire strips were pulled and the tires from both vans blew out. One van flipped over while the other one skidded to a halt against a tree.

"Crash and burn, motherfuckers," I said to myself as I stepped from my vehicle.

The Honda did some kind of *The Fast and the Furious: Tokyo Drift* kind of maneuver to avoid the same fate as the vans. Trigga jumped from the front seat shooting first. Valentino's and Stiff's men let off a round of AKs that had him jumping behind the trees for cover. The vans emptied out as I pulled a Mack 11 from behind me and joined the melee. My focus was solely on the nigga behind the trees until I saw Phenom gunning for me. I took one in the shoulder. I stopped, dropped, and rolled all the while returning fire.

Gravel from the roadway cut into my skin. The smell of gasoline and oil assaulted my senses. That big gorilla-made nigga, Big Jake, had taken down three of Stiff's men I could see, with his bare hands. Speedy was known in Brixton for being just that. His speed was like some crackhead shit and the fact that the nigga's Joker-like laugh was close to me had me turning on my back to let off rounds at him. I looked up and saw that I was moments away from meeting his shank, but the shots backed him up off me.

I jumped up and finally took cover behind one of Valentino's men's Hummers. "Why don't you just let me get my vengeance, Phenom, and this can be all over?" I shouted above the firefight.

I could see Anika putting a hurting on one of Valentino's men who made the mistake of underestimating her because she was a woman. That nigga was crazy. I would have shot that bitch first since she was just as crazy as her husband. But that was his battle.

"Vengeance? Nigga, you kidding me? You been taking from my family for too long, Dante. The gig is up, my nigga. You about to be DOA for real in the motherfucker," Phenom venomously shouted back at me.

My heart beat heavy in my chest and my dick hardened at the thought of bloodshed. I lived for that shit. Palm got sweaty but that didn't loosen the grip on my gun. That monster inside of me needed to be fed. "Talk is cheap, motherfucker. Let's make it happen," I said then laughed as I moved from behind the Hummer.

A movement out the corner of my eye caught my attention. I saw Trigga just as he saw me. Making as quick roll down the steep hill, I avoided the heat of his bullets and returned the favor. As soon as I did, that young pussy they called Ray-Ray bucked the system. Lithe little bitch jumped up and slid over the hood of the Hummer guns blazing like she was in the Wild Wild West. Yeah, I saw Anika all in her. There was a frown on her faced that was etched in pure hatred. Her hair flew wild around her face as her feet hit the ground. This wild bitch had no regard for her own life and I intended to make her pay for it. She had two Sig Sauers which were no match for my Mack 11. I let go with a round in her direction, sprayed that shit like a street sweeper to catch her little boyfriend, too.

"Okay, you two on some Bonnie and Clyde shit I see," I roared. "Come harder or go the fuck home as you motherfuckers in America say," I yelled with a laugh.

She wasn't stupid and took cover underneath the Hummer, quickly sliding out on the other side. Phenom was coming for me from the other side of the hill. I looked up and saw that Anika was flanking him. Hey, I was a lot of things, but stupid wasn't one of them. I only wanted one motherfucker anyway. As bullets chased me, I chased Trigga through the wooded area. I could hear running feet crunching the brush behind me. I made zigzag patterns as I ran. A bullet grazed my left ear to let me know that time was of the essence. I kept Trigga in my vision as the young killer ran like he was on a mission. He knew this land so I knew wherever he was leading me, I didn't want to go.

I dropped my gun and pulled out another one. My pace never slowed down as I aimed the tranquilizer and hit my target between the shoulders. His body hit the ground seconds later like a lump of coal. I slid to a halt as I looked down at him. I believed if he could have he would have tried to swing up at me as I turned him over. I could see the light draining from his eyes slowly.

"There is always more than one way to skin a cat," I told him with glee on my face. "And you, my li'l nigga, are about to get skinned alive."

Chapter 26

Ray-Ray

Everything in me was trembling as I stood outside the room they had Trigga in. The door was cracked just enough for me to see inside. They had him sitting the chair in the middle of a massive room with no windows. It reminded me of what a big stock room in a warehouse would look like minus the crates of merchandise. Only a pendant light hung from the ceiling as Valentino, Stiff, Kim, and Dante surrounded Trigga. I gritted my teeth at the sight of his bloodied face. His hands were tied behind his back as they each took turns taking a pound of flesh in the one-sided ass whooping they were giving him.

He coughed then spit up blood. "This some real lame shit. Four of you for a li'l nigga such as I? I would be impressed, but the way my fucks are set up is I don't give 'em to pussy niggas like y'all," Trigga spoke in a deep voice.

Even with the odds stacked against him, he was fucking with them. But my boy was hurt. I could see in the way he could barely hold up his head. The fact that he was coughing up blood made my soul cry. I have to take y'all back to the moments right after Dante had snatched him.

My heart was beating a mile a second as I watched Trigga being thrown in the back of a trunk. I didn't know if he was dead or alive and that ate my insides up. I saw Stiff and Valentino hop back in the car with Dante in the back and speed away. I ran full speed ahead, my gun aimed perfectly as I tried my best to shoot and hit at least one target in the black car as it sped away from the scene.

"They're gone," sounded next to me.

I didn't readily recognize a nigga's voice so my gun turned on Mirror who stood emotionless as he gazed down at me. Just like his cousin, he had light eyes, only his were so gray they looked silver, which was a stark contrast to his dark skin. My gun was right at his head and he didn't move. I was pissed at him for stating the obvious and even angrier that Trigga was gone. My hands trembled and teeth grinded as I dropped my hand and ran past Phenom, Anika, and Chyna.

"They got him," was all I said as I made my way back toward the vehicles we'd had to abandon because of the tire strips in the road.

The keys were still in the ignition of the Honda. Big Jake and Gina were finishing off one of the goons who had attacked us. People were calling me but I wasn't listening to them. I hopped in the driver's seat of the Honda.

"Diamond, wait," Anika called at me to no avail.

Her pleas for me not to go on some Rambo-style mission fell on deaf ears. I backed the car in reverse like I was a part of the Indy 500. I didn't even remember how Chyna, Speedy, and Gina had jumped in the car. I peeled out and burned rubber in the direction that I'd seen them take Trigga.

"Do you even know where you're going?" Chyna asked me.

"Trig got a tracker on his phone, Ray-Ray," Gina chimed in.

Speedy asked, "How'd they catch the blimey bastard, eh?"

I knew about the tracker on his phone, which was why I grabbed the Honda and sped off after them. I hit the GPS touch screen, tapped his name and number and listened as it told me where to go. They were headed to Southlake Parkway in Morrow. I drove like I was the only one on the road. I ignored every traffic sign and traffic light until I made my way my destination. I made a sharp turn onto Southlake Parkway off of Mt. Zion, passing the Shell gas station and sped down the narrow two-way street. Chyna screamed out as I almost made a head-on collision with a big rig coming the opposite way. I'd sped around another car that was going too slow.

"Bloody fucking hell, Diamond. The fuck you learn how to drive, blood?" Speedy squeaked. "Got her bloody license from a Cracker Jack box, yeah?"

"Slow down, Ray-Ray. You gon' kill us," Gina whined.

I whipped the Honda into a skid as I turned down another one-way road.

"Your destination is on the right," the GPS told me.

I hit the brakes hard as my hands gripped the steering wheel to the point my knuckles were turning white. Chyna jerked forward on the front seat and I could see that the sudden stop had caused Gina and Speedy to do the same in the back. I knew I was too upset to think rationally or clearly but all I could think about was Trigga never coming back. The limp way his body had fallen into that trunk didn't give me any indication of whether he was dead or alive. He couldn't be dead my mind kept chanting over and over as tears fell rapidly down my face. I stared straight ahead at the car I'd seen speed off with him. The doors were all opened and so was the trunk.

"We gon' sit here or we gon' go get him?" Gina spoke up.

I wasn't talking to nobody. I was in my own head, trying to figure out what my life would be like with no Trigga and I just couldn't imagine it. Couldn't handle the thought that I would never see that nigga again. Crazy as it sounded, I wanted to be back at the crib with him threatening to choke the shit out of me. At least I'd know he was alive and breathing.

It wasn't until I saw a black Navigator make a quick turn in behind me that I got out of the truck. Jake had jumped out of the Navi before it even stopped, rushing up behind me.

"Yo, my nigga in there?" he called out to ask me.

I didn't answer him either. Just made my way down the concrete stairs toward the steel doors.

"Diamond, get the fuck away from in front of the doors," Phenom yelled at me.

My anger had blinded me. Trigga's first rule of thumb was to never stand directly in front of the enemy's door. They had the advantage because you couldn't see what they were preparing to do. And sure enough a second after I moved, shotgun shells blew the doors off the hinges. We all dived for cover as gunmen filed out of the doors like a horde of rats. The broken pieces of glass on the ground tore into my elbows as I rolled. I flipped onto my back and let my burners loose. While most people would have aimed for head and chest shots, all I could hear was Trigga in my head.

"Never do what a nigga expects you to do. Do the opposite and catch them off their game every time, li'l shawty."

I started busting niggas in the knee caps and watched them crumble where they stood. That move allowed the rest of my team to come in and do what they did best. When I saw the trunk to the Honda pop open and little feet take off running toward an open window, I smiled. I'd been so hell bent on getting to Trigga that it never crossed my mind Ghost would pull something as such. But that was how Trigga had built her. I prayed I didn't live to regret my lapse in judgment. Then, I turned my attention back to the fight.

"Nothing like getting ya hands dirty with fresh kills, my nigga. The snapping of a nigga's neck will forever give me pleasure," Big Jake boomed.

"That was a sticky wicket wouldn't ya say, bruv?" Speedy asked as he started crip walking over his fresh kill.

That nigga was forever dancing and grabbing his nuts after filleting a ma'fucker.

Gina frowned as she looked up at Jake then took a baseball bat to a nigga's skull. "Ew, Jake. Don't be talking 'bout snapping niggas' necks and talking 'bout shit giving you pleasure that ain't me. That's my job, nigga."

Although Big Jake chuckled, judging by the glance he gave me, we both knew she was serious, which was why he picked the woman he loved up and kissed her passionately like he really just hadn't twisted a man's neck almost clear off. To my left Chyna was going through the same window I'd saw little Pastry shoes–clad feet go through no more than five minutes earlier. Mirror and Phenom were taking on incoming firefight as more men from the Italian Cartel and the Black Sicilians rolled in.

When I saw that no more men were exiting the building, I jumped up and made a run for it. Once inside the warehouse type building, I caught my breath but stayed on guard. The halls were empty and shit was too quiet for my liking. The buzzing sounds of industrial fans serenaded my ears until I turned to walk down a set of stairs that led to a corridor that had one hall before you got to the door at the end. I quickly trotted down the long walkway. I saw Ghost cut the corner with Chyna in tow.

They'd found a way into the building before I'd gotten in. My cousin turned to look at me and the look in her eyes was the same look I had just moments before I got to exact some revenge on the nigga who had stolen and raped me. Only hers was a deeper look of loathing. Not only had Dante stolen her innocence but he'd stolen her womb as well.

Two months after we'd rescued her from that nigga's house, Chyna found out she was pregnant. The days that followed were the hardest times in our camp. Phenom almost lost his grip with humanity as Anika and her daughter decided if she would keep Dante's demon spawn or abort it. In the end, Chyna chose to get her womb vacuumed and scraped of any child who would be born of the most traumatic experience of her life. The family never spoke of it again because, well, it was better that way. Chyna had an agenda and she wouldn't be denied it.

Back to the present, I watched as the men took turns kicking and beating on a boy who would forever be the only person who would have my heart the way he does. I accidentally hit the wall on the side of the door. Saw the men look up and then Dante motion for Stiff to see what the noise was. I made a mad dash down the corridor and quickly bent the corner of the hall I'd seen earlier. My heart was beating so fast and hard that it hurt, but he didn't see me. I peeped around the corner to see him walk a few paces, look around, and then go back in the room.

Although I'd made a stupid mistake, in the end, it worked out in my favor because the dumbass left the door open. I rushed down to the other end of the hall, hoping I could find another way to the door. Luck was on my side as I made my way back to the room from the opposite direction. I knew I'd said earlier that if I'd had to choose between his life and mine, I'd let him leave this hell on earth, but screw that. Just the thought of those niggas trying to take him out like they had earned the right to end his life had me on a suicide mission.

I got down on my stomach like I was in the army. Used my elbows and knees to move. As stupid as it may have sounded, I felt like a snake as I army crawled my way into the room. With their backs turned and the fact that they were on the other side of the room, it was easier than I thought it would be. The room was big and with the dim lighting it was easy for me to do. Not to mention they were so focused on torturing Trigga that they didn't have time to pay attention to me. I looked across the room. There in the big air vent, I could see an outline of a little figure anxiously awaiting her right to save the man she saw as her father.

"You little cocky piece of shit," Valentino spoke as he wiped the bloody spit Trigga had hawked in his face. He pulled out his gun and placed it in the center of Trigga's head.

"Hold ya head, Val. I wanna make sure this little motherfucker feel every kind of pain imaginable before we send him to join his folks," Stiff added.

Trigga slowly held his head back up and eyed Stiff. "What the fuck is that you know about my folks, sir? I'd suggest you not speak on shit you don't know about, nigga, unless you telling me you know about it."

Only those closest to Trigga could hear the threat laced in his voice. His parents would always be a sensitive topic and he held no prisoners when it came to avenging them. Stiff balled his lips and brought a steel baseball bat down over Trigga's thighs. I watched Trigga's hands ball into tight fists behind his back, right along with him gritting his teeth. His face screwed up in what I knew was pain, but he didn't let out one sound, not even a moan.

"We shouldn't play with him," Kim stated. "We should kill him and be done."

Valentino laughed. "Ease up, Kim. It ain't like this little black motherfucker can do shit to us now anyway. Tough little monkey," Valentino commented then laughed again.

"Just like his daddy. Took two bullets to the head to kill that fucker," Dante added then sent a fist flying into Trigga's face that I was sure loosened some teeth.

Trigga's low guttural laugh was all that could be heard. "That's all you got?"

It took all I had not to throw caution to the wind, but I had to wait for the right moment or shit could go all wrong. Had to wait for the signal before making a move. I kept watching as three overgrown niggas did whatever they could break an eighteen-year-old kid to his bare minimum. Seeing blood leak from Trigga's face, ears, and nose would forever be my undoing. I may not have even known what being a true killer meant until that very moment. I watched on as Kim did a Jet Li kick to Trigga's chest that sent the chair he was tied to flying backward. After that, Stiff sat the chair back up and Dante went to work on Trigga's face again. Valentino picked up a razor and as his hand rubbed at the place an ear used to be, I knew I'd seen enough.

"You gotta wake up every day ready to die more than the next nigga," I remembered Phenom schooling me. "You ready to die, Diamond?"

That day I'd been rebellious, didn't understand the knowledge he was dropping on me until now. My attention turned to the tiny outline of a little girl in the shadows. Three sharpened pencils rolled from the vent across the steel gray stain concrete floor.

"What the fuck was that?" Dante asked as the three men looked down at the floor, wondering why pencils were rolling toward them.

Trigga's head slowly rose looking into the direction where the pencils had come from then started to laugh.

Stiff turned to him and asked, "The fuck you laughing at?"

"Tell me something," he taunted. "You niggas afraid of ghosts?" he calmly asked them.

Dante was confused and so was Valentino. Stiff had raised the bat and was aiming at Trigga's knees this time until the light in the room went out. Someone must have cut the power from outside, which was good, but for only a second since I could hear the roaring noise of the generators. Dim lights around the room flickered on. I could hear her little feet rush from the shadows, saw when the little Ghost jumped from a chair onto Valentino's back and shoved a pencil directly into his carotid artery on both sides of his neck. She pulled the pencil out quickly, dropped to the floor, and rolled smoothly out of the way of spraying gunfire. She was good, just as her father, Trigga, had trained her to be. Valentino's life spurted from him as he tried futilely to use his hands to stop the bleeding.

Stiff didn't know what was going on. "Yo, what the fuck, man? I thought you said this shit was secure," he yelled at Dante's retreating back.

While the lights had been out, Dante had managed to make his way to the door. There was nothing I could do about that at the moment. I had other shit to worry about. Stiff was trying to figure out what was going on while Kim quickly turned his attention back to Trigga. I took that as my cue and took Kim out in one shot. The bullet caught him in the back of the skull. Kim and Dante were the deadliest of the men in the room besides Trigga. And since Dante had already run for cover, I had to take Kim out. Next came Stiff. I aimed my Sig and took his left knee out. He fell down to his knees, right near Trigga's feet.

Ghost scurried across the room like a little ninja, stuck a sharpened pencil into his back where his kidneys were. She fell back and used her feet to mule kick the homemade weapon through. She was quick on her feet as she jumped back up and took another pencil through his neck then eyes. When Stiff's's body finally hit the floor, Trigga used his feet to drill the pencil clear through his skull. I left my hiding place and went to rush across the room. I was halfway to Trigga when a bullet blessed my thigh. I screamed out and turned to see Kim's men closing in on us from the hall. I hadn't counted on them getting passed my fam, but when I saw Mirror fighting like Michael Jai White as he gave a roundhouse kick that damn near took one of Kim's men's head off, I knew I was covered. Jake was bringing up the rear. I guessed he'd gotten tired of using his hands as a weapon, but then I saw the blood dripping from them and knew he had been injured.

Anika's machetes had men running for the hills as she took out body parts, any part that she could get to she cut it including heads. I saw one roll and Gina kick it out the way.

"Ew, that's nasty as hell," she said with a frown.

Crazy thing was she had just shoved a screwdriver-like shank through one of Kim's men's skull. I didn't see Speedy but I could hear that nigga's laughter and knew he was doing what he did best, cutting niggas up.

"Oi! That shit was gives a whole new meaning to Asian takeout," he yelled then started to sing. "'Nobody wanna see you rising. When you do they don't even like it. They just wanna see you deep in crisis.'"

"Cut the theatrics, Moseif, and get to your agenda," Phenom's voice came from somewhere to stop Speedy's wild singing.

I could see Ghost running back to her hiding place because we were outnumbered. I loved the little girl because she was both brilliant and resilient. I rushed across the room to Trigga.

"Yo, li'l shawty, what took you so long?" he asked as I untied his hands.

"Had to make sure we got the timing right. Didn't want to add another bullet hole to you."

I moved around to the front of him and caught his heavy body on mine before he could hit the floor.

"Can you believe this motherfucker used a tranquilizer on a nigga?" He was joking, but I was afraid.

Whatever had been in that tranquilizer had him sluggish. I'd never seen him as weak in body as he was in that moment. His weight was threatening to cripple me, but there would be no way I would let his body hit the ground. Well, that had been my plan, until shotguns shells came flying at us. I took as much of his weight on me as I could, grabbed for my gun, and was set to return fire until Dante's feet connected to my face. It was almost lights out for a bitch. My vision became blurry. Head started to swim and I could taste the coppery faint hint of blood, but some kind of way, I remained conscious. Dante grabbed me by my leg and slung me across the room into a wall like I was a rag doll.

A yelp of blinding pain escaped my lips as my back slammed against the concrete. I wanted to move but couldn't fast enough. My gun had flown one way and I another. But none of that mattered at the moment, Dante was standing over Trigga with the sawed of shotty aimed at his chest.

"Time to go night night, nigga." Dante arrogantly poked fun at him before cocking the gun.

Shit started to get crazy in that moment. I took a running leap for my gun at the same time Ghost came charging from her hiding place. She was still a little girl after all. And in her mind she was about to watch the only parent she had left be murdered. Too much had fallen on her. In that moment I'd hated we ever trained her to be the fighter she was. She ran full speed ahead toward Dante, her little fist raised with her sharpened pencil ready to do damage, only to have him turn and send a full blast of the shotgun into her chest. Her little body went flying backward.

"Ahhhhhhhh, no!" That was all I could scream, all I could muster. "Ghost, no!"

I watched in horror as her little body spazzed and it looked like she was convulsing. Her eyes rolled to the back of her head as blood started to seep from her lips. Trigga used a leg sweep to take Dante off his feet. If he had been weak before, seeing Ghost take that hit to the chest gave him strength like never before. I saw Trigga jump from the floor. I rushed over to Ghost and picked her little body up. Hot tears rushed down my face as I turned her over. She kept twitching in my arms.

I knew Dante and Trigga were fighting behind me because I could hear their grunts and groans.

"Chasity! Chas," I screamed out to her. "Oh God, oh God. I'm so sorry, Chas."

All I got for a response were coughs and twitching. I was so distraught that it took me a moment to realize that I didn't see any blood on her shirt. I laid her flat and ripped her shirt open. A shotgun blast behind me caught my attention.

Trigga was now standing over Dante. "Night night, nigga," he growled out, cocked the shotty, and was about to shoot him again until I turned to see Chyna.

"That's my kill, cuzzo," she told Trigga. "Been waiting for a long time for this moment."

On her closed fists were black gloves with barbed wire. In her hand was a shank that I knew only Speedy would have made for her. It looked like some shit from *Edward Scissorhands*.

"You took something from me I could never get back, Dante Orlando, so I take something from you that you can never get back: your life."

There was a coldness in my cousin's eyes, but also a sadness. By default he left her with no choice but to kill her first child. No matter what Dame had done to me, I was damn glad that nigga didn't leave his demon seed in me. I would have never known what to do with myself or the child if he had.

ENGA was live and in full effect as our whole team walked into the room and surrounded a dying Dante in the middle of the floor. Anika was body blocking Phenom because even though he'd promised his daughter she could kill the bastard, in his eyes was a father's love and the need to kill the man who had violated his daughter. Chyna climbed over Dante and straddled his lap. He was trying to talk but couldn't thanks to that hole in his stomach courtesy of the shotgun blast from Trigga.

Chyna proceeded to pull Dante's exposed intestines from his guts with a smile on her face. She then stood and used the shank in her hand to mercilessly jam it into his dick over and over and over until blood drenched her glove-covered hands. It would have been nice to hear that nigga's screams and yells, but the more he tried the more he choked himself to death. Once she was done, she cut away the front of his pants. The sight of his mangled dick made all the men except Phenom turn away.

"Bloody hell, mate. That's some fussy shit, yeah?" Speedy groaned.

She looked at my aunt, her mother, with tears in her eyes. Anika nodded. Chyna turned back and around and proceeded to cut his dick off all the while this nigga was still alive. Chyna leaned over and shoved Dante's dick and balls, what was left of it, into his mouth. Then she stood and beat his face with the barbwire gloves until holes riddled his once handsome face. Punch after punch turned his face into what looked like ground beef. She did that nigga dirty, but no dirtier than he had done her. Chyna beat him until she started sobbing loudly and it broke my heart.

I wondered what she was doing when she moved behind him. My curiosity was satisfied when I watched her pull a wire from her shirt pocket and wrap it around both her hands. She placed it around that nigga's throat and pulled for dear life. I swear I heard skin and cartilage tear as the wire severed his head. It was as if she'd had a nervous breakdown all before our eyes with the way her sobs got louder and louder. She didn't stop pulling until Dante's neck sat detached from his body.

Once she was sure the deed had been done, she released her grip and her shoulders slumped as her head dropped. Her chin sat against her chest while she cried loudly. Phenom walked over and scooped his daughter into his arms, cradling her to his chest like the little girl she was. DOA was no more. There would be no rise from grave for DOA.

It wasn't until Trigga turned his bloodied and beaten face in my direction that I realized I was cradling Ghost's head in my hand as her limp body lay on the floor.. He rushed over to us as quick as he could and took her from me.

"You made her a bulletproof vest?" I asked him.

"Couldn't risk losing her," was all he said as he ripped the vest away from her body.

Although the pellet shots didn't penetrate the vest, her chest was still bruised badly from where the shot had landed.

"She still need to see a doctor, Kwame. The blast knocked her out cold. Could have broken something," I told him.

His lips were swollen; eyes almost shut damn near as he stared at me. He wrapped an arm around my neck and pulled me close to him. "I'm sorry," he said to me.

"Me too and no matter what, I still love you," I admitted to him.

Nothing really needed to be said between us. We'd survived another day and finally, finally we could have some peace. He kissed the top of my head. I smiled through the tears and looked up at him, wanted to say something, but his kiss stopped anything I may have wanted to say.

ENGA, we hood misfits, are here to stay.

Chapter 27

Trigga

Inked on my left arm next to the names JAMIR, FATIMA, and ASSATA, was the reminder from Sun Tzu that he who wishes to fight must first count the costs. In this long battle, naw this nonstop war against enemies who were simple kills and others who were far from weak, that cost in life was no doubt great. Each and every one who was a part of ENGA had lost a lot and never was going to get back what was taken. That's why we all fought so hard feel me?

Old world law, an eye for an eye had nothing on what we did and still do to avenge what was lost. That was why ENGA doesn't just belong to us, it belonged to every misfit in the hood, overseas, even in the 'burbs, who had been taken from and looking for survival and vengeance. That was why ENGA was now inked between my shoulder blades like two wings of death, because me and mine were the bringers of justice.

Everything after the final big show, that final battle with the last of DOA and that pussy-ass nigga Dante, changed everything for us. But let me take it slow on the rewind.

I was dragged out of the room by my family. We didn't exit the way we'd come in. I guess, during all the melee, they'd found other exits in the building. Through it all, a nigga was fighting to keep a hold of Chasity. Someone had taken her from my arms because I was too weak to hold her and stand on my own. I saw it all, saw how she was thrown back, saw the way the bulletproof jacket I had made just for her took the brunt of the force, but still giving her harm. My li'l street solider was still battle bruised from it and I needed to get to her.

"Calm down, bro, I'll get you to her but let's ride up outta here, fam; stop screaming," Jake explained to me.

My dazed eyes glanced up at him and I noticed that his brown eyes and eyebrows where furrowed as he studied me in concern. He had said I was screaming and I didn't even know it. Whatever the fuck was put in me from that tranquilizer was fucking me up big time.

"Just hurry and get him out of here. Dante poisoned him and if we don't move out fast enough . . ." Anika's voice cut off as if she was going to cry.

That shit right there had me shocked. Would I be missed if I was gone for real? Was I really poisoned? The answer to that hit me hard when it felt like several razors were slashing my insides out. Sweat beaded at my temples and my fists twisted in agony. I tried to hold on and not punk the fuck out but as we moved down the hallway, the smell of smoke from Dante's body being lit up, had me stopping Jake in his tracks so I could empty my stomach.

"Trigga!" sounded behind me and I tried to turn to look at Diamond but damn if the world wasn't hazy.

"Go right, and through that door, hurry!" Phenom bellowed out.

Damn, his voice was so fucking loud that it felt like he'd put one of those bullhorns directly to my ear and said what he had. That whirring movement picked up again as they rushed me out of the room. I felt myself struggling again, calling to Chastity, which had us slowing down again. I didn't mean too but shit had me in my old zone again. It had me seeing my baby sister being gunned down again, which had me ready to rip heads off again.

"I'm okay, dad!" Chasity's small weak voice hit me but didn't resister.

Little did I realize I had broken free of Jake's hold and went after a set of Dante's goons in a fit of rage. I found strength from somewhere as I fought with my bare hands. Their blood coated me and my fam as they also fought. The little strength I'd mustered up to fight was quickly dwindling. As we rushed to leave the building, Phenom told me that in another part of the building they'd found several rooms that had kids, girls and boys of all ages locked up. Some dead from drugs and others dead from whatever violence was done to their bodies. He and the rest of the team had already released those that had been strong enough to run.

"There are more in there. I'm not sure we can save them all," Anika said after she had mumbled a prayer.

"We have to save as many as we can," Phenom said as we made our way through the building back to area where they'd seen the kids before.

"Dominique," Diamond screamed and rushed around me to get into one of the rooms.

She moved so fast that it made me stumbled and fall to the floor. Jake grabbed me up and threw me back over his shoulder as if I were a bag.

"Diamond, baby, we have to go," Anika pleaded.

"No! She's still breathing, look. She ain't dead; please?" Diamond pleaded.

"Ray-Ray, let's go! Dat bitch was the one who got you locked up; come on this is Trigga, our Trigga; we gotta go please. Please! We can't lose him," Gina wailed out, rushing forward to pull on Diamond's arm.

From how everything sounded, Diamond was conflicted and I could tell she wanted to save me more, but also save that chick. Lying on the bed, Dominique looked like a pale, pasty, and sweaty ghost with puke caked on her face. Needles lay around her and it was clear shawty had ODed or was coming damn close to it.

The sound of boots walking forward was all I heard with that of Speedy's accented voice. "Step back, ma. I got her. Maybe Anika can help her, too. Seen it done before, mate."

"Only if we move fast, please. Trigga is my main priority right now," Anika sounded.

My uncle's voice bellowed out, "Grab her and be out! We don't have time for this shit."

That was when everything sped up for me. We rode out of the storage house and headed past several spots in the A to Phenom's and Anika's true home hidden in the forest of GA. Medics surrounded me. All I heard was beeping of machines and I knew my heart stopped several times before it picked back up and beat normally again.

The sounds of Ghost begging me to not leave her, with that of Diamond's cussing, screaming, "Don't you punk the fuck out, nigga! You betta than this," she would cry one minute, then, "Don't leave me!" would surrounded me in my white chamber of my mind the next.

In it, I saw my fam again. Each one smiling at me for what I had done for them. We had did what I had planned long ago as a kid scraping in the streets, breaking into cars just to sleep in the back seats, or finding abandoned old homes to sleep in until the state got me. I had come a long way from murdering for a nigga who had been the one who murdered them. All around me was my fam. I was ready to go. My work was done.

But the sound of the voices around me kept pulling at me. Jake's deep yells, with that of Speedy's then Gina's had my attention. It was the touch of my uncle's hand though, Diamond's lips on mine, Gina's sobs, with the sound of Jake breaking stuff in the room and Chas's hug that had me waking up in my bed. The sound of my pops and mom talking to me from the grave gave me a reality check.

They said that my time wasn't done. Said, my new family needed me more than they did. Told me that my purpose was beyond vengeance for them, they told me to accept it and remember them always. It hurt hard for me to hear that, but they were right. My fam, my new fam needed me too. I could never let another nigga hurt my girls, which always included Gina, Diamond, Chasity, and now my cousin Chyna and I for damn sure couldn't leave my homies hangin'. Through this knowledge I continued to learn that shit is crazy in this life. In all my teachings, a nigga was the bringer of chaos and now finally it was righting its course.

Glancing at everyone, I knew there was more to do. Maybe not now, but later, and I had to be that nigga Trigga for when that day arrived.

Epilogue

Trigga

A week later, still weak and healing from whatever that shit Dante had pumped in my system, I stood outside in the rain of the place that made me who I was in some sense. Flowers rested at the broken down door of my parents' old home. My mind reflected back over my journey in this. I had to visit my parents' place before I made a visit to my old stomping grounds. Just needed to visit the place I'd spent the first few years of my life. There would never be any place like home and over the years I'd come by there to sit and think plenty of times. But there was no time to be nostalgic. I had other work to finish.

Later on that same day, I stood at one of the trap houses of Dame's old empire. It was one of the places where Dante had been holed up before he died.

"This is the spot, blood? Don't look like shit at all," Speedy sounded off to the far right of me.

A quietness was in me as I stared at the house that used to be just a chill spot for Dame's goons to leave product and pick up money. It was just a quaint little ranch-style house that had been remodeled to fit that nigga's liking. Painted red with black bars on the window, the house stood out to those who knew what went on inside.

"Yeah, this used to be a torture chamber," I quietly responded.

Jake chuckled. "Compared to his mansion that used to be hell on earth, I'd say this was definitely the old torture chamber." he added. "Shit feels like years already. You ready?" Jake asked.

We all stood with hoodies on. All black everything. Ghost was on my left in between Jake and me. Diamond and Gina stood on the left of me holding hands. Behind me was Speedy and Chyna, our new misfits. Man, life was on some crazy shit and everything had come full circle.

We all walked forward, climbing the fence as a black car waited behind us. In it was Phenom, Anika, and Diamond's best friend, Dominique, who we'd learned had been kidnapped, and forced to into Dante's sick game. Behind that car, sat my cousin Mirror in his SUV. Seemed like the Trap was quiet for the most part, but word had gotten back to us that we needed to check out one of Dame's old spot. Kids were missing after taking Dante down, a lot of them. Way more than the ones we'd found in the old warehouse.

Not to mention, people had been talking about the man who'd set up shop in Dame's old spot. Nobody should have been in Dame's old habitat. And since we knew for a fact Dante was dead, we made it our business to see what was going on. Mirror had been watching the house for a few days so we knew the time when the man inside would be there alone. Everyone gave her a reassuring nod before we rushed into the house. We had to be quick as we didn't know who or what was waiting for us on the other side. The sound of clicking, like someone was typing, caught my attention.

You would have thought whoever it was on the inside would have had enough sense to guard themselves with men at all times. Resting a finger against my lips, I pointed to spots for everyone to position and I moved forward, finding an opening that lead to one of Dame's old offices.

Carefully stepping through, my Timbs thumped against the floor as I spotted the man I'd come to finish off. If he'd been smart, he would have gone back to London after we offed Dante. But the love of money was the root of all evil. And human trafficking brought in scores of money.

"I knew he wouldn't take you down so easily. How'd you like that tranquilizer? Was my idea, mate," S.B. taunted me from behind the desk.

He sat there like he had no worries that we had basically just ambushed him. For a second, I got anxious. Started to think that me and my fam had walked into a trap. The itching of my fingers had me holding my Glock and I stepped forward to see Dante's handler sitting at a dirty desk with a laptop on his lap. He was dressed in a gray vest with matching pants. No shirt was under the vest and he smirked at me, rubbing his black beard as if studying me. I could see that I had fucked him up badly the last time he and I had met. Which was apparent by the wounds marking his arms and neck. I wasn't even done either.

"I knew you weren't dead," I quietly said.

"Yeah, just like I knew you weren't, two men cut from the same cloth, mate. But you greatly underestimated my power, little cunt. Question: you ever know what my name means?" S.B. asked.

There was a crazy look in his eyes. One that said he wasn't afraid to die, and another that said he wouldn't mind fucking you on the way to death.

His question made my rub my chin and laugh at his cocky shit. See, I hated games. Hated when people felt like they were bigger than the game. Ain't shit this cat had done ever impressed me much. For one thing, I never underestimated him, which was why we were led here. Just because Dante was dead didn't mean his sick plans died with him. Every nigga had an agenda. We knew

Dante's game plan was still going on and it seemed this sick pervert was the reason.

"Yeah, son of a bitch." The sound of my Glock going off, a clean bullet zipping forward and hitting him right in the middle of his face, gave me pure satisfaction.

I didn't have the time or the patience to do the song and dance with him. I stepped forward, snatched the laptop off the desk. I knew all the information on the missing kids, teens, and even adults would be there. S.B., or Street Butcher as he was known back in the UK, was a part of Dante's sick global operation, which included human trafficking. Nobody paid attention to that shit in the United States because not many people knew what human trafficking was. We were a part of the lucky few who had people, like my unk and African queen Anika, guiding and teaching us along the way.

Now we knew that Dame wasn't just selling pussy or pimping as it was known in the hood. He was a human trafficker. What he had been doing had a name. Diamond was there just like the rest of my fam. All there just in case we needed backup. But it was the way she was holding her own that made me see her in a different light. Jake had told me that she was the one who initiated finding me when those niggas had taken me. They all had been there but it is was Ray-Ray who was the first to go in guns blazing trying to get to me. That tripped me out, still did, especially with being successful in how she came for me.

Wasn't sure how I felt about it outside of being pissed that she put herself in harm's way yet again and pride because it looked like ma was coming into her power. Something had clicked in her and she was becoming one with the streets. Was crazy, especially with watching her become a natural in how she handled her role. Glancing at S.B.'s dead body, li'l shawty motioned for me to come and I did.

The effects of the tranquilizer was still slowing me down for now. Anika had explained that it was going to take a month to get the rest of it out of me, until then I wouldn't be as fast as I normally was, which was why I had to take a moment to breathe to get myself together. Jake had walked out and come back in with two big cans of gasoline.

"You know what time it is, blood," Speedy quipped then cackled like he was the Joker as he rubbed his hands together.

"Time to light up the sky," Jake added on.

"You two always ready to cause mayhem," I told my boys who were more like my brothers.

"Says the man who's the enforcer of chaos," Jake responded then laughed.

Heading out, the rest of our crew got in our ride and I gave Phenom and Anika the intel we all had. I dropped my hoodie let Diamond do the honors of torching a part of our past. She struck a match and then tossed it where the gasoline trail was. I took her hand as we rushed for the truck. Once I made sure she was in, I hopped in behind her as the flames started to crackle around the old trap house.

I watched her look out the window of our ride, throw up her middle fingers as if she was saying fuck you to the past. After that, we headed out of the Trap, nodding at people who came out of their house just to see what was going on. We all were legends and there was nothing going to stop us from protecting our people. Relaxing in the ride and heading to the airport, Phenom explained that we were going to break for a bit and chill in Trinidad; one reason was for me to heal and two to take down S.B.'s contact there. So it was still game on.

***

I now lay in bed healing in the birthplace of my mom and unk, Trinidad. Spread out before me was a beautiful view of the ocean and sea. I could hear the waves crashing as I lay between cool sheets. Trinidad was on point. Once we landed, we got to meet the other half of Phenom's network and our family. We then finished off our loose ends and took down S.B.'s contact, moving to send all the trafficked people back to their homes. It had me thinking back to the chaos. Like I heard someplace, change is bred out of chaos. In order for change to come, chaos has to occur first and that's what went down for us all. I was soul tired but alive and kinda glad to be here, especially when I could hear Ghost's laughter. My little soldier had become my damn world. It was crazy as fuck to have these feelings for her like that.

Like she was really my kid and shit. Every time I think on it, it makes me laugh, because I still sometimes felt like a kid myself, but that's what it was. Chasity was a Kweli now and proud to sport that last name, too. I knew that one day she'd grow up and have to pro'ly face the demons of her DNA, but I know without a doubt that she'd kill whatever may come for her on the spot and still be strong because of the lessons I gave her.

It was kinda dope to watch her actually break out of being invisible and playing with my cousins her age and chillin' with Chyna. Was dope watching them both study with their private tutor and train with my unk and Anika. Everything that happened back in that safe house with how Ghost almost died, man, yeah, that killed me; but she let me know off the bat that she didn't want to experience that again. So she dedicated her days training and my unk made sure she spent just as much time being a kid growing up in a family of killers. Chyna reminded me of her mom and a little of Ghost. She was still healing like Diamond and Gina, changed forever from fucking with the devil, but even she now, since being in Trinidad, was opening up and feeling safe to be a teen.

This shit was crazy as I kept saying, but we were getting through it. Both Jake and me were doing online classes with Georgia State. Anika had Diamond and Gina both working on things to better educate themselves and introducing them to college courses. She explained that none of the queens in her crew were stupid. They all had a high school diploma and a degree or degrees.

It was kinda crazy to me but I respected it. Like I told Diamond before, ain't nothing like an intelligent hoodrat with an agenda. They ended up being the baddest broads on the block. Jake and Gina were still stuck at the hip. It was kinda dope seeing them together but on some real, Gina was softening my nigga. But it was all good because he was healing her at the same time.

As for Speedy. Nigga was still clownish as fuck. He was also taking college classes with us and starting a party all over the island. Nigga was forever finding ways to cut niggas who came funny at him for taking their broads or just being who he was, which had us always saving his ass from starting another war. Dominque was still healing from the bullshit she fell in with Dante. She broke down everything he had planned once he had killed us.

She gave us locations to where more drugs, money, kids, and people were hidden, in which Phenom and Anika sent out teams to go check it out. We thought trusting her was going to be hard. But, once she and Gina went Worldstar with it again, it seemed that even they got mad cool, especially after she started flirting with Speedy. Crazy shit was, Dominique's parents had washed their hands of her. Phenom and Anika had gone back to her parents under the guise of working for a clinic that specialized in helping girls who had been through what she had, but her father wanted no part of her back in his home because she had caused them too much trouble, too much embarrassment. None of us understood the motherfucking method to their madness, but we wasn't about to leave her assed out. This group kept growing but stayed small and stronger than ever.

As for me and Diamond, yeah. Because of everything and who was around me, a nigga had changed but I was still a Trigga happy nigga, still waiting on death. Though, I was really glad to be here, I was damn sure happier right now because of the feel of a soft thigh sliding over my waist.

Hands ran over my chest, the scent of papaya and vanilla had my senses awakening in desire. Licking my lips, my heavy lids lifted to glance into familiar doe eyes and a sexy smile. When the lips that belonged to that smile brushed mine, I knew this healing was going to be on point. Tongues danced. My hands moved from on the side of me to scooping up the naked juicy ass that straddled me. A soft groan let me know that I could continue what needed to go down and I let out a deep growl the moment my dick hit silky, tight bliss.

Was no doubt that who was on me had a pussy for kings. I knew when I expanded within her that my dick was made just for this queen.

"Ooo damn, Kwame," melted from her lips and had me carefully leaning up to scrape my teeth against her nipples.

I liked her titties. They felt like they fit my needs just right, just like she did. Crazy part of this all, in this moment right now, I could feel that ping of pain in my chest again, and I welcomed it just like my unk had taught me, sort of. The moment I did, that pain turned into something that empowered me and had me going deeper, flipping her onto her back and throwing her leg over her shoulder.

I knew the moment she tensed that I had scared her and I ain't mean to but she felt so damn good, I had to have her pinned like I did. So to wipe away her fear, I let my hips circle eight in that shit, just like I learned from a skilled broad back in Armando's crib long ago. I let my internal rhythm glide in and out teaching her to relax and accept all the thickness and length I had to give. The moment she creamed against my nuts, I knew I had her, especially when she arched and gripped my shoulders.

"So tell me again. Say it again, Kwame."

A smirk spread across my face, I let my locs brush against her supple skin then with one slow winding thrust I had her toes pointing to the heavens and her head digging into the pillows.

"You're my queen, my jaguar like I was taught to look for. We got an authentic connection, Diamond. Ride or die with the same agendas."

Though something in me said her agenda was to lock me down and a nigga wasn't sure he was ready for that, I was slowly learning to dig her being my main. Did I love her? I probably did, but I ain't figured that shit out yet.

A quaking tightness from her body had a nigga fisting the bed sheets. Once she gave a silky laugh, I knew that she knew that I was about to bust with her.

So, I dropped down to kiss her lips and let her fingers hold on to my neck and locs as she whispered, "I love you, Kwame. Oooo, Trigga!"

I kissed then snaked and flicked my tongue around where she had tatted my name, finding my way down between her cushiony thighs to sample her slit. Both hands wrapped around her thighs to hold her in place as she shook and almost ripped the bed apart. I ain't ever eat pussy except twice, just to learn and to get my skills tight. From how I was eatin' her and from how fucking good she tasted, I knew I was doing shit right especially when she went sliding off the bed unto the floor with a thud and begged for more. I always was told that I could roll the fuck outta my tongue.

We stayed at each other's bodies until the sun set and rose again, ignoring dinner. I let the peace of the island, and our victories take me to the heavens, even as gunfire sounded in the distance. This life was ours to make it how we wanted, but what it never was going to do was hold us hostage. We got our happy ending. We are the misfits in the streets. The ones who take what you took first. We never sleep and in this game, even as we gain and grow, it's always one thing to remember: every nigga got an agenda . . . even those closest to you. One.

ORDER FORM
URBAN BOOKS, LLC
97 N18th Street
Wyandanch, NY 11798

Name (please print): ___________________________________

Address: ___________________________________

City/State: ___________________________________

Zip: ___________________________________

QTY	TITLES	PRICE

Shipping and handling: add $3.50 for 1st book, then $1.75 for each additional book.

Please send a check payable to:

Urban Books, LLC

Please allow 4-6 weeks for delivery

ORDER FORM
URBAN BOOKS, LLC
97 N18th Street
Wyandanch, NY 11798

Name (please print): ___________________________

Address: ___________________________

City/State: ___________________________

Zip: ___________________________

QTY	TITLES	PRICE

Shipping and handling: add $3.50 for 1st book, then $1.75 for each additional book.

Please send a check payable to:

Urban Books, LLC

Please allow 4-6 weeks for delivery